The
Creepers

The Creepers

John Creasey

PERENNIAL LIBRARY

Harper & Row, Publishers, New York
Cambridge, Philadelphia, San Francisco, Washington
London, Mexico City, São Paulo, Singapore, Sydney

A different version of this story was published in England under the title *Inspector West Cries Wolf*. A hardcover edition of *The Creepers* was published in the United States in 1952 by Harper & Brothers.

THE CREEPERS. Copyright 1952 by John Creasey. Copyright © renewed 1980 by Diana Creasey, Colin John Creasey, Martin John Creasey and Richard John Creasey. All rights reserved. Printed in the United States of America. No part of this book may be used or reproduced in any manner whatsoever without written permission except in the case of brief quotations embodied in critical articles and reviews. For information address Harper & Row, Publishers, Inc., 10 East 53rd Street, New York, N.Y. 10022. Published simultaneously in Canada by Fitzhenry & Whiteside Limited, Toronto.

First PERENNIAL LIBRARY edition published 1987.

Library of Congress Cataloging-in-Publication Data
Creasey, John.
    The creepers.
    I. Title.
PR6005.R517C7   1987   823'.912   87-45034
ISBN 0-06-080889-6 (pbk.)

87 88 89 90 91 OPM 10 9 8 7 6 5 4 3 2 1

1

Night Call

The bell rang harshly through the darkness.

Roger West heard nothing as he lay on his back, sleeping, snoring faintly.

His wife woke with a start, heard the jangling, discordant note, said: "Oh, no!" and struggled up on her pillow, then leaned across her husband and groped for the telephone. She touched the shiny surface of the instrument, lifted it, and let it drop. The ringing stopped; the telephone fell heavily to the floor. The sound of a voice came from it, distorted and inhuman. *"Hallo. Hallo. Hallo."* Janet pushed the bedclothes back and scrambled out. The bed creaked. Through the window she could see the glow of a lamp in the main road: there were no street lamps alight in Bell Street. She stretched out her hand to touch the bedpost, moving her bare feet cautiously, while Roger made a gulping noise and turned over.

"Hallo. Hallo. Roger. Roger—what the devil's the matter? Roger!"

"Oh, be quiet," Janet whispered absurdly.

She could make out the shape of the bed and the table against the cream-colored walls. She bent down and groped about the carpet until she touched the telephone. Kneeling, she picked up the receiver and said softly into the earpiece: "What is it?" The man at the other end spoke to someone near him.

"I don't like this. Someone's lifted the receiver, but there's no answer."

A pause; and then the man spoke again.

"Surely Lobo can't have—"

Janet didn't hear the rest of the words clearly. The name "Lobo" went through her like a sharp pain. She exclaimed: "*No!*" much more loudly, and glanced up and about the dark room as if it held some menace she hadn't noticed.

Roger stirred.

"Someone spoke," said the man at the other end of the telephone. "Bill, send a patrol car—"

Janet put the telephone the right way round, and spoke urgently. "It's all right, this is Mrs. West."

Roger wasn't snoring; the bed creaked again.

"Everything all right, Mrs. West?" The voice of the other man was brisk.

"Yes. Yes, of course. Can't you let him have any rest? He wasn't in until half-past two, he hasn't had any real sleep for two days and nights. It's killing him."

The other chuckled; the first note of relief since the harsh ringing.

"It'll take more than the loss of his beauty sleep to kill Handsome. I'm sorry, Mrs. West, but I must speak to him. It's Cortland speaking."

"How on earth can you expect him to get results?"

"He'll get results all right," said Superintendent Cortland of the Criminal Investigation Department. "Wake him, please, this is urgent."

Outside, a clock began to strike. One—two—three—four. Four, that was all; Roger had been asleep for little more than an hour. Janet stood up, supporting herself against the bed, and Roger said huskily:

"What is it?"

"Cortland."

"Who? Oh. Tell him to—" Roger broke off; his voice was hoarse and thick.

"Roger, he mentioned—Lobo."

Silence fell upon the room, until West sat up, clothes and bed rustling. There was a click as he switched on the light by the side of the bed. Janet, in a flimsy nightdress, still leaned against it with the receiver in her hand, her hair awry, and a thick lock falling over her cheek and right eye. She brushed it away. Without make-up, she was pale but wholesome; good to see. Roger, his fair hair tousled, handsome face unshaven, eyes bleary, looked at her as he stretched out his hand for the instrument.

"Who mentioned Lobo?"

"Cortland."

"If he told you—"

"No, I heard him talking to someone else."

"Oh." Roger took the receiver and grunted: "Now what's up?" Cortland might be his superior officer, but just then he would have growled at the Chief Constable, the Home Secretary, or anyone who shared any responsibility for the police.

3

The subdued light of the bedside lamp made the room seem cozy; but it still had dark, shadowy corners. Janet looked toward them, and then to the window and into the silence of the night.

Silence? Someone walked outside with slow, steady footsteps; and to her imagination, stimulated by the sudden waking and the name of Lobo, there seemed something ominous about those footsteps. She looked at Roger. He was listening, and Cortland's voice made a meaningless jumble of sound to Janet, but judging from the set expression on Roger's face there was nothing meaningless about what he said.

Janet went across to the fireplace, took a box of matches off the mantel-shelf, bent down and lit the gas under the kettle. On a small stool was a tray, set for morning tea; and there were biscuits. As the gas hissed, she heard Roger say quietly:

"Yes, I'll be there in twenty minutes or so."

He put the receiver back slowly and smoothed down his hair, looking all the time at Janet. Her reflection in the darkened mirror above the fireplace seemed shadowy—ghostly—and enhanced her frightened expression. He got out of bed and began to take off his pajamas.

"Sorry, darling. It can't be helped. When it's over, I'll have a few days off."

"Is it Lobo?"

"There's some talk about him, but it's probably another false trail." Roger laughed on a strained note, not all due to his tiredness. "I wish I knew who first scared you about Lobo. I'd wring his neck. I'll go and brush my teeth, won't be a minute."

When he returned to the bedroom, the tea was

4

made and Janet was sitting up in bed looking toward the window. She gave a convulsive shiver. The steady footsteps still sounded in the street. Roger went to the window and looked out.

"It's a copper," he said. "They're patrolling the whole district. Been too many creepers about lately, Lobo's set the fashion. You go to sleep and forget all about Lobo. Half the stories about him are just newspaper stuff. Anything for a sensation and a punch on the nose for Scotland Yard. Forget it."

Janet didn't speak as she poured out the tea.

"Good night, sir." The policeman saluted as he approached the car which Roger was backing out of the small drive of his Bell Street house.

"Good night. Keep a special eye on my place, won't you?"

"That's why I'm here, sir."

"Thanks." Roger let the car snort out of the gate, then swung toward the main road. He drove swiftly through the deserted streets. A few lights were on in the main thoroughfares; off them, there was the darkness of London's night—darkness which he hated because it made the work of thieves so much easier; that of the police, much harder. Fuel shortage was a curse; crime throve on the gloom.

His headlamps relieved it. The light shone on the big glass windows of shops, the blank fronts of houses, the grimy gray stone of a church. He ignored the one-way sign at Sloane Square, turned right and met no traffic on the twisting streets which led to Buckingham Palace Road. The pale white block of Airways House showed up, then the high wall alongside Victoria Station. Once or twice he saw a policeman, but no one else was about. He swept up Victoria Street, and saw the twin towers of Westminster Abbey outlined against the cloudy sky; then the lighted clock of Big Ben, a beacon. The small light at the top of the tower was on.

"They're still sitting," he murmured. "What's worse? Being a policeman or a Member of Parliament?" He grinned wryly to himself as he drove round Parliament Square, crossed the wide, dim-lighted emptiness of Whitehall, and went down the narrow street into Scotland Yard. Two policemen on gate duty saluted. Several cars were parked in the Yard itself. He hurried up the steps, through the old building, along the narrow passage connecting it with the new, then went up to the first floor in the lift. He passed no one; even the Yard seemed to be asleep.

Light framed a doorway not far from the lift.

He went into the room. It was small, rectangular, and barely furnished; two desks, telephones, odd chairs, some reference books, a patch of carpet, and a fireplace all showed up brightly in the light of a single powerful lamp which hung from the ceiling over the desk at the far end. There, Cortland sat in his shirt sleeves, massive, unshaven, dark hair and stubble turning gray, a cigarette drooping from the corner of his thick lips. He had little eyes, half closed with fatigue, and a broad nose. His hands, palms downward on the desk as his big stomach pressed against the edge, looked like bunches of red bananas. If you wanted an ideal "type" for a bad man, you had only to glance at Superintendent Herbert Cortland.

6

Sitting at a corner of the desk, fresh-eyed, clean-shaven, alert-looking, was Detective Inspector William Sloan. His short, fair hair was brushed and oiled, and he looked as if he had just come out of a bath. Sloan was one of the younger and more promising men of the Yard.

"So you finally got here," Cortland growled.

It was twenty-five minutes to five.

"Sorry." Roger pulled up another chair. "But if you've got the man, ten minutes doesn't make much difference. Has he talked?"

"No," said Sloan.

"You must be sleep-walking," Cortland said. He had a rather thin voice, unexpected and disappointing in a big man. "They never talk. But he's got the mark, he's one of Lobo's men. The fifth we've picked up, and this time we're going to get something from him."

"Have we had him through our hands before?"

"No. That's the biggest piece of trouble. None of them has been through our hands, but they're all clever creepers. Experts. Roger, we've got to get Lobo."

Roger took a cigarette from Cortland's packet, lit it and grinned.

"I'll buy you a gramophone. You've been saying that without a stop for eighteen months. Lobo probably has a good laugh every time you think of him. What did this chap do tonight? The usual?"

Sloan winked at him, unnoticed by Cortland as he answered:

"He did four houses, and we caught him coming out of the fourth. He'd all the stuff from the four places on him. We can send him down for three years, and if there's any common sense at the Old

7

Bailey, he'll get seven. He worked exactly the same way as Lobo's other men. Found a small window open, wriggled through, ransacked the house from top to bottom, went through the pockets and handbags in the room where the people were sleeping, and got out without raising an alarm. It was sheer luck we caught him."

"Who actually caught him?"

"Quinn—a youngster in 21 Division."

"Tell P. C. Quinn it was luck, and then listen to what he says about you in the canteen," said Roger. "One of your troubles is that you won't give credit where credit's due, and there's a lot due this time. Did Quinn get hurt?"

"No. This creeper had a knife like they all do, but didn't have time to use it. He didn't even get it out of his belt."

"Something to be thankful for," Sloan said.

"It's the first time we've caught one of Lobo's men without someone getting cut up." Roger commented. "If he didn't use knives, I'd have a soft spot for Lobo. He's got Flannel-Foot licked to a frazzle, and does a neat, clean job. And he even uses a trade mark."

"That makes him crazy," Sloan interjected.

"Not crazy enough for us to catch him."

"So you'd have a soft spot for him," growled Cortland. "He's fixed nine hundred and twenty-three neat, clean jobs in eighteen months. I wouldn't have a soft spot for him if he'd only done a couple of dozen! You don't take Lobo seriously enough, Roger. You never have. It's all very well to be flippant sometimes, but this man's as bad as they come."

"Flippancy withdrawn," Roger said. "The question is, are we any nearer to catching Lobo himself, or aren't we? Could this chap Quinn caught, be Lobo?"

"You'd better form your own opinion," said Cortland. "I shall be surprised if he is, more surprised if we get a quick squeak out of him. I haven't got the report yet, but we'll have it sent downstairs for us. Let's get going."

He stood up, towering above the others, a man of six feet four—so tall that he looked huge, not fat. He shrugged himself into his coat, while Bill Sloan opened the door. They walked downstairs, their footsteps sounding loud but dull on the stone floors, to the little room where the thief was waiting. A uniformed constable stood outside the door, and opened it with jangling keys as the C.I.D. men arrived. Roger smiled his thanks, Cortland grunted, Sloan said: "Thanks." The room beyond was brightly lighted, and the first man they saw was a police sergeant, standing with his back to the window, his thumbs hooked in his belt, his bare head making him look undressed: no man of the uniformed branch seemed properly clad without his helmet.

Sitting on an upright chair, hunched up, his hands clasped in front of him and looking like a diminutive Uriah Heep, was the prisoner. At first sight, he seemed old—middle-aged, at least. When Roger drew nearer, he saw that it was a youngish, fair-haired man—a man with thinning, straw-colored hair and an incipient bald patch. He was dressed in a dark suit, and wore shoes with enormous rubber soles covered with flannel—shoes which made little or no sound when a man was moving about. He didn't raise his head, but

9

glanced upward at the three C.I.D. men. That gave him a furtive, foxy expression. His face was pale, his features thin; he looked half starved.

"Has he said anything?" Cortland asked the sergeant.

"Not a word, sir."

"Where do you think this nonsense will get you?" Cortland asked roughly. "What's your name?"

The prisoner looked down at the floor.

"You're going to talk before you're through," growled Cortland. "Don't make any mistake, you're going to talk." He gripped the man's shoulder.

Roger said quietly, in a voice that was almost friendly:

"Let me see your left hand, will you?"

The prisoner clasped his hands together even more tightly, and looked like a suppliant praying, but aware that he had no grounds to expect an answer to his prayer. Cortland shook him roughly, proof that the Superintendent was tired out. Roger said: "Easy." Cortland glared. the prisoner slowly unclasped his hands. It was as if he were making a great physical effort, as if his hands were locked together by some invisible force. He still looked down at the floor, but once he shot a swift, raking glance at Roger; in that moment he seemed to come alive.

Roger held out his right hand.

The prisoner, hands parted at last, still held them resting on his thin legs, bunched, like claws. Slowly, he held out his left hand, but didn't open it. On the tips of the little and third fingers were tiny pieces of a proprietary brand of sticking plaster; on the other were slight traces of where similar plaster had been pulled off. Instead of wearing gloves to prevent making prints, he had used plaster; a modern improvement. Cortland said: "If you don't get a move on, we'll make you," but nothing hastened the man's movements. There was no apparent reason for his reluctance, because others had already seen the palm of his left hand; but the need for hiding it from everyone had been drummed into him so thoroughly that it was an ordeal to show it.

He turned the hand, palm upward, finger still clenched.

Roger took it gently, and pulled the fingers back; he didn't have to ue force. The hand was thin and bony, and very cold, although it was warm in the room. At last the palm was exposed, shining palely in the bright light; and in the center of the palm was a pinkish mark. It was the shape of a wolf's head, mouth open, fangs showing. Although it was what he had expected to see, Roger felt a twinge of repugnance, a stab not unrelated to fear.

It was the fifth time he had seen the mark of the wolf—the mark of Lobo.

2

The Knife

"Take him over to Cannon Row," Cortland instructed the sergeant. "We shall have him up for remand in the morning."

"Yes, sir."

Sloan was already opening the door. Only Roger looked back at the thief. He sat in exactly the same position, and his hands were clenched tightly again. Roger smiled into the weak eyes; the man turned away quickly.

The three went into the room next door. There were a few upright chairs against the walls, a table in the middle, and a long bench along one wall. On the small table were dozens of everyday oddments, such as a man might carry in his pockets. A cheap watch, loose silver, some creased and crumpled pound and ten-shilling notes, three Yale keys, a comb in a small leather case, two small dice, the two-spot upward, like beady black eyes. There were pieces of string, bus tickets, the return half of a railway ticket, the program of a greyhound race meeting and a small penknife. None of these was remarkable, but at one end of the orderly array was a game knife with a small, white handle. The blade was four or five inches long and an inch and a half wide at the base. It tapered toward a sharp point, and glittered brightly. Even from the door, Roger saw that the cutting edge and the point had been recently sharpened.

"I wonder if we'll have any better luck tracing that one," he said.

"The maker's name has been ground out, so we shan't," Cortland answered gruffly. "There isn't a thing they forget. It's the first time we've picked up a railway ticket, but that doesn't help much. It's dated three days ago, and was bought at Waterloo. Return half, from Hounslow."

Roger said: "Well, you never know." He crossed to the long bench. There, in similar orderly array, were the proceeds of the thief's haul. It was not impressive. Several small brooches, rings and pairs of earrings, cuff links, a few silver oddments, three gold sovereigns, seven watches, several little wads of one-pound notes and some silver. Roger doubted whether the total value was more than three hundred pounds.

"He didn't get much," Sloan ventured.

Cortland rounded on him.

"Multiply that lot by a thousand, and you'll find that it comes to plenty. Lobo's got away with two or three hundred thousand pounds' worth since he started. All small stuff, all easily negotiable, he doesn't have any trouble disposing of it. Don't you get Roger's habit of taking it lightly."

Sloan didn't answer; Cortland could make himself unpleasant.

"It makes me mad. Every time we catch one, it's

the same. Nothing to identify the man by; he won't give his name. We haven't traced one of them to their home. That swine hasn't opened his mouth once since he was caught—and he'll keep silent in the dock tomorrow, won't speak to a soul until he's under remand and awaiting trial. Then he'll talk fast enough—to other prisoners. We'll have him up at the Old Bailey, and no one will get a squeak out of him, he won't even plead. Next time he opens his mouth, it will be on the Moor, or wherever they send him. Once was bad enough, but this will be the fifth time. We've got to get Lobo, and nothing's going to stop us."

Roger said: "We'll get him, when we stop being hidebound by rules and regulations."

"What's in your mind?"

"Supposing we hadn't pulled this man in? Supposing Quinn had let him go, and followed him. Or even supposing he were to escape now. We might—"

"Not on your life." Cortland's voice rose to a squeak. "We don't want any of that funny stuff. I thought you'd given that up, years ago. That would give Lobo another man to work with, and he'd have a bigger laugh on us than ever. Anyhow, it'd be impossible even if there were any sense in it"

Roger shrugged.

"We've picked up one man tonight, but half a dozen others and Lobo himself might still be working," Sloan said. "They probably are, he usually sends everyone out for a night and then rests for a week. Going to have another shot at this one, Roger?"

"Just before he goes into the dock, that's their

time of least resistance," Roger said. "I'm going home."

Cortland raised no objection, just looked as if he wished he could.

In Hampstead, that same night, a small man with big rubber, flannel-covered soles on his shoes, dressed in dark clothes exactly like the prisoner's, squeezed through the fanlight of a small, detached house in a quiet avenue. There was little wind; a rustle of leaves made the only sound. The man himself seemed to be of rubber; he made no noise, even less than the breeze outside. He stood at the foot of the stairs, which faced the front door, listening.

He heard nothing.

In ten minutes he had cleared the downstairs rooms of everything that might be easily sold, and a small heap of loot was placed on a hall table. As he crept upstairs he held a small torch with a big top in his left hand.

Five doors led off the landing; two of them stood open. He glanced inside. One was a bathroom, the other a small, unoccupied bedroom. He opened the third door, without a sound, and the glow of his torch spread inside. It shone on pale walls with colored animals pasted on to them, and on to a boy who lay in a small bed, sleeping on his side.

The man drew back and closed the door gently.

The next room was large—a bedroom. A man and woman lay sleeping in twin beds, facing each other. The light was poor, but good enough for the creeper thief to see the woman's dark hair and the man's face, which was turned toward him. He stood in the doorway, looking at the dressing table, where some trinkets glowed faintly. He crossed to them, picked up two rings, a jeweled comb, a small *diamanté* watch, and a diamond pendant. He took a wedge of cotton wool from one pocket, wrapped each up, and slipped it into a capacious pocket inside his coat.

Only the steady breathing of the two sleepers touched the silence.

The creeper tiptoed toward the beds. The woman's handbag stood on a bedside table between the two. The man's clothes were folded over a chair at the foot of his bed. The thief ran through the pockets, found the wallet, and put it with the rest of his haul. Then, almost touching each bed because the gap between them was narrow, he approached the bedside table.

Downstairs, a clock struck four.

He opened the handbag; the catch made a slight noise, the first he'd caused. He glanced down at the man, but saw no sign that he was awake; men and women were in a different world in these dark, witching hours. Inside the handbag was a gold compact, and the thief's eyes glistened. He wrapped it up and put it in with the others. There was a purse, also; he didn't trouble to open it, just slipped it into the pocket with the wallet, and turned round.

The man's hand shot out, and grabbed his wrist.

The thief spun round. The "sleeping" man sat up sharply, face set, eyes glittering.

"That's got you, my beauty! Julie!"

The woman didn't move; the thief stood as if he were paralyzed, looking down, still shining the torch into the man's face.

"Julie!"

16

The woman blinked and stirred.

"Julie, don't get excited. I've caught a burglar. Nip out and telephone 999. That's all—just dial 999."

"*Tony!*" The woman sat up, clutching the neck of her nightdress, staring wildly at the little man who stood between the beds looking down at her husband.

"*Hurry*, old girl." The man spoke to the thief in a harsh voice. "Don't try any tricks, or I'll break your arm."

The thief didn't speak.

The woman pushed back the bedclothes, and as she did so the thief dropped the torch to the floor; the light went out. The man in bed snapped: "Don't move! Put on the light, Julie, *Julie!* Put on the light!"

She fumbled with the bedside lamp, and as the light came on she saw the steel blade of a knife glittering in the thief's hand. She screamed. Her husband tugged at the thief, then swung his free hand wildly to try to fend off the sweeping blow. He failed. The knife slashed across his face once, then again, lower. And after the second cut the thief swung round, and the wife cowered back, her mouth wide open, her eyes pools of terror, the neck of her nightdress gaping.

The thief swung the knife downward; buried it in the gentle swell of the left breast; drew it out with a sucking sound as she moaned and sank down. The killer reached the landing, stared at the nursery door; it didn't open, there was only the moaning sound from the bedroom. He sped down the stairs.

As he opened the front door, a light came on at a

house opposite. The thief paused to sweep the oddments from the table into his pocket, then ran out without closing the door. There were trees in the road; trees, darkness, great shadows; but the light streamed out from across the road, a window went up and a man shouted: "Here, you!"

The thief ran, ignoring the call.

"Stop! Stop thief!" shouted the neighbor.

The thief sped on, silently.

It was half-past six when Roger reached the Bell Street house. Dawn spread softly over the eastern sky; in half an hour, it would be broad daylight. The October morning was crisp, not really cold. He drove the car into the drive and left it standing outside the garage. He was desperately tired. That wasn't just because of the Lobo job; there was always too much to do.

Janet was awake.

"What time is it, Roger?"

"Turn over and go to sleep again," Roger said. "You've an hour, yet. Call me at nine sharp."

"Must I?"

"Yes. I want to be at Bow Street by a quarter to ten. Hardly worth undressing again."

"You'll feel much better if you do."

"Oh, well." Roger tumbled out of his clothes, and as he climbed into bed, heard a soft, cooing voice from across the landing.

"Scoopy," came the gentle voice. "Scoopy, you awake?"

Janet called: "Go to sleep, Richard!"

There was no answer; only silence in the house, and from the main road the rumble of early-morning traffic, the roar of the early buses begin-

18

ning to feed the City and the West End with workers. Roger pulled the clothes over him. Janet, snug and warm, lay on her back. He rested his hand on her softness, and smiled in the dim light. She didn't smile or look at him.

"Not often the Fish is awake first."

"He may go off again. You go to sleep."

"Don't forget, nine fifteen—no, nine o'clock. Not a minute later." He mumbled the words; sleep was already slurring his mind and his tongue. He thought vaguely of Martin, called Scoopy, and of Richard, who were in separate rooms because when they slept together they were awake and noisy so early; of Janet's cozy, seductive warmth; of being tired when he wished he were wide awake. He didn't notice that Janet kept herself stiff and did not move toward him.

The telephone bell rang.

He caught his breath. Janet started.

"*No!*" she exclaimed. "No, not again. I won't answer it. They're crazy!"

Brrrr-brrrr; brrrr-brrrr; brrrr-brrrr.

Another voice came from the landing. "Mummy, Mummy! Telephone's ringing."

"Go to sleep, Scoopy!"

The noise jangled and jarred through Roger's head; he knew it would be impossible to sleep until he'd answered it. He struggled up. Janet leaned across him, but he got the receiver off first.

"Who is it?"

"Sorry," said Bill Sloan. "I think you'd better come out again. Not here—17 Division. It's a nasty job."

"What kind of nasty?"

"From all accounts, Lobo's worst. A double

murder. Shall I send a car for you? I haven't called Cortland yet, I thought you'd rather get there first, but I'll have to tell him soon."

"I'll go," Roger said. "Never mind a car."

"Daddy, is it time to get up?" Scoopy called. His voice sounded nearer; his small, sturdy, pajama-clad figure appeared in the doorway. Behind him was a second, smaller figure, equally tousled; both looked pale in the light from the bedroom, and both looked eager.

Janet said: "It's like being married to a machine."

Roger said: "Darling, the next few days will seem like being single. Lobo's really cut over the traces this time."

Martin called Scoopy, and Richard stared, round-eyed, still sleepy; they were puzzled by the way their mother's face changed, by the look in her eyes; and by the way their father leaned across the bed, took her shoulders, and drew her face close to his.

"Murder?" she asked.

"Yes."

"Let's play *murder*," said Scoopy, soft-voiced, as he turned and took Richard into the larger nursery.

3

The Orphan

A child stood at the window of 17 Maybury Avenue, Hampstead, watching as Roger West parked his car in front of three others that were outside the house. The boy was pale, his rounded blue eyes looked like Richard's. Sight of him made Roger miss a step. Behind the boy, with her back to Roger, stood a woman in a red dressing gown, talking to an elderly man who held a cup of tea. The woman's arm was bent, as if she also held one.

The window was open.

"Here is another one," said the child clearly.

"Peter, you must come away from that window!" the woman cried. She turned, showing hair in curlers and a distraught face. "Oh, why are the police such fools? Why don't they let me take him home? It's not right, while upstairs—"

"Steady, Dorothy," said the man.

Roger approached the front door, which stood open. A uniformed policeman inside the hall came forward quickly. The house was small, timbered, charming for all the fact that it aped the Elizabethan period. The garden was well-tended, bright with late dahlias and early chrysanthemums, and had trim, neatly edged lawns. It faced west; the sun rose behind it, shining gold upon two tall elms which stood by the side of the timbered garage.

"Morning, sir," greeted the constable.

"Morning." Roger ran his hand over his stubble, and saw Sloan coming downstairs. The door leading to the front room was closed. "What the devil are you keeping that kid here for?" Roger demanded.

"Not me—Wilson's in charge from the Division, and you know what he's like. Not that it's doing the kid any harm; he doesn't realize what's happened."

"Oh, doesn't he?"

Roger pushed past Sloan and ran upstairs. Every door on the landing stood wide open, and two men with a camera were standing in one doorway. As Roger reached the top, a bright flash came and the camera clicked.

"Finished?" asked Roger.

"Yes, sir, from here."

Roger went inside, and saw the two bodies, just where the neighbor from across the road had found them. The woman, a crumpled heap by the far side of her bed, face showing. There was thick, coagulated blood on her breasts and the night-dress; also over one hand, which lay limply on the carpet. The man was still in bed; bedclothes covered him from the waist downward. There was one cut across his cheeks and another across his throat; the bed was a shambles.

A big, thick-set man with iron-gray hair stood by the window, and nodded as Roger approached.

"Now Lobo's gone too far," said Superintendent Wilson.

The man was a prosy fool.

"He's always gone too far. Any special reason for keeping that kid downstairs?" Roger was abrupt.

"Well, yes. I wanted you to have a word with him. You're good with kids. He was awake when the neighbor came in, so he might have caught a glimpse of the killer. If we leave him too long, he'll either forget or embellish it with a lot of fancies."

"Oh," said Roger. "Sorry, you're right. How are things going up here?"

"It doesn't look as if we're going to get much to work on," said Wilson. "No dabs, he must have worn gloves or tape. Entrance was forced through the fanlight, it was a Lobo job all right. The neighbor saw the man come out of the house, but can't describe him, except that he was small, had big feet, and ran like a hare." That description would have fitted any of Lobo's men. "The neighbor's downstairs with his wife. A Colonel Hambledon."

"I'll have a word with the boy," Roger said. He went downstairs again, regretting his abruptness with Wilson, who had more imagination than he had credit for. Sloan was on the staircase.

"Want me, Roger?"

"Not yet, thanks. Oh, yes—what's the child's name?"

"Peter."

"Thanks." Roger rubbed his stinging eyes and brushed his hair down with his right hand, then went into the front room. The woman in the red dressing gown looked older than she had through the window. The man was tall, and stood erect. He was dressed, but without a collar or tie. He had a

23

gray mustache, a long, thin face, bristly with whitish stubble, and bright gray eyes.

Peter still stood by the window, looking at the newcomer.

"Hallo, Peter," Roger said. "Good morning, sir." He nodded to the Colonel and his wife, and approached the boy. "You're having a rough time, aren't you?"

The rounded eyes were so like Richard's.

"Are you a detective, too?"

"Yes, that's my job."

"Is my Mummy dead? And my Daddy?"

"Look here, why can't you let us take him to our place?" asked Hambledon. "We'll gladly look after him, until—"

Roger said: "Very soon. Peter, come here, will you?" He sat on the arm of a chair as Peter came forward, solemnly, as if the knowledge of death had already been revealed to him, although probably no one here had told him frankly. Roger tried to think what he would say to Richard; or what he ought to say. Hiding facts was useless; simplicity would probably serve him best.

Mrs. Hambledon said: "Peter, later on, we'll—"

Peter didn't look away from Roger.

"Please, are they dead?"

"Yes," Roger said quietly. "I'm terribly sorry, Peter. How old are you?"

"Six and a bit." A year older than Scoopy, two years older than Richard. The clear treble voice was quite steady. "Did a wicked man kill them?"

"*Oh.*" That was a strangled gasp from the woman. The Colonel stepped across and put his arm about her shoulders, while those rounded, questioning, demanding eyes glowed at Roger.

"Yes, Peter."

"I hate him." There was no emphasis.

"We do, too. Do you go to school?"

"Oh, yes, every day, at St. Wilfrid's."

"Do you like it?"

"Yes, it's very nice, especially in the afternoons, when we have drawing."

"My boy Scoopy likes drawing, too. Have you anyone at St. Wilfrid's who's called Scoopy?"

"No, I'm afraid we haven't," said Peter politely. "It's rather a funny name, isn't it?"

"I'll tell you how he got it, one day," Roger promised. "Did you wake up earlier than usual, this morning?"

"Oh, yes, *lots* earlier."

"Why?"

"I thought I heard something, and I did," said Peter. "It was Colonel Hambledon coming in. I heard him run up the stairs, didn't I, Colonel Hambledon?"

"Harrrumph."

"And did you open the door, to see who it was?"

"Well, I was just going to," said Peter. "And then I didn't. I—I just didn't." He set his lips, as if he were determined not to say why. "It wasn't wrong not to, was it?"

"Of course not. Did you hear anything before that?"

"I don't remember."

"Your Mummy or Daddy talking to anyone, or anything like that, I mean?"

"Oh, no, I'm *sure* I didn't," said Peter. "The last time I saw Mummy was when she came in. She comes in every night late, just before she goes to bed, and sometimes I wake up. I did last night."

The woman stifled a sob. Hambledon said: "Dorothy, please don't." Peter didn't look at either of them.

Roger paused; words just wouldn't come, and the back of his throat seemed to close up. Someone walked across the room above, and the glass lampshade rattled slightly. Another car pulled up outside.

"When did you see Daddy?"

"When he took me to school, yesterday morning," said Peter. "He always takes me to school, on the way to the station. It's not far."

"Well, Colonel Hambledon is going to take you this morning, old chap. Where does your Grandma live?"

"Well, Granny Lee, that's Mummy's mummy, lives an awful long way away. Somewhere in Scotland. I went there last summer on holiday, when Mummy and Daddy went away to France. Daddy's mummy lives in London."

"Does she often come here?"

"Yes, nearly every week."

"And do you like her?"

"Oh, *yes!*" For the first time, Peter's eyes lit up. "She always brings me something nice, and she plays the piano, too. Like Mummy. Is—is Mummy *really* dead?"

"Yes, Peter."

"I *hate* that man," said Peter, and suddenly tears filled his eyes. "I hate him, *hate him!* If I could find him, I'd kill *him*, too. I hate him!"

Keep to the prosaic; be like Wilson.

"I expect you do. Are you hungry, old chap?"

It worked.

"I suppose I am," said Peter, thoughtfully.

"Then Mrs. Hambledon will take you to her house and find you some breakfast. I expect it will be a pretty good breakfast, too. If you want to know anything, just ask her, and she'll tell you if she can."

"Thank you. Are you going to stay here for very long?"

"I shall be in and out all day, I expect, and detectives will be here all the time."

"That's good," said Peter. "What did you say your little boy's name was?"

Roger stood in the window, with Colonel Hambledon by his side, watching Peter walk sturdily across the road, holding the woman's hand. A car hid them from sight, but Roger continued to stare until they came in sight again, near the front door of the Colonel's house. A newspaper boy came cycling along, whistling shrilly, and in the distance, milk bottles rattled.

The Colonel coughed.

"Can I get you anything? Cup of tea?"

"No, thanks. Have you talked with our people yet?"

"Yes. They said they'd let me know if they wanted me again. Stayed to be with the boy. Er—hrrrmph. Wouldn't have told him like that myself, not straight out, but I think you were right. Nice kid, Peter. Everyone likes him. Hrrrmph." The Colonel had some difficulty getting his words out. "Anything at all we can do, glad to. Only too glad. His grandmother, Mrs. Graham, will be—well, imagine. But she'll take it well. Know her slightly—like a village, this part of Hampstead, you know. Hrrrmph. Someone will have to tell her."

"We'll look after that."

"Good. Ah—you'll get the devil, won't you?"

"Yes, we'll get him," Roger said savagely. "We'll get him, after this."

The little thief sat in a corner of the room at Bow Street, hands clasped and pressing into his belly, his head on his chest. It flashed through Roger's mind that the man might be a cretin. Ugly thought. *Was* this pose assumed? Or was there something mentally wrong with all the men who worked for Lobo? That notion was fantastic; they were too quick, too cunning, talked too freely when they were in jail. The pose was cunningly taught, adeptly learned, to slip on and off like a cloak. If he could make this man talk, it might be the end of Lobo.

He stood in front of the little man, and barked: "Stand up." The man obeyed. "We've had enough of this nonsense. You've got to talk. What's your name?"

The man didn't answer.

Roger said: "Silence will only make things worse for you. You were caught at Golder's Green, just after three-thirty this morning. You realize that, don't you? We know the time you were caught, what time you paid your calls, where you went."

The pale eyes didn't turn toward him; there was no movement of the small head or the thin lips.

"And we know you killed them," Roger said.

The head jerked up; an expression—was it fear or just surprise?—sprang into the weak eyes. The man dropped his hand by his side, and stood very stiff and still. Only a sergeant was in the small,

28

bare room with them, standing quietly by the door, showing no interest.

"Two murders," Roger said. "You're in line for the long drop, whether you talk or not. You'd better think fast, see if you can prove it was someone else. You can't, can you? You're so frightened of your boss that you won't say a word. You'll let yourself hang before you give him away. And a lot of people will be glad to see you hang. *I* shall, for one. I'll be there in good time to see you take your last walk, and see you drop. Ever watch a hanging?"

The little man licked his lips.

"One of Lobo's men did the job last night. You're one of them. You were in the vicinity. A knife like yours was used. Did you know there was blood between the blade and the handle of your knife?"

The man's tongue poked out again, and sneaked back.

"So it looks as if your knife was used. You were certainly near the place. A man and a woman were murdered with a knife—slashed and stabbed. There'll be a public outcry for the murderer. There won't be any rest until he's hanged. You fit in with everything. Get that into your thick head. Any jury would convict you on the evidence. Didn't Lobo warn you what would happen when you used that knife? You were seen, too, by a man across the road. It's a clear case. There might be a chance for you to get a lifer, if you tell us about Lobo and the other man. It'll be your only chance. Why did you kill? Does Lobo order you to kill rather than be caught?"

There was no answer.

Roger said: "Listen to me. In ten minutes you'll

29

be in the dock. We've two charges we can prefer. The first one, that you were caught leaving a house with stolen goods in your pocket. The other, that you committed a double murder last night. You can please yourself which one it is. If you don't speak now, it'll be the second. If you start to talk, it'll be the first. Did you kill that couple?"

No answer.

Roger thought: I'm making a hell of a job of this, I'm half asleep. He lit a cigarette, and the faded little eyes seemed to move in line with the light. He drew in the smoke, blew it over the thin, straw-colored hair; the man's head hardly came up to his chin.

"One of Lobo's men did that job last night. Understand that? We know it was one of his men, and you've been caught, red-handed, on another job. I wonder how that happened? We don't often catch one of his men—and in the past, we've always been tipped off. Ah! That makes you think, doesn't it?"

The little man darted him a swift, frightened look, licked his lips again, and spoke.

"I didn't kill anyone. I didn't!"

4

The Squeak

Roger said: "Wait a minute. Sergeant, have the next case called, will you, I want ten minutes." He tried not to show his excitement. "So you've come to your senses, have you? But saying you didn't kill the couple isn't enough, we want a lot more. What's your name?"

"I—"

"Your name!" Roger gripped the man's shoulder and pressed tightly, his excitement rising; this was the first squeak of any kind from a Lobo man; sensational. "Let's have it, and don't waste time."

"I'm—Morgan." There was a slight lilt in the man's voice; it was Welsh, with an overtone of Cockney. "Dai Morgan. I didn't kill no one last night, I swear it. Was—*was* I shopped?"

Roger released him, and shrugged. Cortland and others wouldn't approve of this, they'd say he'd talked too freely; and that lying so as to get information was bad. But if this man thought his Boss had shopped him, there was no telling how much he would say.

"How do you think we'd have caught you, if you weren't shopped? You're the fifth we've had in our hands, and last night there was the fifth tip-off from Lobo, or from someone who works for Lobo. How old are you?"

"Thirty-one. I—"

"You're getting old for this job. The others were much younger than you, not much more than boys. They all went off the active list. They had a busted ankle, a weak arm—something which prevented them from doing their job the way Lobo wanted it done. He thought the best thing was to shop them. Are you married?"

Morgan nodded; his eyes were bright and fearful as he stared up into Roger's.

"Any kids?"

"Three."

"Nice thing for a wife and family to know that the old man's going to be strung up. And that's—"

"I never used the knife last night!"

"You've used it before."

"I—I never did no harm with it," muttered Morgan. "Only scared people, that's all. I'm not a killer. I tell you I'm not a killer, you've got it all wrong! I never really hurt no one with that knife. Anyway—"

He gulped, and broke off.

"Anyway, what?"

Morgan said: "We get a different knife for every job, that's what. We never have the same knife for two jobs running, ony one o' the same kind. I—"

"Yes, Lobo framed you nicely," said Roger, and grinned. "He fixed you up with a bloodstained knife. Oh, the blood didn't show, it had been washed off. But you can't wash blood away between the blade and the handle. Some always sticks. We found plenty in yours—Lobo's good, isn't he? Have you let him down lately? Done something he doesn't approve of? Come on, let's hear it?"

"I—I dunno. I just dunno."

There had been no tip-off; but there had been blood on this man's knife. Roger had built up a convincing story, worked on the man's fears, turned Lobo into Morgan's deadly enemy, and made him desperately afraid of hanging; the rope was the one thing which frightened all crooks. Roger didn't feel tired, now; he hadn't really felt tired since he had talked to Peter.

He said: "Where do you get the knives from?"

"They're given to us."

"Where? Who from? I want the truth, it's the only thing that might save you."

"I'm talking, aren't I?" Morgan shivered, and his hands were clenched in front of him, as if instinctively trying to conceal the sign of the wolf. "We're told what streets to work, and given the knives, a couple of hours before we start the job. We don't get any more warning than that—we're given a packet and everything's inside."

"How many are there of you?"

"I dunno. I tell you I dunno! There's only two I work wiv. There's plenty more, must be, but I only know two. We live at—"

He hesitated, and gulped hard; as if a mental picture of Lobo had sprung to his mind, and he was more afraid of the man whom he served than of death. Roger didn't force him, then; just waited. Policemen passed along the passage, and someone called out: "Next case!"

Morgan muttered: "We're at Ma Dingle's place."

"Just the three of you?"

"Yeh, that's right."

"How long have you been at the game?"

"Coupla years."

"Before you worked with Lobo?"

Morgan shook his head. "Not really."

"How did he get hold of you?"

"I was in the ring," Morgan said. "Never got any-where, I didn't get a chance, that was the trouble. I was hard up. Then—then I was offered a job. Cleaning the ruddy streets! Catch me sweepin' up other people's muck! There was only one way to make a living. I started out as a dip. I was okay, I could run fast if there was any trouble. Then—"

He stopped and closed his eyes, as if an old, ugly vision had come to his mind. He stood quite still, his left hand clenched and raised near his chest. Slowly, he opened his hand and his eyes, at the same time. He looked between the clawed fingers, toward the sign of the wolf. He shivered, as if he had suddenly turned cold; and once he started there was no way of stopping him. He shook from head to foot, and his teeth began to chatter.

Roger took his arm and led him to a chair, but he shook as he sat down; and kept shaking.

"Can I get anything?" the policeman asked.

"Yes. Whisky or brandy."

The shaking was as violent as ever when the po-liceman returned with a tot of whisky. Roger held it to Morgan's lips. Teeth chattered against the glass as the man sipped. He choked; a little of the whisky spilled out, and ran down his chin and neck. But he swallowed some, paused, then drank again.

34

Gradually, the spasm passed.

Roger gave him a cigarette; he took it gratefully, and drew in the smoke as if his life depended upon it.

"What was all that about?" Roger asked quietly.

"You—you dunno wot you're doing to me," Morgan muttered. The cockney whine was very pronounced, now. "You dunno wot *'e'll* do, guv'nor. There was one of the mob wot threatened to squeak, once. 'Is wife was—" he broke off, and shivered again. "You dunno nothin' about Lobo. That's a fact, you don't know a thing."

Roger said: "We're learning. He can't get at you while you're here. We'll look after your wife and the kids, too—don't worry about them. Remember, I'm trying to save your neck. It won't be easy. I shan't be able to do it unless you tell me everything you know. You're one of three of the gang living at Ma Dingle's. You get a packet, with your orders and the knife. Now, let's go on from there. What do you do with the stuff when you've finished your night's job?"

" 'E collects it."

"Lobo himself?"

"I dunno. It's nearly always the same man," Morgan said. "An' that's all, until we get orders for the next job."

"And how did you get mixed up with Lobo?"

"I started work wiv one of the race gangs," Morgan said. "Louey's mob. They wasn't so 'ot. Bein' a little squirt, they used me as a dip. You know 'ow easy it is at the races. Then Louey's mob got broke up. I was out o'work again, and didn't know wot to turn to next. That's 'ow I started. I didn't know Lobo then. Two years ago, it was—nearly two years. Cove told me 'e 'ad a job for me. Livin' in. It was in the country, but if you arst me what part, I can't tell you. Taken out there in a closed car, I was. That's where I met the ovver two. They was there, trainin'. We was at school again. We learned 'ow to get through small winders, how to break in—proper school for crooks, worse'n Borstal. That's all I can tell yer, guv'nor, except—"

"Yes?"

Morgan muttered: "Gimme anovver drink, will yer?"

Roger gave him the glass; he finished the whisky, and sighed heavily.

"Ta. Except that we was told never to open our mouths. If we split, our wives an' the kids would get theirs. We didn't argue about that. Got fifteen quid a week, we did, and only worked one night a week. Easy money. We didn't like the knives—*I* didn't, anyway." He shot a furtive glance at Roger, as if wondering whether that went home. "We was told to use the knives to slash ourselves free, not ter kill. I never killed no one, guv'nor!"

"Who taught you at this place?"

Morgan said: "There was two or free of them— old-timers, they were. Did they know the job or didn't they! Lived at this 'ouse in the country, and we never knoo their proper names. One was called Mike, another Loppy, the third one was Tich. Like a mountain, Tich was. Big as Cortland. Mike, Loppy, and Tich," he repeated, and shivered again. "That's all I can tell yer, Guv'nor, I don't know an- nuver fing—an' I never killed no one!"

He stopped speaking, but his breath came gust- ily.

There was another heavy tap at the door. "Won't

be able to wait much longer, sir, the last case but one is already being heard."

"All right," Roger called. "Use the breaking and entering charge." He turned to Morgan. "You'll be safe from Lobo if you keep your head. Don't say anything in court. No one else is going to know you've started to squeak. Your wife might drop into trouble if Lobo suspects, remember. We'll do what we can for you—but you'll have to talk when we want you to."

Morgan said: "Sure, okay. I'm glad it's over. I'm glad it's over, see? I 'ope you get Lobo."

The police asked for an eight-day remand, in custody; the policecourt proceedings were over in three minutes, and Morgan didn't utter a word.

"No," said Roger, when he was with Cortland at Scotland Yard. "I shouldn't pull Ma Dingle in, or either of the men who live there. I'd just watch 'em. Get the Division to put their best man on it. Better still, draft a good tailer from another Division, one who's never worked in the East End and won't be recognized. The next time either of the men goes out on a job, nab him. When we've got them both, we can start on Ma Dingle. If we pull her in now, Lobo will know that Morgan's squeaked. He'd know we've picked up a lot of odds and ends, too. If we wait for a bit, we can work on the new angle. The big chap Tich, Loppy, Mike, and the country house—the whole works. We can watch Ma's and see who goes there with the next orders, too."

Cortland said: "I suppose you're right."

"Ma may be clear of this job. She probably

knows why her lodgers go out at night, but you can't bring a case against her on the strength of that. We want another good man tracing Morgan's family and his movements over the past two years. There's no big hurry. The quieter we move the better, for the time being. We mustn't botch this chance."

"We're on the way home." Cortland would soon be overconfident. "I didn't think you'd make the beggar talk. Nice work, Handsome! You've been crying wolf so often we've come to look on this job as yours. I think it should be. Care to take over completely and drop everything else?"

Roger blinked. "Are you retiring?"

Cortland laughed. "You know what I mean. It's a full-time job from now on. I was talking to the A.C. about it this morning. He agreed we should have to assign one man with nothing else to worry him. Ready to play?"

"Of course I'll play."

It was a bright morning; a few clouds drifted sluggishly across the sky, and a gentle wind stirred the trees along the Embankment as Roger drove home. Mixed thoughts teased his mind. Of Peter; the dead man and woman; Morgan; his fear for his "wife and kids"; and of Janet and the boys. He was glad, in one way, that he would be able to give all his time to this case; sorry in another. Sorry chiefly because Janet would have to know; if he didn't tell her, she would first suspect and then become sure of the truth. Being the wife of a policeman in days when crimes of violence were increasing wasn't exactly easy. Janet had become increasingly nervous of late; and the Press reports of Lobo and the free use of a knife scared her.

He was suffering from reaction after the all-night session, too. He was really too tired to drive.

After talking to Morgan and breaking through that hard crust of resistance, he had felt on top of the world; the feeling had lingered while he was with the buoyant Cortland. Now, a change of mood set in. Lobo wasn't going to be easy to trace. It would be a long business, there was no telling how many more crimes Lobo or his men would commit. How many more Peters—

That was wallowing in sentiment.

He pulled up outside the Bell Street house just before one o'clock. Scoopy and Richard, both in their school blazers, came rushing out. Scoopy had a toy pistol in his hand, Richard had a thumb in his mouth and, tucked beneath his arm, a book. The book dropped, and fell open; it was a story of Red Riding Hood—and a wolf stared up at Roger.

He stood absolutely still.

"Can we go for a ride?" asked Scoopy, hopefully. "Just a *lickle* one."

"Er—not now, old chap. Sorry. I'm tired out."

"Oh, *please.*" Scoopy pleaded with insistent eyes, and Richard, taking out his thumb and examining it, reflected aloud and sadly that "Daddy's too tired." Janet came hurrying from the kitchen, and a sleek Talbot drew up outside the house.

In a flash, both boys were tearing toward the gate, crying: "Uncle Mark, Uncle Mark!"

Janet called: "Mark, take them round for ten minutes, will you?"

"I've no choice," the Talbot's driver called back. The boys were clambering into the seat next to him, chattering excitedly. He waved, and the car moved off.

39

"That couldn't have happened better," Janet said. "Roger, you look worn out. Have you had anything to eat?" Her voice was sharp.

"Er—yes. Canteen. I—"

"You're not going back this afternoon, are you?"

Roger grinned. "No. Night shift for a bit."

"Oh," said Janet. "I'm not sure that I like that. Anyhow we can talk about it later. I want you to be in bed before the boys get back." Yes, her voice was sharp. He supposed the strain was becoming too great for her.

Mark Lessing, closest and oldest friend of the Wests, kept the boys out for twenty minutes, and returned only just in time to drive them to school for the afternoon session. On his way back from there, he stopped at a newspaper shop for an early edition of the *Evening Cry*. The front page headlines were about the Hampstead murder; and Lobo. Roger was mentioned as being in charge of the investigations. Mark murmured to himself: "There won't be a chance for me in this job," and folded the paper, but sat in contemplation for a few minutes before he returned to Bell Street.

His interest in crime had started long before he had come to know Roger; they'd met when Roger was a young and hopeful detective sergeant. Four slim volumes of criminal cases and two thicker ones on criminal technology stood to Mark's credit; he was more than a dabbler in criminal investigation. He was also director of several companies, and a collector of old china, which he always claimed to be his first love. A bachelor of forty—a year and a half older than Roger—occasionally he had worked with Roger. This time, if he read the signs aright, his chief job would be to soothe and to reassure Janet; she needed reassuring.

She was in the kitchen.

" 'Lo, Jan. Where's the great man?"

"In bed—and he's going to stay there until he wakes up. I don't care who telephones him. Have you an evening paper, Mark?"

"Yes."

"What really happened last night? I missed the news on the radio. Was it very bad?"

"Yes. Pretty nasty." Mark handed her the paper, and she immediately saw the picture of Peter, beside his parents, on the front page; and she saw the name Lobo in one of the headlines. She read tensely, while Mark, interpreting the signs correctly, put on a kettle for tea.

Janet laid the paper aside.

"He's in charge of it all, now. Mark, Lobo frightens me."

"Others have, in the past," said Mark, "and Roger's always come out on top. That's the advantage of having a tidy little organization behind you. He isn't fighting by himself, you know." He spoke seriously; Janet was in no mood for superficial comfort. "He'll go all out on this, especially since he saw that boy—as he must have done by now. Jan, my sister was saying that she hadn't seen you for a long time. How about spending a week or two with her?"

"I can't take the boys away from school," Janet said. She smiled into Mark's face; he was an impressive-looking man, with clear-cut features, a rather sallow complexion and, to strangers at first meeting, an aloof manner and a haughty expression; more distinguished than handsome, the graying hair at his temples gave him a touch of dignity.

"And you wouldn't if you could! Well, I'm free for a bit. I'll stand by."

"He's going on night shift—he thinks there'll be more doing at night, with Lobo."

"Call it night and day, you'll be safer. Like me to move in, until it's over?"

"Can you?"

"Of course." He knew that she was nervous not only for Roger but also for herself and the boys. And from what he knew of Lobo, she had good reason.

5

Night Shift

Roger pushed open the door of his office and found Bill Sloan sitting at one of the five yellow desks, his feet up on a chair, a mass of papers in front of him, and, on another desk, an array of photographs.

"Working overtime?" Roger asked dryly.

"I couldn't miss this. If you want me on the Lobo job, you've only to ask Cortland. He's agreed that I can work with you."

"Good. What's the picture gallery for?"

Sloan stood up, and they looked at the photographs together. All were of men, most of villainous-looking men but some as ordinary as anyone who might sit next to you in a train. There were nineteen.

"All the six-feet-four-inchers we've got in Records," Sloan said. "Morgan told you that Tich, at the country house, was as big as Cortland, who is six-four. I thought you'd like to start on these, and if Morgan identifies one as Tich, it will give us a lead. If he doesn't, we can do the six-feet-three mob. Be more of them," he added. "All right?"

"Fine. What else is cooking?"

"We've put Taggart on to Ma Dingle. Remember him? That youngster from 13 Division who did a good job on the Waderson case. He'd applied for a transfer to the Yard, and I think he's as good as we can find. He's got a room in a house opposite Ma's. He's a big chap, too, and looks a docker to a T. All right?"

Roger nodded; trust Sloan!

"I told him that he might get something tonight, but I doubt if he will," Sloan said. "After last night's show, Lobo's men won't fancy going out too soon. He'll probably keep them in for a week or two, until the fuss has died down. The papers have had a Roman holiday on it," he added grimly. "We are not popular. Usual line—Lobo has been active for eighteen months, and the police are as far away from catching him as ever."

"We can ride that. Before this is over, we're going to get our knuckles rapped good and hard." Roger lit a cigarette. "But I don't think you're right about tonight. Lobo will know that his men have the jitters. What's the best thing to do, if you have a car smash or trouble with a forced landing? Drive on or go up again. Lobo will probably send most of his men out tonight."

"Hm. Possible." Sloan wasn't convinced.

"And the man we want first is the one who takes the packets round to the wolves. I've been thinking about Ma Dingle's. The Rose & Crown is almost opposite, isn't it?"

"Yes."

"And thinking about Lobo," Roger said. "He isn't

44

exactly popular with the gangs and the small fry. A lot of 'em can't earn a living because he's cornered so much of the market. We could probably safely look in at the Rose & Crown without anyone giving us away."

"I doubt it," Sloan said dubiously.

"What's on around there, these days?"

"Not much. It's been pretty quiet. There was that coining job, ten days ago—we found the den in Marsten Street, remember? Birds were flown. We could go and have a look at that, and pop into the pub on the way out. Suit you?"

"Yes, we'll do that."

Roger drove. On the way to the East End, they said very little. They had arranged with the Division to visit the coiners' den in Marsten Street, and would be treading on no one's toes. As they went through the silent city, with the tall gray buildings in utter darkness although it was not yet nine o'clock, Roger said: "Have you found Morgan's family?"

"No, not yet. I've left that to the Divisions."

"That's all right."

There was light and life, garish brightness, and not a little noise in the East End—near Aldgate Station and in the Mile End Road. Farther along, shops disappeared and houses lined the broad thoroughfare. They passed a huge concrete block, the Troy Cinema, and turned down a road on the right; Marsten Street. They had the keys to a small house, one of a terrace in that mean, narrow street. They went inside and looked round the dingy rooms; and at the tools, molds, furnace, and equipment, which had been left there by the police after the place had been raided. Ten minutes later, they left the house and drove to the Rose & Crown, a small public house on the corner by crossroads. The mean streets leading from the crossroads all looked exactly the same. They were lighted by gas, which burned dimly in the street lamps. Radio music came from dozens of little houses; a babble of talk and laughter from the pub itself.

Ma Dingle's, a lodginghouse of the cheapest type, could be seen from here. A lamppost was immediately outside it, lighting up the drab front door, which opened straight on to the pavement.

"Nicely placed," Roger said. "We'll go and have one." They pushed open the door of the crowded public bar, and were met by a fug of tobacco smoke, a strong smell of beer, a babble of talk which sounded three times as loud as it had outside. Two or three men glanced at the newcomers —and immediately stopped talking. Elbows poked gently into ribs, heads turned, silence fell for a moment upon everyone in turn—then talk started up again. But now it was forced. Roger grinned as he went to the bar, where a little man in shirt sleeves held four glasses in one hand and pulled the beer-tap handle with the other. He glanced up.

"You're busy tonight, Fred," said Roger.

"Yeh. Too busy. Got some customers we could do without." Fred had a spurious cultured accent, a drooping mustache and watery eyes. "What do you want?"

"Two brown ales."

"Well, I can't refuse to serve you," said Fred. "The law's the law. I always believe in obeying it, whether I like it or not." He pushed the four filled glasses to a burly docker standing next to Roger,

46

and then served the brown ales. "I haven't done anything, Mr. West."

"If you go on protesting like this, I'll think you have," said Roger. "But I've really come about something you haven't done."

Behind him, a man said: "If that ain't like the ruddy dicks!"

"You haven't told us all you could about the mob from Number 57," Roger said. "How much slush did you change for them, Fred?"

"I never changed any slush for anyone, this is an 'onest house, and you know it. Pity you don't go where there is some work for you to do."

"And where ought I to be now?" asked Roger.

"Never heard of 'Ampstead?"

"Oh, that job. Bad business." Roger shrugged. "It's a good thing for you and your friends, Fred, that we're short-handed at the Yard and the Divisions—if we weren't we shouldn't have to cut ourselves in two. Can you honestly tell me that you've never had anyone from Number 57?"

"Not to recognize them."

"What a liar you are." Roger drank. "But you sell good beer, Fred." He turned from the bar and surveyed the crowd; that would be expected of him. He recognized three old lags, men who were probably at work and would be picked up sooner or later for another lagging. Most of the others were dockers, stevedores, or foremen from the neighboring docks; several lascars huddled together in one corner and drank steadily. They were little, ugly, dark-skinned men. There weren't many women here; the Rose & Crown was as much club as pub, and women weren't encouraged. Two middle-aged and staid matrons were sipping brown ale in a corner, one of them smoking a long cigar.

A car passed outside, and went on.

Roger said to Sloan: "If we hear a car stop, we'll drink up and go. Have another?"

"My turn." Sloan went up to the bar, and a little man by the door, with a narrow face and a squint, motioned toward it with his right hand. Roger affected not to notice. The man motioned again, and Roger, knowing that several people were watching him covertly, paid no attention. The man with the squint went outside.

Sloan came back.

"Squinty Lowe wants to see me," Roger said.

"You can't trust him, you know."

Roger grinned. "We're agreed about that, but he may have something. We'll go when we've finished this one, whether the car's arrived or not."

"Right." They didn't hurry over their drinks, but smoked another cigarette before going, waving above the heads of the crowd to Fred. Even before the door closed behind them, the conversation in the public bar became freer and louder.

Squinty was standing by the window, in the shadows, only just visible.

"What is it?" asked Roger.

"You'll do right by me, 'Andsome, won't yet?" Squinty had a hoarse, throaty voice. "You wouldn't sell me aht, would yer?"

"No. But what I do depends on what you've got, Squinty."

"It's big, 'Andsome. If it wasn't, I'd 'ave told one o' the Division boys, but this is too big for them pikers. S'a fact. After Lobo, aincha?"

Roger kept his voice steady: "We're always after

Lobo. But Lobo doesn't let squirts like you know his business, Squinty."

"There's no need ter be rude." The little man tried to assume a lofty tone. "Listen, 'Andsome, I got sunnink for yer. I was at Bow Street s'mornin'. Didn't you see me?"

"No. What was the charge?"

"Nar be decent, 'Andsome! I 'aven't bin charged wiv' anyfink for monfs. S'a fact. Goin' strite, I am. No, I was up because I 'ad a whisper that one o' Lobo's men would be in the dock. So 'e was—remember the guy that wouldn't open 'is trap?"

Roger said quietly: "Squinty, if you've got something on Lobo, it will be worth plenty. Did you recognize the man?"

"That's exactly wot I want ter tell yer." The throaty voice was so faint now that Roger had to bend down to hear it; and warm, beery breath fanned his cheek. "Yes, I rekernized 'im. 'E doesn't live a farsand miles from 'ere, eivver, 'e—"

Then Sloan shouted: "*Roger!*"

The cry came loudly, smashing the quiet of the night, breaking across Squinty's words. Squinty drew back. Roger swung round toward Sloan, who was by the car, and saw a small man darting across the road, away from him. In the faint light from the sidelights of his car, he saw something glitter: a knife.

"After him!" cried Sloan.

The man was halfway across the road, swerving away from them, toward the crossroads. Squinty swung round and began to run in the opposite direction. The man with the knife veered right, with Sloan and Roger in pursuit; they could just hear the soft padding of his footsteps. His small figure cast a grotesquely large shadow. His feet looked enormous, like the feet of all Lobo's men. At the corner, Roger was a yard in front of Sloan.

He slowed down.

"We'll get him. Hurry!" Sloan gasped.

Roger said: "Keep after him." He turned and ran back. He could hear Squinty's footsteps as the copper's nark scurried from danger. The noise from the pub had stilled; the crowd had heard the shout. The door opened and a shaft of light shot out.

A man called: "Shut that blurry door!"

The door banged.

A hundred yards along the road, Squinty appeared beneath a lighted lamp, looking over his shoulder, as if he were frightened of being followed. Sloan's footsteps pounded in the distance.

Roger reached the car, wondering whether he had guessed right. Squinty drew near the dark stretch of Marsten Street, between two lamps—and then Roger saw another figure, crossing the road in Squinty's wake; a man with big feet.

Roger bellowed: *"Squinty! Squinty!"*

He pulled the front door of the car open, slid inside and let in the clutch; but with his back toward Squinty he couldn't see what was happening. He reversed to the corner and swung round. The headlights blazed out and showed Squinty, still running; and a man running after him.

The man behind Squinty raised his right arm; the flash of his knife showed in the headlamps' beams. The knife fell. Even above the roar of the engine, Roger fancied that he heard Squinty scream.

He saw him pitch forward on his face.

The man with the knife leaped over him and raced onward. He was less than seventy yards away. Between him and the main road there was one turning to the right, the side of the road he was already on. He ran with his head forward, the knife still in his hand and moving with the movements of his arm; the knife no longer glistened.

Squinty's body loomed up, a dark shape; and fell behind.

The man swung round the corner.

Roger took the turning wide, headlights shone on the tiny houses, making the windows gleam. A man and a girl came walking toward the car. The girl drew back, her arms up, her face terrified. The little man sped past them; neither made any attempt to stop him. But the killer couldn't escape, hadn't a chance against the car.

Ten yards separated them.

Roger jammed on the brakes and pushed open the door at the same time. The door banged back. He leaped out, a few feet behind his quarry. The headlights still showed everything vividly. The man was on the half-turn, his knife hand raised to strike again.

Roger went down, hands stretched out for the man's ankles, caught one and pulled. The man fell, the knife hit the pavement and rattled loudly. Roger maintained his grip, scrambled nearer, shifted his hold to the man's right arm.

Triumph . . .

Then Roger heard a soft, padding sound behind him. He screwed his head round, in time to see another man, with his right arm raised. He didn't know whether the weapon was a knife or a bludgeon. He had time to shout once—and then a

51

heavy blow fell on the back of his head. His grip on the killer's arm relaxed. He didn't lose consciousness, but was dazed and lay still, fearful.

He heard a car move off: his own car.

6

Laughing Stock

A girl knelt by Roger's side, her hands moving slowly about his head. He felt pain when she pressed just above the nape of the neck. A man was holding his right hand, thumb on the pulse. Other people were approaching, and a police whistle sounded.

"I hope he's okay," the girl said.

"Sure, he's fine. Wonder who—"

The police whistle sounded again, and it was possible to distinguish the heavy thump of the policeman's footsteps. By the time he arrived, a little crowd had gathered round Roger. The doors of the nearby houses were open, and people stood in the doorways or at the windows, dubious about coming farther; just watching.

Roger raised his head.

"Look, he's coming round."

"I'm all right. Thanks."

The man and the girl helped him to sit up, as the constable drew near, shining his torch.

"What's all this?"

Roger said: "Get a call out for a Morris twelve, black saloon, number SY 812, and hurry."

"*What* number?"

"Yes, you're right, a Yard car—SY 812. There are two men in it—Lobo's men?"

The girl gasped: "Lobo!"

The crowd was growing. Roger sat against the wall of a house, beneath a lighted window. A car pulled up and added the beam of its headlights to the glow: Roger closed his eyes against the glare.

A man on the fringe of the crowd called: "Strike a light! That's West."

"'Oo?"

"'Andsome West—of the Yard!" The man began to laugh, others tittered, the girl said indignantly that it was nothing to laugh at, look at his head.

"That's just wot I am larfin' at, duckie. Caught a proper packet, 'Andsome 'as." The tittering became deep-throated laughter, the laughter of malicious enjoyment. Roger's right hand strayed to the back of his head, and he felt the warm blood. His head ached, but apart from feeling sick, he was all right. He stood up, and the girl helped him. He swayed. The policeman had gone hurrying off, but two others were approaching.

Then Sloan arrived.

"Did you find Squinty?" Roger asked.

"Yes. He's had it." Sloan's voice was harsh. "Sergeant, clear these laughing hyenas away." He glowered round at the chortling men on the fringe of the crowd. "How is it, Roger?"

"I'll do. Who's with Squinty?"

"Two men off the beat." Sloan didn't ask pointless questions, and the uniformed men cleared the crowd; or at least kept the people on the move. The girl's boyfriend began to agitate for her to come away. Sloan took their names and addresses, as well as a brief statement. Two police cars arrived, and set off immediately on a hunt for Roger's car. The tall man who had started the laughter was holding a little meeting farther along the road, telling his crowd what a joke it was—Handsome West knocked out and his car stolen. Someone said: "Murder," and the joke seemed to turn sour.

By half-past ten, Squinty was in the morgue attached to Divisional Headquarters; and outwardly, everything was normal in the East End.

The police surgeon, a squat, dour man, patted down the sticking plaster on the back of Roger's head, and said there was nothing to worry about, except a headache. He packed up his kit, and left the office of the Divisional Superintendent. On the desk was the knife which the first man had dropped; the only clue. The Superintendent had little to say, but sent for some tea. It arrived in large, thick mugs, was dark brown and sickly sweet.

Sloan came in.

"Nothing much doing," he said glumly. "I lost my chap—sorry, Roger, he showed me a clean pair of heels. What the devil happened your end?"

"I thought there might be two of them, I didn't reckon on the third."

"What made you think there were two?"

Roger shrugged. "I couldn't see why there should be one by himself, making so much noise that we couldn't miss him. I thought there might be another watching Squinty."

Sloan said: "Hmm."

Roger went on: "They had someone at Bow Street who knew Squinty was there. They also knew Squinty could name Morgan, and that he was a nark. So they watched him, and when he waited outside the pub for us, went for him. They probably thought we went to the Rose & Crown to see him."

The Superintendent said: "They're getting too clever. And we haven't a clue."

"Oh, haven't—" began Sloan.

"We shall have." Roger broke in, and Sloan stopped; not even the Divisional Super was to know what they had learned about Ma Dingle's place. "We'd better get back to the Yard, Bill."

"You don't want to see Squinty?"

"No. What was the wound like?"

"Neck. Those knives are like razors."

"Yes. And from now on, we're going to carry a gun apiece. Any news hounds downstairs?"

"Shoals of them."

"Oh, well, let's face 'em."

The hall of the police station was crowded with Fleet Street men, most of them familiar and usually friendly to Roger. They greeted him noisily.

A gangling man with his hat on the back of his head, said: "Had a nasty crack, Handsome?"

"Nothing to worry about, you needn't make a hero out of me."

The man laughed. "Okay, we won't. Going to buy a new car?"

There was a general chuckle. That car loss was going to take some living down.

"That's right, rub it in. You can get just what

happened from the Back Room Inspector. I'm in a hurry. You know it was Lobo's men, I suppose?"

"Sure?" Half a dozen put the question.

"Dead sure."

"Why, that's fine. Anything we can do..."

A car was waiting for Roger outside, a sergeant drove him and Sloan back to the Yard. Roger was glad that he passed no one in the wide, echoing passages. The photographs were still laid out on the desk, and he studied them again, rubbing his chin. It was midnight. He scribbled out a report in longhand, put it in the basket on his desk for the typist next morning, and said: "We'll go and see Morgan, I think. They haven't moved him to Brixton yet, have they?"

"No, he's across at the Row."

With the nineteen photographs under his arm, Roger led the way to Cannon Row. The night-duty sergeant was drinking a cup of tea; everyone seemed to be drinking tea. He called a constable, who walked along the cell passage, keys jangling. Morgan was in the end cell, apparently asleep, lying on his back with his hands clasped on his chest. He stirred as the keys jangled and scraped in the lock. By the time the two Yard men were inside, he was blinking up at them.

"Want—want me, guv'nor?"

"Yes, Morgan. How are your eyes?"

"Eyes? They're okay. Why, what did you think was the matter with them?"

"I want you to have a look at these," Roger said. He handed the bundle of photographs to Morgan as the creeper sat up. Morgan looked intently at them, without raising any protest or arguing. He put one after the other aside, shaking his head.

57

Roger watched him closely; Morgan couldn't be trusted, might pass one over although he recognized the man; but he would give himself away, under close scrutiny. He turned down sixteen of them, without batting an eyelid; then stopped at the seventeenth. He glanced upward, and drew in his breath; then looked downward, as if he were going to refuse to speak again. Roger said nothing, Sloan moved.

Morgan said: "That's Tich. You know, Tich."

"It's building up," Sloan said, tautly.

"If we can believe him."

"He's too scared of the rope to play the fool now. Didn't you see the way he started when he first saw that one?"

Roger said, "Yes. Probably you're right."

The man whom Morgan had picked out was a beetle-browed giant, and even in the full-face photograph, his cauliflower ears showed up, thick and ugly. He had a thin little mouth and a flattened nose. They went to *Records*, for his dossier. His name was Carney; he had served three sentences, the last five years ago, for breaking and entering, one for robbery with violence. There was no record of what he had done during the past five years; he'd either run straight or fooled the police.

His last known address was Ma Dingle's.

"Better pay her a visit," Sloan said.

"No, not yet."

"It can't do any harm. Lobo will think that Squinty squealed before he was killed. It won't affect Morgan, or his family. No need to be squeamish now."

Roger said: "You've got it all wrong, Bill. I'm not

squeamish about anything in this job. But if Ma Dingle's deeply involved, she'll be more use to us later. We want to catch that messenger, he's important. Find out from Taggart if two little men are still with her, that's the first job."

"He won't report until morning."

"That's time enough. Better find someone else to help him, Bill. He can't do night and day shift, and Ma's will have to be watched all the time. I—"

The telephone bell rang on his desk.

He pulled the instrument toward him. "Hallo?" He waited. "Yes...Oh, you've found it, have you? Is it all right?...Well, that's something....Yes, drive it round for me, will you?"

He rang off.

"So they've got your car," Sloan said superfluously.

"And perhaps they've given us another line," said Roger slowly. "It was stranded at Hounslow, Heath—near the barracks. Remember that Morgan had a return ticket to Hounslow? We'll tackle him about that in the morning. Get the Hounslow police on the line for me, will you?"

Sloan put in the call; Roger read through Tich Carney's record again. The man had been a docker, and had drifted into crime during the depression days of the early thirties; that depression had a lot to answer for, it had given birth to as much crime as either of the wars, although no one ever thought of saying so.

There was a note, saying: "The man has good intelligence, a quick, alert mind, although his appearance and general manner are uncouth." That was worth knowing.

"Hounslow," Sloan said.

"Thanks. . . . Yes, West here. . . . Thanks, there is an urgent job you can do for us. I'm sending up a photograph and dossier of a man named Carney, a big chap, six feet four inches. He might be living somewhere in your district. . . . Yes, it's urgent, the Lobo job." He smiled. "We all do!"

"I'll send a messenger over at once," said Sloan. "What else are you going to do tonight, Roger?"

Roger said: "I want to find out where Lobo's been busy."

"So you still think he'll have a night out."

"You can kick me if he doesn't, Bill."

Between the hours of two-thirty and four-thirty, that morning, there were thirty-one burglaries in the Greater London district; twenty-five of them had all the hallmarks of a Lobo job. No one was hurt; the haul was comparatively small. It had obviously been a gesture of defiance.

No one was caught.

Morgan said he'd been out that week to do some jobs at Hounslow, gone by Southern Region train, and returned by bus. That was disappointing. There was no record of Carney at Hounslow, but the local police promised to study the photograph during the day. That was at half-past seven in the morning. As Roger put the telephone back on its cradle, Sloan came in with a sheaf of newspapers.

Roger groaned. "Must you?"

"They've done you proud," Sloan grimaced.

"I know. Lobo makes off in Yard man's car. Won't the public love it? Won't Chatsworth be pleased in the morning? Not to mention Cortland." Roger opened the *Daily Photo*, and winced. There were

60

pictures of his car; of himself; even of the sticking plaster on the back of his head. The headlines smirked at him. He glanced through the other papers. By far the worst was *The Record;* the editor had a personal grievance, for his house had been ransacked, months before, by a Lobo man. He had written a second, brief, biting editorial:

We all know that Scotland Yard is overworked. We are constantly being told that police control of traffic is a most important part of their duties. We wonder whether Chief Inspector West, whose car was used by a murderer in a brutal crime committed under the eyes of the police, thinks that the traffic control is satisfactory. This latest daring attack by a sinister gang shows up the ineffectiveness of the police countermeasures against the crime wave. We suggest that they spend less time on harassing respectable citizens over minor traffic offenses, and more time hunting down these ruthless murderers.

Sloan scanned it, and shrugged. "He's working it up nicely. Lobo hasn't paid anyone a second visit yet, has he?"

"And will he please start on a certain editor?" Roger chuckled, and yawned. "Bill, he's more than half justified. We've done a lousy job on Lobo. But it's reaching its climax, we'll see it through before long. Now I think I'll go home."

Janet glanced at the front page of the *Daily Photo,* and exclaimed: "Look!"

Mark, who was watching the toast, turned and saw the picture of the back of Roger's head.

"I knew it would be like this. I shan't have a minute's peace until this case is finished."

Mark said: "You know, if you go on like this, Roger will start wishing he hadn't got to come home."

"Nonsense!"

"It isn't nonsense. You know what he's like on a big job. He thinks, eats, and sleeps the case, and he likes to talk it over with you. If you're going to fly into hysterics every time he gets his name in the papers—"

"Who's flying into hysterics?"

"You're not far from it."

"You're worse than Roger! I hate this case, his job, Scotland Yard, everything to do with it. I tell you I can't stand it if this goes on much longer. I'm never sure whether he'll come back. *Look!* This happened just after a murder, he was actually attacked by a murderer!"

"You've got to pull yourself together, Jan. I can't understand you, you're not usually—"

"It's always like this. A few days of peace, and then some damnable thing crops up. He doesn't get half enough sleep. He hasn't had a day off for weeks, Sundays and Mondays are all the same to him. The boys hardly set eyes on him. He'll crack up, and we—Mark! The *toast!*"

Flames were blazing up from the gas grill. Mark grabbed the handle of the toaster, winced, pulled it out, and dropped it. Burning black toast fell to the coconut matting on the floor. They bent down to grab it, and their heads banged together. Janet gasped, stood up, and kicked the toast under the sink. Smoke and the smell of burning filled the small, spick-and-span kitchen.

Janet turned and ran out of the room. Halfway along the passage from the stairs, Scoopy called: "Mummy. Mummy, I—"

He broke off; and soon appeared in the kitchen doorway, looking puzzled and grave.

"Mummy's crying," he announced. "Did you say something nasty to her?"

"The toast burned, old chap. It was my fault."

"She *often* burns the toast," said Scoopy simply. "I wonder why she's crying." He caught sight of the *Daily Photo*. "Look, that's Daddy's car!" He grabbed the paper and swung round, wildly excited. "Richard. Rich! Daddy's car is in the paper, come and see!"

Upstairs, Janet shouted at Richard: "Go away, don't pester me. Go away!"

Mark frowned and brushed his hair out of his eyes, and then saw that the front door was open. Roger came in. Scoopy had reached the foot of the stairs and was on the way up; he didn't see Roger, who closed the door quietly and came along to the kitchen. He made no comment about the smell of burning, his face was set, his eyes bloodshot.

"I was on the porch. How long has Janet been going on like that?"

"When did you come in?"

"There was some talk about hysterics."

"Then you heard most of it," said Mark. "I don't get it, Roger, she isn't usually like this."

"No. Only on a morning when I've a head like a kicking horse."

"The picture of your head patched up started the show," Mark pointed out. "It can't be much fun for Janet, and you don't seem to have had a lot of time off lately."

"I haven't. If we had two hundred more men in the C.I.D. branch we'd be able to live like human beings. But I can't understand Janet. She wouldn't take a holiday without me, this year, nothing would move her. Now it's my fault that she didn't go away." He forced a smile. "I'll go up and see her."

"If I were you I'd leave her alone for a bit," Mark said. "I—hallo, telephone. Shall I go?"

"Have another shot at the toast," said Roger. He went off , unsmiling. Scoopy and Richard were on the landing, pages of the *Daily Photo* spread about them. Scoopy was spelling out the words of the comic strip, Richard was gurgling with laughter for some obscure reason certainly not connected with the cartoons. The telephone went on and on ringing until Roger crossed to the sitting room and snatched it up. Just before he'd left Scotland Yard, the first report of Lobo activities had come in; this was probably to report more.

"Hallo?"

A woman said: "May I speak with Mrs. West, please."

"Can I take a message? She's engaged."

"Who is that?"

"Roger West speaking."

There was a pause; Roger thought of Janet and the outburst, heard Richard's gurgling laughter, and Scoopy calling "no!" in an agonized voice. So Richard had been plotting some practical joke and was now reaping the harvest of it, for he cried out in turn, "Don't hit me!"

"Chief *Inspector* West?" asked the woman. She had a lilting voice; a voice to remember and to like, and he imagined that she was young.

"That's right."

"I'm thrilled to speak to you," said the woman, and Roger frowned; she was going to gush, he disliked gushing. "I really am delighted, Inspector. I didn't think you'd be at home. You probably know me, though, I've had several conversations with your wife on the telephone. She sounds so charming. But, of course, she must be charming. A talented detective like you wouldn't marry an ordinary woman, would he?"

She wasn't simply gushing; Roger concentrated, the quarrel between the boys sounding loud in the distance.

"Who are you?" he asked. "And what message can I give to my wife?"

"My name is Lobo. *Surely* Mrs. West has told you about our conversations. *Miss* Lobo. And I've telephoned two or three times recently, just to tell her that she really must persuade you to take more rest. No one can go on working at your pressure without breaking down, or meeting with and accident or something like that. I know she would hate you to get hurt. I'm really disappointed that she hasn't said anything to you about it. Perhaps it's because you're so seldom home, and there are so many things to do when you have an hour with the family. How are your two little boys, by the way?"

Roger said: "They're fine, thanks." He wanted her to go on; but his knuckles were white where he gripped the telephone.

"I'm so glad. Boys are boisterous but such good fun. Did you hear about that poor child whose parents were killed last night? It must be terrible to be orphaned, mustn't it? So final, if you can understand me."

Janet screamed: "Stop fighting. *Stop fighting!*"

Mark appeared in the doorway. Roger pointed to the telephone, then to the window, made faces at him. Mark started, puzzled—then suddenly realized that Roger wanted the call traced, wanted him to call the Yard from next door. He ran out. Scoopy and Richard came hurrying downstairs, silent, a little scared.

"So the message I'd like you to give Mrs. West is just that she must keep you home more often—especially at night," said the woman with the lilting voice. "I must go now—or you'll find out where I'm calling from, won't you?"

7

News of Carney

Mark hadn't reached the gate. Roger tapped at the window, and beckoned as he put the receiver down. Mark came hurrying back, Scoopy and Richard whispered their secrets in the hall. "She's gone," Roger said, as Mark came in.

"Who's she?"

"Half the cause of Janet's trouble, I think," Roger said. "Aren't the boys gong to school today?"

"It's *Saturday*," came in chorus.

"Of course it is, I forgot. Stay down here and amuse Uncle Mark for a few minutes."

Roger went upstairs, and found Janet lying across the bed, her face buried in her arms. He closed the door quietly. She wasn't crying now. He went to her and rested a hand on her shoulder. "How often has Lobo's woman telephoned, Janet?"

She stiffened and raised her head.

"You know?"

"She came through just now. Why didn't you tell me you were being worried?"

"I didn't want to, you've so much on your mind."

Janet sat up, and groped for a handkerchief; he gave her one. "She's called me three times in the last two days. Always from a kiosk, it wasn't any use having the call traced. I knew that, or I would have called the office. What—what did she say?"

"Pretty much the same stuff she's said to you, I fancy. It's only an effort to get me jittery."

Janet sniffed. "Yes, of course. I've tired to tell myself that, but—Roger, I just can't stand this pressure any more. I hate being like this, shouting at the boys, always being in a bad temper, but—I can't help myself. You're so tired when you get home, or else you bring work with you. We never spend time together, it's work, work, work. And it's no use pretending. Lobo scares me. When that woman called herself Miss Lobo, I nearly dropped the telephone. I hate the boys' picture books with wolves in them. It's becoming an obsession, and—"

She began to cry again.

"It won't last long," he assured her gently. "Jan, why don't you go away for a bit, and take the boys? There's nothing I can do about it, I've got to go on working until we catch Lobo."

"I'm going to stay here. If anything happens, at least I'll be where I ought to be."

"I don't get it, Jan. There have been worse jobs than Lobo. You were going to pieces before he became really savage—long before the murders. Until then, it was just another job, and it got you down. Is there anything else?"

"No. No, it's just that my nerves are on edge all the time. I'll be all right. Mark's promised to move in, until you've caught Lobo. I'll feel safer if there's a man in the house at night. I can't rely on you."

It didn't sound like Janet speaking. He felt suddenly resentful, and his head throbbed.

She stood up and went to look at herself in the
mirror. "Oh, I look dreadful! Roger, go down and
apologize to Mark for me, and tell him I'll be down
in a few minutes."

"Right." His resentment melted. He put his
hands on her shoulders and drew her to him; and
she resisted. Not strongly; no more than she had
done a dozen times in the past, at the beginning or
even near the end of a tiff. But this was more than
a tiff. He wanted her to yield against him, and she
held herself stiff. Even when he kissed her, there
was no response. He forced himself to pull her hair
gently, an old intimate gesture, and hurried downstairs. The boys were hard at work on a train set
which Scoopy had managed to keep in fair repair
since Christmas.

"How is she?" asked Mark.

"She'll be down in a minute. It was that damned
woman who telephoned with some nonsense
threats. One more reason for wanting to get Lobo.
Er—Mark."

"Yes?"

"I'm very glad you're staying. Thanks. If you
think there's anything else I can do, tell me. I have
been away a lot lately. Too much. I suppose, in a
way, Janet's jealous of the Yard."

"That's understandable, isn't it?"

Roger said: "I suppose it is."

Memory of those few minutes in the bedroom
worried him. The daytime noises were unfamiliar,
while he lay in bed trying to sleep. The vacuum
droning, the boys playing in the garden, hushed
now and again when Janet or Mark called out to

them. But there was no real quiet. He was a long time getting to sleep, and he kept thinking about the way Janet had stiffened when he had tried to kiss her. It went deeper than ordinary nervousness; Janet had lived through too many dangerous periods to be affected like this.

Was it just that she was tired? It must be. Work had to come first; it was absurd to think that Janet was jealous of the Yard. True, they'd spent only two evenings together during the past three weeks, and he was often home late and always rushing off next morning. Get Lobo settled, and perhaps things would ease off.

At four, when he woke, Janet was out with the boys; she wouldn't be back until six. His resentment flared up; he hoped he hid it from Mark.

He was out of the house by five o'clock, on edge to get to the Yard before the day was over. Finish the job. Then worry about Janet.

He went first to his own room. There, Chief Inspector Eddie Day, one of the four men with whom he shared the office, sat at his desk and brooded over some counterfeit five-pound notes. Eddie was a specialist on forgery, and he liked to have a watchmaker's glass screwed into one eye. He was a big man, with a barrel-like stomach, large fat face, conical-shaped head, and small feet. He had protruding teeth, thin gingery hair, and nothing could ever disguise the fact that he had been born within the sound of Bow Bells; his Cockney was as native as any East Ender's, for all his care with his aspirates.

"Hallo, Eddie."

Day took the glass from his eye.

"So you *have* come in," he said. "I've been wondering what's got into you, Handsome. Thought you'd be around, after what happened last night."

"Who's on the warpath?"

"Why, Chatty! Come storming in, half an hour ago, and *I* couldn't tell him where you were. I did my best for you, Handsome, said you'd had a nasty biff last night, maybe you weren't feeling so good. He's pretty mad, and"—Eddie sniffed—"come to think of it, there's reason, isn't there? Fancy letting Lobo drive off in your own car."

"Yes, fancy." It would be easy to get mad at Eddie. Roger went out.

Cortland was alone in his office; he looked up and growled: "And about time." Roger sat down, opposite him. "Had the A.C. on the warpath. He doesn't like these requests for carrying guns."

"Well, I'm going to carry one." Roger offered cigarettes. "What he really means is that the newspapers have upset him, and the Home Office is probably telling him that something must be done. What's cooking?"

"The only two things worth knowing came from Hounslow. They think they know the man Carney. Not on their records, or we'd have him down for that, but the photograph rang a bell with two or three of their men. I told them you'd be there some time this evening. Better call them if you want to go somewhere else."

"I'll go out there. Anything from Taggart?"

"Your two little men are still at Ma Dingle's. They spent a couple of hours at the Rose & Crown at lunchtime. No, they didn't go out last night."

"Where's Chatty now?"

"He won't be in again today—only looked in for

half an hour to blow off steam. He approved of you concentrating on Lobo, but he wants results."

"Did you ever know a time when he didn't? And don't we?"

Cortland looked at him curiously.

"Lobo's got under your skin, hasn't he?"

"In more ways than one. And this is a formal request for a special watch to be kept on Bell Street. They've been worrying my wife with threatening telephone calls."

"Oh, *have* they? You can tell her she needn't worry, Roger. Sorry about it. I—" Cortland broke off as the telephone rang; it was his habit never to say a word to anyone with him, once the telephone had started ringing, until he'd finished with the caller. "Cortland . . . Yes, he's in the office. . . ."

Roger took the telephone.

A man said: "It's Bray of Hounslow, here. I think we've traced your man, Carney. He lives at a country house, not far from Feltham, just on the fringe of our district. He doesn't call himself Carney, he's known as Tich Smith. Shall I make preparations for a raid?"

"Not yet, please." Roger was urgent. "I'll be right there."

Roger first noticed the car on the road between Brentford and Isleworth. He couldn't very well miss it. A gleaming Chrysler convertible, painted pale blue, it purred past him with a woman at the wheel. Even if the car had been unremarkable, he would have looked twice at the woman. You saw a woman like that perhaps once or twice a year; caught a glimpse of her, and she was gone, never quite forgotten but only half-remembered. Beauty,

72

poise, mastery of the car, all combined to make him notice her; so did her hat, a ridiculous thing which seemed to be made wholly of feathers. A cigarette was white against her red lips, and the eye toward him was narrowed, as if to prevent the smoke from getting into it.

He saw the car again, parked near Pears' Soap Factory, at Isleworth. She was opposite a newspaper shop, reading a newspaper. That was a reasonable enough explanation of her stopping there. He tried not to look at her, but couldn't resist a swift glance; and she was looking at him. She didn't smile, yet contrived to be provocative as she peered at him over the top of the newspaper.

He drove on; and thought of Janet.

He didn't see the blue Chrysler again for some time.

Bray, the Hounslow Superintendent, was a big, tidy man, with a large square jaw and a quiet, countryman's voice. He had a comprehensive report ready, typed in triplicate. The house where "Tich Smith" lived was called Morden Lodge. It lay between the Great West Road and Hounslow Heath, and was a hundred yards from a by-road. Several acres of overgrown, weedy grassland, neglected trees, and stunted shrubs surrounded it. There was an orchard, which was carefully tended; Morden Lodge had started as the country home of a wealthy man, had become a hotel, then the house of a market-gardener, then a fruit farm. Just before the war it had been sold to a man named Paterson, a widower, who lived there with his unmarried daughter. Carney appeared to be the odd-job man at the house. There were two other menservants, whose wives also worked there—so there was no excuse for the neglect in the grounds.

Paterson was a jewel merchant in a big way, and traveled to London three or four days each week. A jewel merchant might well be involved in Lobo's jobs, to dispose of the stolen gems.

The household ran three cars. It didn't occur to Roger to ask whether one of them was a blue Chrysler.

Since tracing Carney, Bray had arranged for the house to be watched, sending two men to dig up the roadway nearby, but not too close to rouse suspicions.

"I think we might raid it soon," Bray said.

"Yes, but we can wait a bit." Everyone was in too much of a hurry. "I'd rather watch everyone who comes out of the place, find out more about Paterson and his daughter, that kind of thing. We haven't got much to go on yet."

Bray looked disappointed and disapproving.

"Do you know how long Carney's been there?" asked Roger.

"For some time—a year or two, at least. What's the objection to picking him up right away?"

"We could only hold him on suspicion, and if we do that, we'll warn everyone else connected with the business. We can make sure they don't leave in a hurry, that's our first job. If there's any sign of a general move away from the place, pick 'em up. It means having the grounds watched, of course, can you manage the men for that? I'll look after the trailing."

"I'll do whatever's necessary."

"Thanks. Now I'd like to borrow a man who can take me round," said Roger. "I'd like to know the approaches to the house, where it can best be watched from—the usual stuff."

"I'll get someone." Bray pressed a bell-push. "Here's a map of the house and grounds, I had it drawn this afternoon. All approaches are clearly marked there."

"You're good," said Roger, warmly. "Thanks."

Bray thawed....

Roger drove, a lanky Hounslow plain-clothes man sat next to him. Morden Lodge was fringed by trees, and could be seen from the road only through gaps in a tall hawthorn hedge. It looked a monstrosity in the evening light; Victorian elegance at its worst, with two red-brick turrets, heavy gables, big ugly windows. On one side of the house were stables, which the Hounslow man said were still used for horses; they kept four. The garage was on the other side, and couldn't be seen from the winding road. By-roads surrounded the seven unkempt acres, and three gates led from the grounds to the roads; each was suitable for motor traffic.

After making a complete circuit, they approached the front entrance, where a pair of white gates, in need of paint, stood open. Farther along a brazier glowed red and friendly in the gathering gloom. Bray had been wrong there; if Paterson had a guilty conscience, those pseudo-workmen would cry suspicion.

Roger caught a glimpse of a car turning from the distant main road, but it was soon lost to sight. He couldn't hear the car approaching, so switched on his headlights; the headlights of the other car shone out immediately. He dipped his, and pulled well into the side of the road. The other car came

75

into sight. Dusk shadowed its light blue and partly hid the woman at the wheel.

The red tip of a cigarette glowed near her mouth.

"That's the daughter," said the Hounslow man as the car passed them. "She's hot stuff. I happen to know, because—"

He didn't finish, for a rending crash from behind them cut across his words. Brakes squealed, and as Roger jammed on his, a shot rang out.

8

Beauty in Distress

Roger flung the door open and jumped out, saw the ditch by the side of the road just in time, cleared it, and grabbed the hedge to save himself from falling backwards. The noise had stopped; the silence seemed sinister. He scrambled along by the hedge until he was past the car, then jumped to the road. Precious seconds had been wasted. The Hounslow man was only now getting out of the car; hurry, man! Roger ran toward the bend in the road which hid the blue Chrysler from him. The sudden exertion brought a blinding flash of pain across his head. It went as quickly as it had come, but left a dull ache. He rounded the corner.

The Chrysler blocked the road, a sleek blue shape with the front wheels in the ditch; and the driver leaning back, her eyes closed, her head drooping forward. The detective ran heavily behind him; and someone else was running, across the grounds of Morden Lodge. In the headlights, Roger caught a glimpse of a tall, thin, youthful-looking figure, who turned his red head; then the thick hedge got in the way, and he was hidden from sight.

There was smoke in the car. Fire?

Roger reached it and glanced inside; a cigarette lay on the woman's knees, the tweed of her skirt was smouldering.

"Did you see that fellow?" the Hounslow man asked in a gasping voice.

"Yes, a redhead. See if you—"

Before he could finish, two cyclists drew up; they were dressed as workmen, but he knew they were Bray's men.

He pulled open the door of the Chrysler.

"All of you, after that gunman," Roger pointed. His guide exclaimed: "This way," and began to run. The two cyclists followed him, glancing curiously at the Chrysler, the girl, and the smoke.

"Here!" Roger called. The nearest man nearly fell off his machine. "Take this." Roger handed him his automatic. The man took it without a word, and pedaled off. The gunman might be caught, the superior speed of the cyclists might just do the trick. Roger told himself that but for the throbbing ache in his head, he would have snatched a machine and led the chase; but would he?

He took the driver's cigarette away. It was half smoked and one end was stained with lipstick. He tossed it into the road. A small dark hole in the gray tweed still smoldered. He rubbed the blackened spot with his forefinger, and the woman didn't move. There was a faint overcheck of green and blue on the gray material. Woman, or girl? She looked young, and the glimpse he had caught of her when she passed him on the road hadn't lied; she was beautiful.

Was she hurt?

He saw the bullet hole in the roof the car. The driving window was down, the other closed; so the bullet had come through the one opening. It had been fired by someone standing below the level of the road or it wouldn't have hit the roof, and it certainly hadn't touched her, there was no injury to her face or head, no sign of blood. She'd probably banged her head on the windscreen and been knocked out. He walked round the car; there was just room for him to squeeze past, behind it. The front wheels had lodged at a spot where the ditch was deep and wide.

Only a man crouching in the ditch could have fired that shot. He saw that there was a big stone, at the side of the near-side wheel; that explained the crash. When she had lost control of the wheel, the Chrysler had turned into that stone. The fender was crumpled; there seemed no other damage, but they would have to get a breakdown van to move the car.

She sat with her chin on her breast, and he thought her eyes flickered. She had dark hair, dark eyebrows, dark lashes which swept her cheeks. She breathed gently; he watched the rise and fall of her breast and the movement of her lips. Her make-up was perfect; she looked perfection. Yes, she could have been thrown against the windscreen and knocked out, then swayed backward. But there was no sign of bruising on her forehead. The jolt might have ricked her neck, causing unconsciousness.

The gathering dusk softened the lines of her face, adding beauty to beauty.

He heard nothing, now, except the quiet rustlings of birds and creatures of the hedgerows and the fields. All sounds of pursuit had gone; he'd almost forgotten the chase. No one else appeared to have heard the shot; that was odd, because the house wasn't so far away. Perhaps they were used to shooting rabbits or pigeons; a shot was less remarkable in the country than in a town. This was the country, although it was close to one of the most densely populated dormitory suburbs of London.

He lit a cigarette.

The girl's eyes flickered again, and this time she raised her head and blinked. She didn't look at him, but peered straight ahead. Her eyes were dazed, her expression was blank—until suddenly she started, and fear blazed up in her eyes; or what he took for fear, in that half-light. She darted a glance away from him, then toward him—and she raised her hands, as if to fend off another attack.

Roger said: "It's all right."

She didn't speak, but sat upright and smoothed down her skirts; odd, how women always did that, it was almost a reflex action. Then her hands strayed to her hair, and the ridiculous hat, with its gay, colorful feathers. Why was she wearing a dressy hat with a tweed suit?

"I—I was shot at," she said.

"Yes, some men are chasing the beggar, and he certainly won't come back. Relax."

She didn't relax, but looked round her as if surprised that she was in the ditch. She saw the buckled fender, and grimaced, then fumbled for her handbag. He offered her his case, and thumbed his lighter. Her hands were pale, slim, with long fingers, the nails painted pink.

80

"Thank you."

"Would you like a drink?" asked Roger, and put his hand to his hip pocket, for his whisky flask.

"No. No, I'm all right. I was so scared." She gave a little, forced laugh; but it was as attractive as everything else about her. "I could kick myself for crashing the car! He jumped up from the ditch, I didn't realize anyone was there until he fired at me."

"I shouldn't worry too much about the car."

"You would if it were yours and you'd only had it for ten days!" She laughed more naturally, but ruefully. "I suppose I ought to be thankful it's no worse."

"Some people would really think being fired at was more important than crumpling a wing," Roger said dryly. "Do you know who it was?"

"Heavens, no!"

"So a perfect stranger popped out of the ditch and loosed a round at you. After some target practice, I presume."

She frowned. "I don't understand you."

"It's easy to understand," Roger said. "I think you recognized him. Who hates you well enough to want to murder you, Miss Paterson?"

She drew deeply at the cigarette, held the smoke for a few seconds, then let it trickle slowly between her lips. Her eyes were half closed; and because the light was getting worse, he found it difficult to judge her expression. Then she stretched out her hand and touched the handle of the door.

"I think I'd better get out."

"You'll find it easier on the other side, this is too near the ditch." He watched her slide across the seats and open the other door. When he reached that side of the car, she was standing upright, with a hand resting on the door, and looking along the winding road. The silence was broken by a distant hum of traffic, but there were no nearer sounds. By then, the Hounslow men had either succeeded or failed and one of them should soon be back with the news.

"Who was it?" asked Roger.

"I don't know. Who are you?"

"My name is West. I was passing by when I heard the shooting, and thought I'd better come and see what it was all about. Why don't you tell the truth? You know who it was."

"I don't like being called a liar," said Miss Paterson. But he could see her face more clearly now that she was out of the car; she was smiling, as if he amused and interested her.

Roger shrugged. "All right, keep up the pretense if you think it's a good idea. Have you jilted any passionate young men lately?"

She laughed. "No more than usual."

"Or made anyone particularly jealous? Or do you drive around the countryside with a fortune in your handbag, making it worth a man's while to lie in wait and shoot you?"

"It's quite an ordinary handbag with everyday contents. Would you like to look?" She held it out to him, and he opened the bag deliberately, without watching her, rummaged through the bag and its contents. Compact, lipstick, keys, purse— everything was normal enough. He gave it back.

"Hadn't we better get to the house, and telephone? My men are looking after your displaced lover."

"Who are?" She ignored his guess.

"My men."

"Who are you?"

"I am an Inspector of the Criminal Investigation Department of New Scotland Yard. My special assignment is patrolling the countryside, looking for beautiful young women who might be shot at, rescuing them, and sending my myrmidons to catch their assailants. You see how good Scotland Yard is."

"I'm beginning to appreciate Scotland Yard," said Miss Paterson. "I think we will go to the house."

The gate was a hundred yards farther down the road, and as they drew near it, a man came cycling slowly along, toward them; one of Bray's officers. He stopped, and swung his leg over his machine, touched his cap to Miss Paterson, and said:

"Lost him, I'm afraid, sir."

"Well, he had a good start. Have you done anything about it?"

"We telephoned the station. The others are on the main road, waiting for a patrol car. We got a good look at the beggar," the man added—and Roger saw the girl's lips tighten. "He ran across the main road, in front of a car, and was easy to see in the headlights. Young chap with ginger hair, as you said."

"Good. Did you warn the station that he's armed?"

"Yes, sir."

"That's fine," said Roger. "I'm going up to the house with Miss Paterson. If I'm wanted, send a message there. You might stand guard over the car, and make sure no one comes blinding along and runs into it. I'll send for a breakdown gang. Oh—and send my car up to the house, will you?"

"Very good, sir."

A great bank of clouds was blowing up from the west, and it was much darker—too dark for Roger to see anything except that the banks on either side of the drive were overgrown and unattractive, and that the drive itself was uneven, pitted with holes, and with many loose stones lying on the top. Once, the girl kicked against a stone, and nearly fell. Roger grabbed her arm.

"Thank you." She held on to his arm after that.

"Red-haired men are known to be passionate," said Roger. "How many redheads have you jilted?"

"Isn't that joke getting stale?"

"Is it a joke?"

She said: "Once and for all, I've never seen the man before. The first time I'd ever set eyes on him was when he jumped up from the ditch, and fired. I *did* just notice his ginger hair, but I didn't think about it until your man mentioned it. You may be a policeman, but you don't have to assume that I'm lying to you."

She had a warm voice; "warm" was the word that occurred to him. It was husky; not clear and lilting, like the woman who called herself Miss Lobo. She still held his arm.

He didn't answer.

"Why do you seem so sure that I know him?"

"Young women are so gallant. You'd prefer to maintain a noble silence than betray the hot-blooded young man."

"So you're not convinced?"

"I am not."

She took her hand from his arm, and they

84

walked in silence toward the house. One light glowed from a side window; none at the front. The hideous towers were shrouded by the darkness, now; it looked just a house, not a monstrosity. The lighted window was on the first floor, and the stream of yellow light shone over the roof of the stables and on the branches of several oak trees, which grew close to the stables, some of their boughs stretching out over the roof, protectively. The quiet, with that distant background of traffic noises, seemed to envelop them. Here, the drive was more even, and the top covering was of asphalt. They made little noise as they approached the front door.

"There are two steps," said Miss Paterson coldly.

"Thanks."

Her hand brushed his as they went up the steps; hers was cool; pleasant to touch. She opened her handbag and took out the keys. He shone a torch on to the door. It needed painting; a big pale blister in the brown paint showed ghostly beneath the light. But the brass surround of the lock was brightly polished. She opened the door, and the light shone into a dark space; there was no light anywhere, apart from that from the torch.

"I'll put on a light," she said, and slipped past him. He directed the beam on to her head and shoulders, and the ridiculous hat of colored feathers. Then he moved the torch and shone it on the wall toward which she moved. She pressed down a switch, and light blazed from a glass chandelier above their heads.

Roger had stepped out of the neglected grounds into a home of luxury; one glance was enough to tell him that. The hall was large and high-ceilinged. Great oil paintings in gilt frames hung on the walls; there were three pieces of antique furniture, with a dull finish. A wide staircase, lined with paintings, was carpeted in rich, dark red.

She said: "That's funny," and looked, as well as sounded, puzzled, then turned into a room on the right and pressed down another switch. He waited for her to go in, ahead of him—and as he entered, he saw that this was a lovely, gracious room; with skin rugs on a dark, polished parquet floor. A head with great white teeth snarled up at him from the rug that lay in front of the huge open fireplace.

It was a wolf's head.

9

Morden Lodge

Miss Paterson repeated: "That's funny," stepped past the wolf skin, and pulled an old-fashioned bell rope which hung by the fireplace. Roger glanced round, away from the head, which was so like an enlargement of the tiny red mark in the middle of Morgan's palm. The telephone, dark red, stood on a small table on the other side of the fireplace.

He crossed to it, and murmured: "May I use this?"

"Yes, of course." She seemed to take little notice of him, but looked about the room, as if there were something here which really surprised her. She was more puzzled now than she had been outside. He had to watch her, and so see the beauty of her figure, the grace with which she moved her head. She was superbly sure of herself, and he wondered if he were wrong about her age, after all; she wasn't just a girl.

He looked up the Hounslow police number in his notebook, and dialed it. Miss Paterson waited by the fireplace, and her toe moved about the rug;

near the wolf's head. She touched the head, as if idly; but was she drawing his attention to it? Then she stared toward the door, but no one came. She pulled the bell rope again; he fancied he heard a jangling sound, from some way off; and then the station answered. He asked the operator to arrange for the car to be moved and the road cleared, then told the man to hold on, and looked at the woman.

"What garage do you want to deal with your car?"

"Robey's, please."

"Fix it all with Robey's garage," Roger said. "And tell Mr. Bray that I hope to see him a little later." He rang off, and thrust his hands in his pockets as he looked at Miss Paterson.

Was she expecting someone to answer her ring? Or was she pretending surprise and bewilderment? If it were acting, she was very good indeed. Everything about her suggested that she was on edge, that there was mystery here she couldn't understand. She stopped fiddling with the wolf's head, walked toward the open door, hesitated, then returned, and gave the rope a third tug. Without a word, she managed to fill him with something of the tension she appeared to be feeling herself.

Was something amiss?

There was no answer to the ring.

She said: "I can't understand it. Will you wait here a minute, please?"

"I'm nervous on my own in big houses," said Roger. "May I come with you?"

"If you like." She went out into the hall, and paused at the foot of the stairs, glanced upward, then down a passage which was blocked, halfway along, by a heavy door.

"Wasn't there a light somewhere?" she asked.

"Yes. On the left side of the house, on the first floor. It shone over the stables."

"So father's in." She walked along the passage. It was dark, near the door. She thrust it open quickly, and darkness met them. She walked slowly as the door swung to behind them. Roger took out his torch again. She pressed a switch, and the passage, obviously in the domestic quarters, was flooded with light. The walls glistened with cream paint; the doors shone. The neglect was confined to the grounds, everything inside suggested a well-run household. Several doors led off the passage—and the woman went to the first on the right. She put on another light. This was a kitchen, tiled, bright, spotless. The huge Aga cooker glistened cream, the boiling-plate covers shone, a large dresser was filled with sparkling crockery, the table was covered with plastic. Everything was as spick and span as the kitchen at Bell Street.

"Where on earth have they gone?" She was speaking to herself and seemed to have forgotten that Roger was here. She went to another door, which led to a scullery. Yet a third, presumably leading to the garden, was closed and bolted—and chained. Roger had seldom seen a door better protected against burglary. His gaze strayed to the windows. There were special antiburglar catches there, and the telltale wires of a burglar alarm.

"Has your cook taken French leave?" he asked.

"Cook? No, we—" she broke off, biting her lips. That made her look younger. In the harsh light from the single electric lamp above her head, the texture of her skin seemed beautiful. Her make-up wasn't overdone. She took off her hat and rumpled her hair; that made her even more attractive, more natural. The hat had confined rich, dark tresses, which were glossy and wavy—naturally curly, like Janet's. It was the only thing about her which reminded him of Janet.

"I think I'll go upstairs," she said.

She turned quickly, and pushed past him, as if anxious to lead the way. Now, she hurried. Her footsteps rang out sharply on the lino-covered passage, were muffled on the hall carpet and up the stairs. That made the quiet of the house seem more noticeable.

She ran up the last few stairs.

"Pat!" she called. There was no answer. "*Pat!*" she repeated, and tried the handle of a door on the left. The only light came from the chandelier, but it was bright enough for them to see clearly—and too bright to allow any glow to come from the edges of the closed door.

The door opened, and she stepped inside the room—and then backed away, bumping into him. The hissing intake of her breath was more alarming than a scream.

Roger pushed past her.

He was prepared for anything; for the body of Paterson; anything. There was no body, but the room had been ransacked. The wild confusion contrasted sharply with the order in the rest of the house. Papers were strewn about the floor, books had been pulled from open bookcases and flung down, two tables and a chair lay on their sides, a skin rug was rolled up in a heap and pushed

90

against the fireplace. A bowl of chrysanthemums —beautiful, copper-colored blooms—had been upset, the flowers resting in a pool of water which spread over a walnut table. There were a dozen small pictures on the walls; etchings. Most of them were askew, as if they had been hung by a drunk. The drawers of a large, carved walnut desk were open, the top of the desk was piled high with the contents of the drawers. And the wind, coming through the open window, rustled the papers and the woman's hair, as Roger turned to look at her. He saw only horror on her face.

He went to the window and leaned out. The light shone on the branches of the oak trees and the red tiles of the stable roof. Any agile man could get from the window to the roof without difficulty.

When he turned back, Miss Paterson still stood in the doorway, her hands raised to her breast, her dazed eyes taking in the chaos. Then suddenly she exclaimed: "No!" and rushed toward a corner, went down on her knees and began to tap the paneling near the floor like a demented creature. She ran her forefinger up and down the polished wood, and her breathing was harsh and labored. Then he heard a click; and part of the paneling opened; there was a cavity. Now that she had found what she wanted, she drew back, still on her knees, as if she were fearful of going any further.

Roger approached, and glanced round.

"You—you shouldn't know about this," she said. The words seemed pointless. "I just wanted to find out—"

"Whether the secret hiding place had been rifled. Has it?" Roger went to her side and knelt down. She pulled the panel wide open. There was a recess, actually a steel-lined safe in which a tiny light glowed. Inside were several documents, all of them tied round with red tape. She took them out and flung them aside, as if they were of no account. Then she groped again—and suddenly stopped moving. She closed her eyes; he knew that it was with relief.

"All safe?" he asked dryly.

"I—I think so. You shouldn't be here."

"Don't you usually send for the police when you have a burglary?" He took her wrist, drew her hand away, then groped inside. He touched something soft; probably wash leather, from the feel of it. He drew out a small wash-leather bag, which was tightly tied round the neck with strong cord, and heavily sealed. He weighed it up and down in his hand; there was no rattling sound. He prodded the bag with his fingers, and suspected that whatever was inside was wrapped with cotton wool. This was a jewelbag; dealers very often took their goods about in bags like this; few of them troubled to seal the binding cord.

"You'd better see if everything's there."

"No. No, the seal's intact, there's no need for me to open it. My father will make sure—Pat! Where is he?" She jumped up; fear seemed to take possession of her again, but she had the presence of mind to snatch the bag away from him. She looked round the room, as if expecting her father to materialize from one of the corners. "Pat" was obviously her affectionate diminutive for Paterson.

Then she ran out of the room.

Roger pulled a handkerchief from his pocket, lifted the receiver of the telephone which stood, undisturbed, on a corner of the desk, and dialed the Hounslow station again. This time he spoke to Bray, who said at once: "I'll be out in a couple of jiffs."

"Bring all the equipment," Roger said.

Bray didn't trouble to answer.

Roger closed the panel, closed the window, then found the key of the study on the inside of the door. Handling it with the handkerchief, he took it out; when outside, closed and locked the door and slipped the key into his pocket. Then he went along a wide passage, where lights blazed. He heard the girl moving about, agitatedly. She came from one of the rooms, and hadn't got the jewels now.

"He's not here. No one's here!"

"We haven't looked everywhere yet," Roger said. "Come with me."

She followed him meekly as he explored the house, putting on every light he came across. They found no one in any of the bedrooms; there were two floors, and on the top one the rooms were obviously tenanted by the staff. Clothes were in the wardrobes, personal oddments were in all the rooms. There had been no sudden clear-up before a hurried departure. None of the other rooms had been ransacked.

"A squad will soon be out from Hounslow," Roger said as he led the way to the staircase. "You'd better come down and have a drink."

"I just can't understand it."

"A drink might help you."

"Are you telling me that I'm lying *again?*" she flashed, and looked angry; and in her anger, superb. He shrugged his shoulders and smiled sardonically, and led the way downstairs. There was a cocktail cabinet in the front room; he poured her gin, added a dash of orange, and helped himself to a small whisky and soda. She sipped her drink, still looking dazed. She stood in front of the fireplace, and her right foot began to play with the wolf's head again.

"Do you know of anything that might have called your father away?"

"No. He didn't go to the city today; his secretary came out to see him. There was some urgent business. I don't know much about it, I don't take any interest in his business affairs." She spoke quickly, as if she felt that she had to explain, but found it distasteful.

"Who else should be here?"

"All of the servants. All five of them. It's absurd! They were here when I left, just after lunch. I was so astonished when there was no answer to the bell and when I found the house in darkness. There are usually a lot of lights on. The—the thief must have left the light on in the study." She licked her lips. "I suppose it was one of them who fired at me. He was afraid—"

She broke off.

Roger said dryly: "Any thief who'd been here would have been in a devil of a hurry to get away. He would have kept out of your sight, and scampered off as fast as his legs could carry him when you'd driven past. Unless you saw him before, and recognized—"

"I didn't recognize him!" she flared.

"We won't go into that again now. Have you had any other burglaries here, Miss Paterson?"

"No. Not that I can remember."

"The house is pretty well protected, isn't it?"

"Of course. There are always some jewels here,

94

and Pat thinks it's wise to take precautions—better to be safe than sorry, he's always saying." She bit her lips. "Do you think anything has happened to him?"

"I don't think that the burglar carried him off, if that's what you mean."

"I hardly know what I do mean." She went to the window and looked out. The headlights of a car were coming along the road. Farther away, a glow of light showed where the breakdown crew were already at work on the Chrysler. The newcomer was probably Bray, and he came from the opposite direction, to avoid the road block. The blazing lights turned into the drive and swayed up and down. They reached the house, showed up the long grass of the lawns, the unpruned rose trees, the dead flowers in overgrown flower beds. The neglect outside and the orderliness inside puzzled Roger as much as any other feature.

So much was puzzling; the coincidence came first. From experience he knew better than to scoff at coincidence; the most fantastic things could happen without any relationship, any logical explanation. But it was pretty steep to be asked to believe that the attack had been made on the girl, by chance, just as he had passed: it wasn't reasonable. Yet—she had behaved convincingly. He could, if he liked, read suspicion into some of the things she had said and done, but on the whole she had behaved as if she had been frightened and then alarmed by what she had found.

The car drew up outside.

"Perhaps it's Pat." She swung round from the window eagerly.

"It's probably more policemen. You're going to

find us a nuisance from now on," Roger said. "You needn't go out, I left the front door open.

The car door slammed.

A man walked across the drive and up the steps; Bray wouldn't be by himself, so this wasn't Bray. Roger moved nearer the door. Miss Paterson finished her drink, and followed him, then changed her mind and went to the fireplace; she seemed to love toying with that wolf's head.

Was that another coincidence?

Footsteps sounded inside the hall now, heavy, deliberate; Roger pictured a big man with ponderous gait. It might be Bray, ahead of his squad, after all.

A man called: "Who's about?"

Miss Paterson cried: "Pat!" She ran to the door, but it opened before she reached it, and a man stood on the threshold. He saw Roger, sent him a single, searching glance, then turned to the girl.

"What's amiss, Margaret? Why are all the lights on?" He was tall; he had to bend his head slightly to kiss her on the forehead. He was a big, powerful man, as handsome as she was beautiful, and the likeness between them left no doubt that they were father and daughter. Then: "Who's your friend?" he asked.

But there was nothing friendly in the second glance he gave Roger.

10

"Pat"

"Friend!" exclaimed Margaret. "He's a policeman. Pat, we've had—"

Paterson gripped her arm so tightly that she stopped speaking. He looked all the time at Roger; there was no hiding the hostility in his expression, but was there any nervousness, any hint of fear?

"What are you doing here?"

"Police do come to the scene of a burglary, you know. Although we don't yet know what's happened here," Roger said. "It was probably housebreaking, I fancy it was done before dusk. And it might not even be that. An inside job." He smiled at Paterson, intending to irritate the man, to make him lose his self-control. He did not like the handsome Paterson, and knew that the spontaneous dislike was mutual.

Paterson said: "Did you send for him Margaret?"

"No, I—"

"Then what are you doing here?"

"Pat, I met him at the gate, there was—" she broke off, as if there was too much to explain simply, and she didn't feel equal to the task.

"A man shot at your daughter. She crashed her car. I was passing, and came to the rescue. She was nervous, so I brought her to the house. We found it deserted, and your room ransacked."

"Ransacked?" Paterson's aplomb deserted him, he shot a glance toward the door. Then he tossed his gray Homburg hat into a chair. He wore a gray overcoat, raglan style, concealing a powerful figure. A silk scarf was draped round his neck; he wore one yellow pigskin glove, new and bright, and carried the other.

Headlights blazed at the end of the drive again.

Margaret said: "The bag's safe. I put it in your wardrobe. Pat, Carney's not here, all the staff has gone. The house is empty, and—oh, it's fantastic!" She looked very young, now, the sophisticated young woman had become an ingenuous school-girl. And she had named *Carney*. Roger didn't speak, but that had jolted him.

"I'd better go and see what's happened," said Paterson, and turned and saw the headlights of the other car, which was now very near the house. "Who the devil is this? We don't want visitors. Margaret, go and say—"

"More police, I'm afraid," Roger said.

"More? What right—" Paterson broke off, and shrugged. "Oh, I suppose there's nothing I can do about it now. Margaret, do you mean that none of the staff is here? What about dinner?"

"Nothing's ready, nothing's been done."

"What time did you leave the house?" Roger asked. Bray was getting out of the car, and speaking to the men with him. "Miss Paterson tells me that you didn't go to the office today."

"As a policeman, you'd better get your facts

right. I didn't go this morning, I went this afternoon."

"Was everything normal when you left?"

"Yes. May I see your credentials?"

Bray came in as Roger showed Paterson his card. Paterson looked at it, but made no comment. Bray was eager, and seemed triumphant. Paterson nodded to him distantly, and kept silent while Roger told the Hounslow man what had happened.

Men were waiting in the hall with their equipment: a camera, fingerprint outfit, everything likely to be needed for the investigation. On such a job as this, Bray would be an artist.

"We'd better look round," Bray said, trying to sound casual.

"I'll come with you. Margaret—" Paterson looked at his daughter, frowning as he spoke. "Telephone the Pied Piper, tell them we shall be along to dinner in about an hour's time. Then I should take some aspirin and close your eyes a bit. There's nothing to worry about now."

"I'm all right."

"Do as I say." He spoke as if he knew that his orders would be carried out to the letter; "orders" was exactly the right word. Then he turned, scanned the three men in the hall distastefully, and led the way upstairs. He said nothing when Roger unwrapped the key from his handkerchief and opened the door, but he was the first to go inside. He stood in the middle of the room, looking round, scowling.

"They made a job of it," said Bray. Roger opened the window, and the wind blew in, papers began to float about the room, falling from the desk and then dancing on the floor. Paterson went to the window, and made to close it, but Bray got there first and said:

"Leave it, please. Shut the door, one of you." He glanced inquiringly, almost hopefully, at Roger, who waved a hand, silently telling him to carry on. Roger was intent on Paterson, studying the man, taking in every detail on his face, his manner, his movements. He had short gray hair, very thick; it was cropped at the back and sides, and inclined to curl on top. His cheeks were pale, but not with a sickly pallor. There was a slight red ridge on the bridge of his nose; so for close work, he wore glasses. His regular features had a film star-ish perfection, his lips were red and moist, there was a cleft in his square chin; and he kept a poker face. His gray eyes, which seemed very bright, missed nothing; and he was aware that Roger was studying him. Yet in spite of his composure, Roger felt there was great strain; he didn't find it easy to be so calm.

Bray said: "The quicker we know what's been stolen, if anything, the quicker we'll get it back."

"It will take me some time to check everything. I certainly can't do it myself. The only really valuable things in the room are the jewels, which my daughter says are still in the house." Paterson went to the wall safe in the paneling and peered inside, nodded and stood up. "That fooled them. Hadn't you better start looking for my servants? They're obviously concerned in this."

"Have you any photographs of them?" Bray asked.

"I haven't. There may be some in their rooms." Paterson took off his scarf and ran it through his hands; it made a little swishing sound. "I can give you their names and a description, if that will help. Have you been outside, or in the gymnasium, Chief Inspector?"

"No." Roger thought: Gymnasium rings a bell. Morgan had talked of one.

"Carney, my butler—major-domo, in fact, might conceivably be there, although it isn't likely." The scarf went *swish-swish-swish*, the only indication of Paterson's taut nerves. "I should have said that all my staff was quite reliable, but I suppose I was wrong. It wasn't because I wasn't warned."

Why did he go to the trouble to say that?

"Warned about what?" asked Bray.

His men were already at work, examining the door and the window for fingerprints, studying the window to see how it had been opened, searching the room for any clue.

"I employed ex-convicts," Paterson said coldly.

Bray shrugged his shoulders. "All of the servants?"

"All the men."

Bray's look said: "You fool," but he didn't speak, only turned to the window and began to examine it. Paterson stepped to the desk, his hand hovered about the telephone, and Bray said: "Don't touch that, please!"

"I wish to telephone my secretary."

"Isn't there another telephone?"

Paterson said: "Very well." He went out, and Roger followed him, but the man appeared to ignore his presence, in spite of the fact that Roger was just behind him. In the drawing room, Margaret sat back in an easy chair, but her eyes opened as soon as they entered. "Stay there," Paterson ordered, and went to the telephone. He dialed, while looking out of the window, and had to hold on for some time. He fidgeted impatiently and frowned, but suddenly his face cleared, and he said: "Helen?" He paused.

"Never mind about that. I want you to come to the house immediately. There has been a robbery, and the police want a list of the missing goods.... Yes, please, as quickly as you can.... Oh, finish your dinner, half an hour won't make any difference."

He replaced the receiver, turned, looked at Margaret and said: "What is this about being shot at, Margaret?"

"By a red-haired man," murmured Roger.

Paterson started; it was the second sign of surprise and alarm that he'd shown, reminding Roger of the way he had looked over his shoulder toward the door. This time he flashed a glance at Roger, looked as if he were about to speak, changed his mind, and approached his daughter.

"Did the Chief Inspector help you?"

"Yes, he—"

"I have to thank you, Mr. West." There was no feeling in the words, this was just a polite convention. "It was extremely fortunate that you happened to be passing. Was that just coincidence? Or were you coming to see me?"

Margaret sat up.

Roger said: "Why should you think that I was coming to see you?"

"I thought you might have heard about the burglary at the office," Paterson said calmly. "This is the second attempt to rob me."

"Do you employ ex-convicts at the office, too?"

"No," said Paterson. "No great harm was done, a little ready money was stolen, that's all. But it's odd that the two things should happen so quickly. Hmm." The scarf swished. "Margaret, you're not looking too good. Perhaps we ought to have a snack

102

here, so that you can get to bed early. It would be better for you, and—"

"No, I'm all right." She jumped up, as if anxious to prove it. "Have you looked at the jewels?"

"Not yet."

"You ought to make sure that they're all right," said Margaret. "I'll go and get them." She hurried out, while Paterson swished the scarf, betraying his taut nerves. He looked sharply at Roger, as if Roger's silence was adding to the strain. Margaret's footsteps faded. A policeman ran downstairs to the waiting car, stayed there for a few seconds, and hurried back again. Margaret was away for a long time. Paterson flung the scarf away from him. It fell lightly to the floor, but one corner caught on the seat of a chair, where his hat lay on its side. He didn't look at Roger, who felt that his tactics were paying a good dividend. Paterson had something to hide, was afraid to meet his eye.

Roger took out his cigarette case.

"Will you smoke?"

Paterson glanced at him, then quickly away. "No, I seldom smoke cigarettes. I—West." He braced himself and now looked straight at Roger, challenging and hostile. His eyes were different from his daughter's, gray flecked with green and brown. The whites were muddy now, as they might be if he were tired; a puzzlingly quick change. Yet his movements had been brisk enough. "Did you see this man who shot at my daughter?"

"I caught a glimpse of him."

"Is it true that he had red hair?"

"There isn't much doubt about that."

Paterson looked away again, and muttered: "The fool!"

"Who is?"

"Eh? I didn't speak. I will have one of your cigarettes." Paterson stretched out his hand; it was long and slim, like Margaret's, the nails filbert-shaped and rather too long. "Thanks. Have a drink?"

"No thanks. Why didn't you tell me the truth, Mr. Paterson? There's too much lying in this house. First your daughter and now you. It's bad enough to know a man is trying to kill your daughter, without protecting him. Who is the red-headed man you suspect?"

Paterson said: "I don't think you heard me properly." The cigarette seemed to steady him, he moved away and his hands became still. "As for Margaret lying to you, I doubt very much whether she would do anything of the kind. She's upset—anyone who had been fired at would be upset, wouldn't they? It's the most natural thing in the world. I wonder where she is?" He turned sharply and hurried to the door.

Roger took a step toward him.

Then he saw the face at the window—the face of a young man, at the side of the window, peering in. Roger saw him out of the corner of his eye, and didn't look directly at the window. The man ventured a little nearer; and the light shone on to his bright hair.

Roger hurried out of the room, without looking at the window openly, and turned right, toward the stairs. Paterson was already near the landing, his footsteps thudding. No one was in the hall. Roger slipped into the next room, the door of which was ajar; it was a dining room with paneled walls and heavy dark-oak furniture; Jacobean or reproduction. Only one light burned here, over the fireplace and the portrait of a man. He didn't look toward the portrait, but hurried across the room and stood by the side of the window; it was closed, but the catch wasn't fastened. He inserted his fingers between the bottom of the window and the frame, eased it upward, then pushed. It squeaked a little. He drew back. No one appeared outside. He pushed it farther up, so that he could climb through easily, and peered cautiously toward the drawing room. No one was at that window now, but a slim, boyish figure passed the front door and reached the corner of the house. He looked round before he disappeared.

Roger climbed out.

Upstairs, Paterson called: "Margaret!" There was no answer. Had Margaret really gone upstairs to get the bag of jewels from the wardrobe? They had only her word that the gems were there. There were strong cross currents in this *ménage*, confusing, misleading. Roger's job was to probe gently, searching for weak spots. There were plenty: the abrupt change in Paterson's manner; the girl's sensitiveness about the red-haired man; Paterson's "the young fool!"; and even Margaret's sudden dash from the room.

He reached the corner of the house.

"Margaret!" came Paterson's voice. This time someone else spoke: Bray, or one of his men. The study light still shone on the roof of the stables. The stables were in a walled yard, and the door was on the far side, away from the house. The stalls were some distance away from the entrance, dark shapes without a glimmer of light. Horses stirred; the heavy smell was unpleasant. Roger could make out the shape of a door by the side of the stables; it stood open. He stole toward it, stood for a moment at the foot of a steep flight of stairs. A dim light glowed at the top, so dim that he

105

thought it probably came from a candle, a match, or an electric torch; more likely one of the first two. It revealed a half-open door and the silhouette of a man standing outside it. Roger started up the stairs, then stopped as the man whispered:

"Margaret, are you there? Margaret?"

The answer was whispered; Roger only just heard the sound. The man pushed the door wide open and went in. The door swung to, but didn't close properly. Roger started to mount the stairs, stepping as close to one side as he could, to try to avoid creaking treads. As he crept up he heard more whispering. The light was blotted out by a shadow. He stood near the door listening to a whispered conversation. He gave them a minute or two, then moved forward.

The door was slammed in his face. He heard an exclamation, then the sharp click of the key turned in the lock.

Heavy footsteps sounded in the room beyond.

He put his shoulder to the door and heaved; it didn't yield, there was no easy way of forcing it. He turned and raced downstairs, the thin beam of his torch shining brightly in the darkness. He ran out into the yard and turned between the stables and the house. Here a little light came from the study window. The window of the room above the stables was probably at the back.

He reached the corner in time to see a man staggering beneath the window to get his balance. The man ran off, and Roger yelled: "Bray! Down here. Use the window!"

Then his torch light shone on a thick beech hedge. He was forced to stop, while he swiveled the beam round, looking for a gap. Footsteps sounded heavily, beyond him, along a path; by the time he found the gap, the sound faded. He fancied that he could hear it farther away.

Bray called out from the window of the study: "What is it?" Roger looked up, to see one of the Hounslow men climbing down the side of the house and flashing a much larger torch.

He called: "You got that call out for a red-haired man, didn't you?"

"Yes, of course."

"He's been back," said Roger. "Call your station and tell them he's somewhere about here, will you?" He tried to speak calmly, but was bitterly angry with himself. The other man joined him.

"We'd better see what we can find, sir, hadn't we?"

"Yes. This way." Although it was probably a waste of time, it had to be tried. Other men came hurrying from the back door of the house, and Bray followed them. Torches flashed from one end of a well-tended vegetable garden to the other, and to a wooden gate in another part of the beech hedge. They found a meadow beyond the gate, and, on the far side of the meadow, another by-road. Bray was by Roger's side, here.

"Not much use going on, is there?"

"Afraid not," Roger said. "I thought I was being clever. Sorry. You left someone in the study, I suppose?"

"Oh, yes. Paterson was there, too. He says he can't find his daughter." There was a complaining note in Bray's voice. "I do dislike it when so many things happen at once. Do you say you saw this red-haired chap?"

"Yes. And I know where Margaret Paterson is," Roger said. "Will you go back to the house, and keep Paterson there on some pretext? And lend me a man to stand guard at the stable door while I have another word with her ladyship?"

"Of course."

In the distance they heard Paterson calling: "Margaret!" By the time they reached the path between the house and the stables, he was in the garden, still wearing his coat. He turned toward the little party of policemen, and his voice was almost shrill.

"Have you seen my daughter?"

"I haven't, Mr. Paterson," said Bray. "There's something I'd like you to do for me upstairs. Will you—"

"Damn it, man! My daughter has disappeared."

"She'll come back," Bray said reassuringly. "I shouldn't worry about that, sir. If—"

Roger said: "I'd like you to look in your wardrobe, Mr. Paterson, to find out if that bag of jewels is where she put it. It may be important. We'll look for Miss Paterson."

"You mean you think—" began Paterson, but he didn't finish. He turned toward the corner and the front door, and led the way inside. Bray and two other men followed, Roger and the last of Bray's squad went to the stables.

Roger shone his torch round, heard the horses stamping, and saw an empty stall, with wood piled up against one wall. He found a long-handled ax and took it.

"Shall I need something?" asked the other anxiously.

"Please yourself. I may want to break a door down."

"Then I won't bother, sir."

"I want you to stand at the foot of these stairs," Roger said, as they entered the doorway which led to the upper room. "Stay there, until I call. I don't expect much trouble. Anyhow, she's probably flown by now." The harshness of his voice reflected his savage anger with himself. "By the way, what's your name?"

"Garnett, sir."

"Thanks."

Roger gripped the ax more firmly as he went upstairs. The door was still closed, and a dim yellow light showed at the bottom. Perhaps she was still in the room. He reached the top and drew back his hand to tap—and then the quiet of the stables was broken by a scream. He raised the ax as the cry came again.

"You all right, sir?" Garnett called up.

"Yes." Roger smashed at the door. Two blows shattered the wooden panel near the lock—and the light inside went out. There was no more screaming. He thought he heard heavy, labored breathing in the darkness.

11

The Gymnasium

"Better come up!" Roger called.

"Coming, sir." The bright beam from a big torch shone out, showing the splintered wood, but scarcely penetrating the darkness beyond. The stairs creaked under Garnett's tread. Someone spoke, outside— had the scream been heard? Roger smashed at the panel again, and the door sagged open.

"Careful, sir!"

"Yes. Shine your torch downstairs for a moment." That left the doorway and the tiny landing in darkness, and Roger slipped into the room. He saw the square outline of a window, nearly opposite him, and felt the cold rush of wind coming across the room; so the window was open. "Are you there, Miss Paterson?" He went farther inside, while Garnett hesitated, not sure what to do next. "Just stand at the ready," Roger called. He took out his own torch, bent down, switched it on and rolled it along the floor. The light shone on pale brown boards, and on an Indian club, lying on its side. One Indian club, on its own.

Nothing happened.

He whispered: "See if you can find the switches, they should be near the door. Careful with your own torch."

"Yes, sir."

Roger thought: I came with a gun for this job and gave it away. It's time I went back to school.

"I've got it, sir."

"All right, switch on."

"But—"

"Switch on!"

Bright light shone from the ceiling, coming from pale bluish strips, and showed up the huge room, with the parallel bars, the vaulting horse, everything you would expect to find in a gymnasium. Also, it shone on the fellow to the lonely Indian club. That lay in a doorway on the other side of the room. The smoothed top was stained red—as with blood. And lying near it, crumpled up, skirt rucked above her knees, was Margaret Paterson. He couldn't see her face or her head.

She wasn't hurt.

Her right hand lay on the floor, in the middle of a little smear of blood which had come off the top of the Indian club; or looked as if it had. The room beyond was in darkness. On the floor near Margaret's other hand was a small, flat torch, switched off. Roger made sure that she was breathing, and stood up, looking down at her with a scowl. Garnett approached.

"Is she—"

"She's all right," Roger said. "I'm going into that other room." He approached slowly, and from the side; a man, killer, might be in here. He reached the door, made sure that his shadow wasn't thrown into the small room, thrust the door open, and darted inside.

Only one man was in there; he lay on the floor with his head smashed in.

Roger stretched out his hand and switched on the light of the small room. Men were coming up the stairs, he felt sure that Paterson had heard the scream and was hurrying to investigate. He turned and studied the dead man. It was a little fellow, whose left hand was stretched out, with the palm upwards and the fingers cupped.

Roger forced the fingers open and saw the sign of the wolf on the dirty palm.

He turned back, pushed past Garnett and looked at Margaret. It was the second time that day he had seen her unconscious, or feigning to be so. In spite of all that had happened, she had a fresh beauty.

Then Paterson burst into the room, with Bray on his heels. "Margaret!" Paterson shouted, and hurried toward her.

On the sofa in the drawing room, her cheeks flushed and her blue eyes bright, she made a vivid picture. All she would say was that she had gone into the gymnasium, come upon the body, screamed—and remembered nothing more until she came round, with her father bending over her. Paterson stood by her side, on guard, fending off Roger and the even more insistent Bray.

Roger tried to picture the woman as he had first seen her, so aloof and elusive at the wheel of the Chrysler; and later, looking at him over the top of the newspaper; and then, unconscious in the car and on the floor, with her hand in the blood.

It was half an hour since she had come round

and been brought here. Bray's men had split into two parties, one working in the gymnasium, the other in the study. Apart from hovering about his daughter, Paterson had done one thing willingly— telephoned for a doctor. He had grudgingly identified the dead man as Lake—Loppy Lake, so called because he had a slightly deformed foot which made him limp. As grudgingly, he had named Carney Smith and Mike O'Hara. Roger telephoned the Yard, gave Sloan the names and asked him to search in *Records* for the three men.

O'Hara and Loppy were married.

Bray said for the fifth time: "Miss Paterson, you couldn't have stumbled over the dead body. It was inside the small room, you were in the large one."

"But I did! I went in, fell over it, my torch shone on his head, and I don't know what happened. I remember screaming, that's all. I could scream now!"

A car drew up outside; the night seemed to be filled with cars pulling up and people switching on lights in dark rooms. Roger said: "I'll go." He wanted a few minutes in which to steady his thoughts; and to ease his throbbing head. He touched the sticking plaster; his scalp was more tender today than it had been yesterday. He turned, and glanced down at the wolfskin.

In the hall he lit a cigarette and waited for the caller to reach the porch. That didn't take long. He heard a bell ring in the kitchen, and opened the front door.

The man who blinked in the light from the great chandelier was short and squat. He had a bowler hat pressed low on his head; it made his small ears stick out. He was muffled up in a woolen scarf and a thick overcoat which made him look almost as

113

broad as he was tall. His face was pink; a baby face. He was ludicrous but brisk as he stepped into the hall, swinging a small black case.

"Who are you?" He had a thin, nasal voice.

"Miss Paterson is in the drawing room," Roger said. "Are you Dr. Sorensen?"

"Yes." Sorensen had big eyes; pale gray, quite his best feature. They were steady and calm. "Who are you? Where is Carney? What's the trouble?" He didn't seem interested in any answer, but went straight to the drawing room, a further indication that he was familiar with the house. "What's been happening here? Nothing much the matter with her, is there?"

"Mr. Paterson thought it worth sending for you."

Sorensen sniffed and opened the drawing-room door. Roger stayed outside. Paterson would ask, and the doctor would insist, that Margaret be allowed to rest before she was questioned any further. Roger went upstairs. Garnett and another man were in the study; it looked much tidier than it had an hour before.

"Anything?" asked Roger.

"Not worth calling anything. The window was opened from inside. There are marks where the beggar climbed out, none where he climbed in. You can always tell." Roger didn't question that. "He probably had sticking plaster on his fingers, it's a pro's job. He was in a hurry, too. Left a lot of things that would be worth something to him, sir—he was looking for some special thing, no doubt o' that."

"Yes. Nothing else?"

"No, sir."

"Thanks." Roger went out, and hurried to the room where Margaret had been after snatching the

114

wash-leather bag. The light here was still on, although most of them had been switched off. It was a man's bedroom, furnished bleakly in ultra-modern style—a cold cubist room. The furniture was of limed oak; all the fittings were of chromium. The wardrobe door stood open. Roger glanced inside; a small electric lamp, operated by the door, shone on the wash-leather bag. He picked it up and weighed it in his hands; if it contained jewels, they were worth a fortune. He laughed: his first laugh for some time. A fortune, lying in a wardrobe; Paterson hadn't troubled to pick it up! He inspected the seal more closely; it was a monogram mark, and looked like "J.P." The wax was red; the cord, blue. He put it in his pocket and hurried out. Now he could have a quick look round by himself. He went into room after room. Most were furnished in modern style, sternly utilitarian. He found no photographs in the servants' rooms, and ran through their clothes. There was nothing of interest. He searched for crackman's tools and any sign of the wolf, and the only thing that caught his eye was a small, bright-handled soldering iron in the bottom drawer of the chest in Carney Smith's room. Soldering? No, it was a branding iron. The end was darkened, as with fire, and he pressed it hard on to the edge of a *Sporting Times* which was folded on a chair.

A faint impression of a wolf's head showed.

There were no other tools; nothing else to connect anyone in the household with Lobo.

Margaret's room was next to her father's. High-ceilinged, spacious, it was modern without being austere, and the curtains and furnishings were bright and gay, everything here was for comfort.

Roger's feet sank into the pile of a Persian carpet. He looked quickly through the wardrobe and every other piece of furniture and possible hiding place; he found nothing about Lobo, but there was a photograph album which made his eyes widen.

Margaret's vitality glowed from the glossy surface of the photographs. She was shown in the garden, aboard ship, on the sands, in her car, with dogs and horses, in brief swim suits, in evening dress, at parties; only once was she alone. Usually different men were with her, all young, boyish and looking carefree.

There were also some loose photographs; he selected one of her, one of Paterson, then looked at the youths again; but ginger hair wouldn't show up in a photograph.

He studied the postcard picture of Margaret before putting it, with Paterson's, in his pocket. He went downstairs and outside. The wind had now reached a half-gale; it was whining through the trees; as he turned the corner toward the stables a strong gust took his breath away. After that, it was calm until he reached the open door of the staircase to the gymnasium. Here, too late, there was plenty of light. He hurried up the stairs. Lake's body was still in the small room; the bathroom. There were three showers and one foot-bath; this place had been fitted up regardless of expense. The two Hounslow men who were working looked up, but didn't stop what they were doing—measuring the distance between the dead man's deformed foot and the door. One of them was on his knees, with a tape measure, the other had a pad, held against the wall, and pencil at the ready.

"Three feet, eight, and five sixteenths," the man

on his knees said. "That's the lot for that. Anything you want us for, sir?"

"Nearly through?"

"Another ten minutes, and you can take him away. The doctor wants to see him again before he goes, though—he looked in, but couldn't stay. Think it was the red-haired chap, sir? Or—"

"Could be." There was no point in telling the man that it was a silly remark. "Is there anything here that you wouldn't expect to find in a gymnasium?"

The man gave a sly grin, and nodded toward the corpse.

"Apart from that."

"Nothing at all, sir. Are you looking for anything in particular?"

"You've probably heard them called housebreaking implements," Roger said, and won another grin from the man.

"Nothing like that—except the ax. You didn't mean that, did you?" The ax stood by the door, near the head of the stairs.

"No, I didn't mean that. I'd like a picture of every print you find here, it doesn't matter how old, sent to the Yard by special messenger. Will you arrange that with Superintendent Bray? And if there's a photograph of Carney Smith or anyone else, add that to the prints."

"Very good, sir."

Roger nodded, and went off and stared into the blustery night. He didn't like his mood. He was leaving too much to Bray; what was worse, he was glad to do it. And he had no patience with the methodical, routine work which the men were doing. Routine brought more results than any other method, it was invaluable, and yet—this job wasn't going to be solved by routine methods. You couldn't fit that girl into routine; or have a ready answer to the fantastic coincidence of this affair blowing up just as he had passed the gate and the girl had passed him. If he could find a satisfactory explanation of that, he would feel happier.

Another gust of wind howled between the stables and the house.

He was restless, dissatisfied with himself, fighting against depression. He didn't often feel that way. Although Carney and the other servants had flown, he was much farther ahead with the case than there had been any reason for hoping before he'd left the Yard. Paterson was nursing a guilty secret; Margaret a secret of some kind; Lobo's men had undoubtedly been trained here. He wouldn't tackle Paterson about that yet; let the man stew for a bit. Yes, there was plenty of reason for satisfaction if not for congratulation, yet he remained restless and worried.

It was not because of the case; or Lobo.

He'd better face the truth; Janet had upset him badly, and was constantly in his mind. He couldn't understand why she was so jumpy. It wasn't simply fear of Lobo, there was something else in her mind, and she hadn't wanted to tell him. Janet being secretive was a new and unpalatable factor. Until he got things cleared up at home, he was likely to make mistakes through lack of concentration. She had plenty of reason for complaint, because he'd been working at such high pressure.

Why not telephone her?

At one time, he'd called up whenever there was a few minutes break in his night work; of late, he'd let the habit fall into disuse. That was his fault, and—

yes, he'd telephone her! He hurried back to the house and closed the door behind him. Brrr! It was colder outside than he'd thought, but it was warm here. He hurried upstairs, past the drawing room where Paterson was talking. The decision to telephone Janet had lifted a load off his mind, he felt exhilarated, no longer doubted that Janet was the explanation of his gloom. He smiled broadly and clapped his hands together as he entered the study, making Garnett and the other Hounslow man look round in surprise.

"Found something?" Garnett asked eagerly.

"Eh? Oh, no. But on the whole, this is a good night's work, something to be pleased about. How are you doing here?"

"We're finished—just waiting to report."

"Wait downstairs, will you, Mr. Bray will be ready soon."

The wind howled against the window, which was now closed. The detectives gathered up their equipment and notebooks, and went out. Roger clapped his hands together again, laughed at himself, snatched up the telephone, and dialed the Bell Street number. Good! It was free, the *brrr-brrr* had a comforting effect. Janet would answer, of course, and—

"Hallo." It was a woman; not Janet.

"Hallo, is Mrs. West there?"

"I'm afraid she's out. Who is—oh, that's Mr. West, isn't it?" He recognized the West Country burr of a neighbor who sometimes sat in for them, looking after the boys while they went out for the evening; it was six months since they'd had a living-in-maid. "She's gone to the West End, Mr. West, with Mr. Lessing."

"Oh. Oh, yes, of course, she told me she would probably be out." That was a lie; but the disappointment in that "oh" might give Mrs. Wrigley wrong ideas. "It's nice of you to sit in for us. Any trouble from the boys?"

"No, they're fast asleep, they're never any trouble."

Roger forced a laugh. "You should ask Janet sometimes! Leave a message and say that I called, will you?"

"Yes, gladly, Mr. West. Good night."

"Good night." He put the telephone down slowly, lit a cigarette, and scowled at the window. There was no reason at all why Janet and Mike shouldn't have an evening out; every reason why they should. Janet needed something to cheer her up, being on her own so much was the chief trouble. It was absurd to feel resentful with Mark of all people, and yet—oh, hell!

Voices sounded downstairs; as if several people were talking at once. Most of the party from the drawing room was coming out. He went to the door and stood with his hand on the handle. Paterson and Margaret came first, Margaret leaning heavily on her father's shoulder. Dr. Sorenson followed, Bray came after them. Only Bray noticed Roger, and came toward him.

They went inside the study, which was still empty.

"Doctor's orders?" asked Roger.

"Yes, she's going to bed. You know, I don't like the atmosphere of this house, West. There's much more wrong than we realize. That girl's story is—"

"Phoney as they come."

"You agree?" Bray's eyes lighted up. "I had a feeling that you didn't approve of he way I questioned her."

"But I did! I was playing the part of Watchful Willy, trying to size them up. You're quite right, there are things we know not of, in this joint." His manner wasn't natural, but Bray was too pleased to notice that. "So many things have happened so quickly that we haven't time to get the right slant on them. We need a breathing space. Still, some things stand out. Carney and the rest of the staff got the wind up and beat it. We'll find out where Paterson and his daughter come in, later on."

"Think there's a chance of holding the daughter?" Bray asked. "She had the opportunity to kill Lake, you know."

"If I didn't know that the redhead had been with her in the gym, I'd say we ought to take her along to the station. But the presence of the boyfriend lets her out, for the time being. That makes a good case for policemen not knowing too much, doesn't it? We can turn our blind eye for a while."

"Er—oh, yes. Yes." Bray gave a rather pained smile and looked at him uncertainly from beneath his bushy eyebrows. "Yes. What do you want to do next?"

"Tackle Paterson and his secretary, when she arrives. Apart from that, the usual routine. Care to get things sorted out from the reports, while I have a go at Paterson?"

Bray looked relieved. "Yes, I'll do that."

"Fine. First I want to speak to the Yard. I need a man." He dialed Whitehall 1212, and soon had Sloan on the line.

He explained briefly, but comprehensively, then added: "Bill, come out here at once, will you, and watch the window immediately above the front porch; it's Margaret Paterson's room, and she might do a flit."

"Right-o."

"I wondered about that," Bray said, when Roger rang off.

"Better be on the safe side." Roger went out, and Bray called for Garnett. Roger walked along the passage, where shadows on the wall told of people moving about in one of the bedrooms—Margaret's. He reached the doorway as Paterson and Sorensen came out.

Paterson, looking around, said: "You're not to worry, Margaret. I'll deal with these fools."

Sorensen caught sight of Roger; his thick lips curved in sardonic humor, his fine eyes gleamed. Roger liked the squat doctor in spite of his unprepossessing appearance. Rule of thumb number one, never let personal liking affect one's judgment; that was the first and most difficult rule of detection. He stepped past Sorensen and glanced round the door. Margaret lay in bed, cheeks flushed, eyes bright, a picture to remember.

He'd gone in just to see her.

Paterson barked: "You're not coming in *here!*"

Roger had to justify himself. "I hope your memory is better in the morning, Miss Paterson."

Paterson almost pushed him out, closed the door firmly, turned the key in the lock and slipped it into his pocket; defiance in every movement.

Sorensen said: "She'll be all right, Pat. Now I must be off, lot of calls to make. People always feel worse at night. Find that with your patients, Inspector?"

"Mine usually get frisky at night."

"I won't come down," Paterson said frigidly.

"No. I'll call in at the Pied Piper." Sorensen bustled off, Paterson ignored Roger and went into his own bedroom. He made as if to close the door; Roger, hands deep in his pockets, stopped him from doing so. Paterson shrugged, went straight to the wardrobe, and looked inside. He frowned, bent down, and groped about the floor. He muttered a sharp imprecation, took out several pairs of shoes and tossed them behind him; two boot boxes, a pair of trees, three pairs of slippers followed. When they were all strewn about the floor, he leaned inside, head and shoulders disappearing as he felt round the wardrobe. At last he withdrew and stood up. His face was pale and his eyes glittered. He looked anywhere but at Roger.

"What's missing?" Roger asked.

Paterson said: "That bag of—damn it, *you* were here all the time! They've been taken from under your very nose. I'll make you suffer for this! They were here, I saw them myself. I thought there was nothing to worry about with the police on the premises. Why—"

Roger said: "Were they so valuable?"

"They were worth—never mind what they were worth!" Paterson's eyes glistened, he seemed really upset for the first time, couldn't pretend any longer. "It's criminal negligence!"

"The negligence was in leaving them in the wardrobe of an unlocked room," said Roger. "Blame yourself, not me. Queer behavior, isn't it? First your daughter and then you behave as if the bag isn't worth tuppence, then you round on me because it's gone. What are those jewels worth?"

"That's my business! It's criminal! I must have

123

those jewels." Paterson's face was red, now, his eyes bloodshot. "They—they weren't mine. I was looking after them for someone else. West, you must find them!"

Roger put his hand into his coat pocket.

"Curiouser and curiouser. Negligence with your own valuables would be odd enough, but with other people's it's—what's the word? Criminal?" He took the bag out, and tossed it into the air, caught it again. "I thought it better not to let them lie about for anyone to pick up. Yes, the seal is intact."

Paterson gulped. "You—you give them to me!" He held out his hand.

"Later. Your daughter seemed satisfied that because the seal isn't broken, the contents haven't been touched. As a policeman, I've different ideas. Clever people can make a seal look as good as new. Have you a list of the contents of the bag?"

"Give that bag to me!"

Roger said quietly: "You don't quite get it. I am a police officer, and I must know whether the contents of this bag are intact. I intend to make sure." He took a penknife from his pocket and opened it, as if he were about to cut the cord. Paterson clenched his hands, looked as if he were prepared to snatch the bag away.

And then Roger was aware of another presence, behind him. Paterson noticed nothing; Roger sensed rather than saw it. He held the knife in one hand and the bag in the other, and repeated quietly: "Have you a list of the contents?"

"I have," said a woman.

Paterson exclaimed: "Helen!" Roger turned

124

slowly, and a woman smiled at him. He was ob-
tuse.

"Who is this, please?"

"My secretary—Helen Wolf," Paterson said.

12

Helpful Miss Wolf

She was short, plump, rotund, and middle-aged. She wore a sealskin coat, which made her look like a furry black ball, and a black felt hat with artificial flowers in it, cupped on top of a head of fluffy, golden hair. Her eyes and her cheeks glowed with good health and good humor. She had a round face with a little button of a nose, a small pointed chin, a wide mouth carelessly daubed with lipstick, and lovely teeth. Under her right arm was a fat, black briefcase, the zip-fastener kind; and she wore yellow gloves, with that outfit!

"Are you Superintendent West?" she asked.

It was the voice of the woman who'd telephoned Janet. Light, lilting, gay; a child's voice, the voice of someone who enjoyed every moment of living. And her name was Wolf.

"I'm Chief Inspector West."

"Is that *higher* than a Superintendent?" asked Helen Wolf, and smiled brightly, ingenuously. "I suppose it doesn't matter. Pat, aren't you lucky—you always fall on your feet! You might have had to deal with an ordinary policeman or someone from Hounslow; instead you have one of the *élite* of Scotland Yard. He'll put everything right in five minutes, won't you, Mr. West?" She held out her hand. "May I check that?"

"We'll do it together," Roger said dryly.

"I only wanted to save you trouble, you must find the routine work so wearying. Isn't he attractive, Pat? Pat! What's the matter? Haven't you had dinner?"

"No. Never mind dinner. I—"

"But I do mind," said Helen Wolf firmly. "Mr. West, I wonder if you're like that? If Mr. Paterson misses a meal, he really feels unwell, it's the poor nutritive value of the food today, I suppose, although he doesn't go short of much." She gave a gay little laugh. "Will this checking wait until I've prepared a snack, Mr. West?" She took a bottle labeled "Bismuth Tablets" from her bag, shook one on to her palm, and gave it to Paterson. "I bet you forgot this, too."

Paterson gulped it down.

"Yes, I'll wait," Roger said.

"I met Dr. Sorensen, he told me that all the servants have left, it *is* a nuisance." She turned to the passage, stripping off her gloves; it was difficult because of the briefcase, and the furry ball began to shake, as if it were a cat, licking itself. "He told me that Margaret isn't well, and has gone to bed. Shall I just pop in and see her?"

Paterson gave her the key, and she hurried along, walking as if her feet were fitted with roller skates. She disappeared into Margaret's room, and her lilting voice rang out; she didn't close the door, but when she reappeared she had taken off her coat and hat, and was poking her fingers through that mass of golden fluff. Round her neck was a bilious-looking yellow scarf, with a black design on it; as she drew nearer Roger felt a chill quiver at the back of his neck; for the design was a series of wolves' heads.

The ends of the scarf rose over her rounded bosom; she looked as if she had much difficulty in keeping any shape at all—and he noticed that she had tiny hands, tiny feet and tiny ankles; but the big calves of her legs were revealed by an old-fashioned knee-length skirt.

"I won't be two jiffs," she said. "You'll have it in the study, Pat, won't you?"

"The study will do." Paterson seemed more sure of himself now, was much more like the man who had first arrived at the house; the woman's arrival had given him confidence.

The study was tidy. He nodded with grudging approval, went to the desk and sat down.

"I hope you won't have to stay here long, West."

"Probably until we've caught the murderer. You don't seem to realize that a man *was* murdered here."

"It's a nuisance," said Paterson, and shrugged. "Well, what questions do you want to ask me?"

"For cold-blooded indifference that would take some beating. I want lists of missing goods, and any information you can give me about your servants' friends and visitors. And—"

"Helen can give you all that." Paterson lit a small, black cheroot.

"And I want to know the name of this red-haired man."

"If I knew the name of the man, I'd tell you." Paterson shrugged again, as if there was nothing more to be said about that. "I'm greatly concerned about my daughter. That fool downstairs seemed to be suggesting that she might have killed Lake. She—"

"She had the opportunity, and she's lied to us as freely as you have."

"That's impertinent!"

"It's the truth. Why are you shielding the redhead? What is he to you? Or to Miss Paterson? Everything points to the fact that he tried to murder your daughter, and did murder Lake. If he didn't do that, then Miss Paterson almost certainly did. There were only two people in the gymnasium."

"Nonsense!" But Paterson wasn't really perturbed.

Roger said: "You can't brush off circumstantial evidence like that. If you don't want to see your daughter held on a murder charge, you'd better name the man."

"I am not going to allow myself to be browbeaten."

"Look here," said Roger, "I have every justification for taking Miss Paterson along to the station for questioning. If you want to save your daughter a lot of unpleasantness, you'll name the man."

"I have no idea who he is," Paterson said firmly, "and as I told you before, I am not going to be browbeaten by you or anyone else. I have some rights in law; so has my daughter. One of them is the benefit of legal advice. I shall take it first thing in the morning, unless you're foolish enough to want to take Margaret away against medical advice. In that case, I should take legal opinion immediately. I don't want to make difficulties, West, but I don't like your manner."

Roger said: "And I don't like your habits."

"What habits?"

"Employing old lags, who—"

"If I choose to help men who have fallen foul of the law and who never get a square deal from the police, that is my affair and my risk," said Paterson. "I am not responsible for what my servants do. Until now, they have behaved extremely well. I shall help them in any way I can, with money, advice, and legal aid. You're not going to ride roughshod over anyone in this affair, West, and the quicker you realize it the better."

"You've a cockeyed opinion of the police. We want justice and we want results. In this case, we want a murderer, and you and your daughter are withholding material evidence about one. That is a criminal offense."

Paterson sat back in his chair and smiled; the change which had come over him since his secretary's arrival was astonishing. There was a change, too, in his appearance; the whites of his eyes were clearer, and there was no hint of shakiness about his hands. The small cheroot was half smoked; he took it out of his mouth and looked at the two inches of gray ash, left it there, and put it back between his lips.

"You have to prove that we're withholding that evidence, and it can't be proved. Don't waste your time trying to frighten me, West."

Roger said: "I've a job to do, and I'm going to do it. Friends of Lobo are enemies of society."

Paterson didn't even blink.

"Friends of whom?"

"A man called Lobo." But the challenge for which he had been building had already fallen flat. "Don't tell me you've never heard of him."

"Lobo," murmured Paterson. "I don't think that

130

—oh!" He started, and the ash dropped from the cheroot. "Do you mean the burglar? The man who is supposed to be responsible for a long series of crimes and that brutal murder in Hampstead? My dear man, have you taken leave of your senses! What has this affair to do with Lobo?"

Roger said: "His men trained here."

"Don't be ridiculous."

"Carney and your other servants trained them."

"I am really beginning to understand why the police seldom get results," said Paterson. "I—"

He started to get up, as the door opened, but Miss Wolf said brightly: "I can manage." She came into the room carrying a large tray; how she had opened the door was a mystery. The tray looked heavy; Roger took it from her, and found that it was. "Thank you so much! You see, the police can be useful when they really try, Pat. You shouldn't be too hard on them, they have a difficult task. Don't you, Mr. West? I think they get results *quite* often. Why, Pat, only the other day I was fined a guinea for parking my car on the wrong side of the road! Be fair." She beamed up into Roger's face. "I thought you'd be hungry, too, Mr. West, so I've brought enough for both of you. I'll go and get the coffee in a few minutes—or do you prefer tea?"

"Coffee will do nicely, thanks."

She took the lids off two dishes. On one was a pile of sandwiches, cut very thin, oozing butter and some kind of spread, on the other, thin slices of ham. She whisked a lace cloth from beneath her arm, spread it over a gate-leg table, and laid the table swiftly. Then she placed chairs on either side of it, and stood back to admire her handiwork.

"You won't starve on that." The lilting voice was

always bright and beguiling. "While you're eating, I'll start checking the things in here. None of the other rooms were touched, were they?"

"I don't think so," Paterson said.

"I expect Mr. West will see that we check everything, and make sure." She busied herself at the desk, but after a few minutes, bobbed up and went downstairs for the coffee. Paterson made no comment while she was out of the room.

The coffee was perfectly made; she poured out two cups, added cream, and sat at the desk again, studying the papers. She seemed incapable of sitting without anything to do. Her cheeks were bright and pretty; yes, she was a pretty creature, in spite of her plumpness; it was impossible to imagine anyone less sinister. But every now and again a corner of the wolf-head scarf fell across the paper on which she was writing, and she flung it back, with a gesture of annoyance. Each time she did that, she looked up at Roger with a beguiling smile.

She jumped up the moment they finished.

"Never mind the tray, I'll clear that away later. We *must* check that bag of jewels, Pat."

Roger took it out of his pocket, and opened his knife again. There was no longer tension in Paterson's manner; he watched the string being cut, and the neck of the bag being pulled open, as if it were of no importance at all. Then why had he made so much fuss before?

Cotton wool was stuffed in the top of the bag.

Roger lifted some out, and felt the first jewel, inside a little roll. As he pulled off the cotton wool, his excitement rose.

It was a diamond, nearly as large as a hazel nut, beautifully cut and polished, which lay on the palm of his hand winking and sparkling in the light as if it were alive. The woman made a tick against a small typewritten list in front of her. Roger picked up his penknife, and deliberately scratched the surface of the diamond; the knife made no impression.

"Oh, it's *real*," said Miss Wolf. "And it's legally in Mr. Paterson's charge, so you won't find anything here that there shouldn't be. Pat, I do declare that he thought you dealt in smuggled gems—or perhaps even stolen goods!" Her laugh trilled out.

Roger put the diamond on a sheet of white blotting paper which dimmed its beauty, and unwrapped an emerald, much larger, rich in green, lambent fire. The diamond was probably the most valuable; the total value of all that he took out could not be far short of fifty thousand pounds. There were two dozen gems at least.

"Nothing missing," crowed Miss Wolf. "I don't think anything is, Pat, anyway. The money's intact, everything! The thief must have been looking for the jewels, and wasn't going to bother with trifles. I suppose he was after the same thing at the office. And that reminds me, you and Margaret will have to move to the office tomorrow, you can't stay here without staff. There are limits, aren't there, Mr. West? Now, you want the full names and old addresses of the servants, and everything else, don't you? Here are the files—we keep a file on everyone who works for us, it's a kind of dossier, really. Here's Carney's; we always called him Carney. You see, he was absolutely frank with us. He served four terms of imprisonment—and unlike so many rogues, he didn't say that he was really innocent, he just said he was tired of a life of crime. Prisons aren't very comfortable, and they are getting so overcrowded. I wonder if he did kill poor Lake? They were never very good friends." '

"I think Carney was a long way from here when Lake was killed," Roger said.

"Well, I suppose you know. Carney has great natural cunning. I never liked him, but he was so able, such a good disciplinarian, intelligent in spite of his looks. Here's Lake's dossier—*he'd* been in prison *five* times. I could never understand it, because he had a good job, he was a skilled mechanic, and wonderful about the house. If a window catch broke or we locked ourselves out and wanted to get in, he was always at hand. He boasted that there wasn't a lock in the country that he couldn't force if he wanted to! He kept the burglar-alarm system in order, too— such a waste, as it was never used. You may think we were unwise to employ jailbirds, Mr. West, but you know the old saying—set a thief to catch a thief, don't you?"

"I've heard it somewhere."

Miss Wolf gurgled. "You've a delicious sense of humor! When Margaret's feeling better, she'll enjoy being with you. You haven't seen Margaret at her best, you know; she's perfectly adorable. The only trouble with her is that she likes a good time, and won't settle down. Are you married, Mr. West?"

"Yes. Didn't you know?"

The innocent blue eyes sparkled at him.

"I believe I did read something about it in one of the papers. Wasn't it mentioned yesterday? Oh, yes! You've two lovely little boys and a most charming wife. One wouldn't expect you to marry an ordinary woman, would one?" The words were almost identical with those she had uttered into the telephone; the voice was exactly the same. He was quite sure that she had threatened Janet, and had talked to him. She knew he realized that, and was laughing at him, because she felt completely secure. Was she a megalomaniac, who thought it safe to behave like this with the police?"

How had she managed to pour Paterson's confidence back into him? Paterson was smoking another cheroot and smiling as if he appreciated the subtlety of her approach.

She jumped up.

"Here are the other dossiers, Mr. West, you can look at them while I take the tray downstairs. More coffee? Shall I bring the brandy up, Pat? You know you always like a little brandy late in the evening." She loaded the tray and fluttered out, pulling the door to with her foot without waiting for Roger to close it.

Paterson stood up, smiling.

"She is a remarkable woman. Quite the most efficient person I've ever employed. Absolutely trustworthy, too, and her knowledge of precious stones is exceptional. You have gathered that I deal in gems, I assume?" The sneer in the voice was unmistakable.

"Part of your time," said Roger.

"I assure you that it is my chief occupation. You know, West, you're quite mistaken if you think I know anything about any roguery my staff might have been up to. They spent a lot of time here on their own, I'm away a great deal. I suppose it *is* possible that the house was used as a kind of training center." His smile broadened. "I admire men with cool nerves! Haven't you done enough here? I should have thought there was plenty for you to do with Carney and the others."

"I want the name of the red-haired man."

135

"Oh, that." Paterson shrugged. "I suppose I shall never convince you that I don't know the fellow. Margaret might know him, of course. She has a host of boyfriends. You'd better ask her again in the morning. I—"

He broke off at a flurry of footsteps approaching. The door burst open and Helen Wolf rushed in, breathing with her mouth wide open, a hand pressed deep into her bosom. "Oh!" she gasped, and drew a deep breath. "Oh, Pat! Pat, she's run away again. Got up and dressed and gone out. What *are* we going to do with her?"

13

Sloan's Night Out

The bed was empty. Margaret's pajamas were in a heap on the floor, her slippers stood by the end of the bed, a hot-water bottle lay on the pillow. The window was wide open. Roger went to it and looked at the roof of the porch beneath. Paterson stood by the door, hands clenched, more angry than worried, and Miss Wolf fluttered about at the wardrobe.

"She's got on the gray overcheck tweeds, Pat—and those old comfortable walking shoes, and-oh! She's packed a bag! Her black evening gown is missing, and all the accessories. That means she intends to stay away for some days again. What are we going to do about that child?"

"So she makes a habit of it," remarked Roger.

"Yes, she's so self-willed. Her father doesn't like her gadding about so much, she was very naughty last week, and she was supposed to stay at home at night for the rest of the month. If it hadn't been for what's happened tonight, she would never have got away, Carney would have stopped her."

Paterson said: "You're a wonderful policeman, West, aren't you?"

Roger shrugged. "She isn't the first woman to run away from us, and she won't be the first we catch."

"Run away from *you?*" gasped Miss Wolf. "Don't be silly, she's run away from her father. I suppose we ought to go and look for her, Pat. But why worry, tonight? She won't come to any harm, and a night out might relieve her high spirits. I'm not a bit sure that this curfew is a good thing for her, it stimulates her mind, she's always trying to find a way to defeat it. I'll telephone round to the usual places, if you like."

"Don't worry," said Roger. "Give me a list of them."

"Shall·I, Pat?"

Paterson said: "We might as well let him earn his salary for once. How on earth he won his reputation, I don't know."

Roger ignored that. "What kind of places does Miss Paterson usually visit?"

"Oh, night clubs," said Miss Wolf. "These silly places where a lot of desiccated have-beens and stupid provincials waste their money and think they're having a good time. I don't know what it is about them that fascinates Margaret, but something does. First, she usually goes to the Plastic Slipper. Then the Can-Can, that's always got a floor show soon after midnight and she loves the dance. After that..."

Bill Sloan thought: Roger's an uncanny beggar, he's right again. He stood some distance from the window and watched Margaret Paterson climb out. There was no light in her room, but that from the drawing room showed her clearly. She had a suitcase which she lowered to the ground on a long strap; she let it fall the last few feet, and it dropped into a flower bed with a dull thud. Then she turned her back on him, while standing on the roof of the porch, went to one side, and gradually lowered herself. She hung a couple of feet from the ground, dropped, stood up and kept close to the wall, looking about her as if she were afraid that she might be seen. Satisfied, she crept away from the porch, but didn't go to the drive. She walked across the long lawn, and Sloan followed her, thirty or forty feet away. She made her way toward the drive from there, and he saw her as she went out of the gate, a dark figure against the white woodwork. Then she turned right, walking boldly, her footsteps ringing out.

Sloan followed, his rubber soles making little noise. She blotted out the rear light of his car, then appeared again, a vague shape in the glow from the side lamp. The surface of the road was pale, and she showed up against it. She didn't look round now. Sloan kept close to the hedge, against which he would be invisible if she did turn her head. The glow of headlights as cars moved along the Great West Road seemed a long way off; he knew that it was the better part of a mile. They passed the brazier, which had become a dull red glow. Margaret stepped out at a good pace; her suitcase couldn't be very heavy.

A church clock, not far away, struck the half hour; ten-thirty. A little farther on a double-decker bus, lights shining brightly, passed the end of the road. A single word floated back to Sloan. *"Damn!"*

She probably knew that was the last bus. She didn't slacken her pace; it took them about twenty minutes to reach the corner. She crossed the road, immediately, but he stayed on the same side. It was well lighted. She changed the case from one hand to the other, and stepped out as if this were high adventure.

Sloan crossed the road; he was fifty yards behind her then. He lit a cigarette, and looked back, but saw no lights shining from Morden Lodge.

Half a mile farther on was a large, white-painted garage. Sloan saw the attendants putting petrol in the tanks of two cars. He picked out the name sign: Robey's Garage. The girl changed the case over again, and began to hum; the lilting tune came back to Sloan; he found himself humming it, too. The wind had dropped, but a sudden gust swept up around him. Margaret clapped her free hand on top of her hat; a little dark hat. She kept her hand there, looking an odd, yet attractive, figure, a silhouette now against the garage lights. Several cars stood on one side, and above them was a sign: Cars for Hire.

"I get it," murmured Sloan.

She reached the garage and went inside. Sloan didn't hang back. She wouldn't know him by sight, he doubted whether she suspected that he had followed her. Anyhow, his job was to make sure he didn't lose her. The light of the garage fell on his face as he heard Margaret say:

"Hallo, George. Can I have a car?"

"'Evenin', Miss Paterson. I thought you wasn't going to do this any more."

"Life's so *dull*, George."

The unseen man chuckled; obviously he was on

her side. He was short and thin, and dressed in white overalls; he glanced up when Sloan appeared. Margaret looked round and smiled; she was likely to smile at any good-looking man, Sloan fancied.

" 'Evening, sir."

"Can I get a taxi here?" asked Sloan.

"Yes, sir. Won't keep you long."

"Where are you going?" asked Margaret. She rubbed her hands together, as if to ease them after the strain of carrying the case. She looked bright eyed and wide awake; it was hard to believe that she had been through so much that night.

"Now, Miss Margaret—" began George.

"Don't be silly, George. Where *are* you going?" she asked Sloan again. "I'm going to drive to the West End. If that would help you—"

"Miss Margaret!"

"Well—" said Sloan. "It's very kind of you and I am going to London. I'm told that I've missed the last bus."

"Oh, you have! Come with me, I like company."

"Miss Margaret, it's silly to drive alone with strange men."

"Isn't he a dear?" asked Margaret; and had Roger heard her, he would have thought that she sounded very much like Miss Wolf. "I shall be all right, George, I know how to look after myself. You won't kidnap me, or anything like that, will you?" She laughed into Sloan's face.

"That wasn't exactly the idea," Sloan said. "On the other hand, if you'd like to be kidnapped—"

"No, not tonight."

George shrugged his shoulders, as if washing his hands of the whole affair, and went outside. He drove a sleek Alvis up to the petrol pump, checked the petrol and oil, and collected Margaret's case, putting it in the back. She put a pound note into his hand; Sloan gave him five shillings.

"Drive straight there," George warned.

Margaret laughed.

She was an excellent driver, and seemed to know the car. Soon they were touching seventy along the straight, wide road. There was little traffic. Small houses on either side were mostly in darkness. They passed the Osterley Hotel, then the factory area. A train was passing over the bridge serving one of the factories, and Margaret slowed down and watched the red-tinged smoke pouring from the funnel.

"Do you like watching trains?" It was the first word she had spoken since they'd driven off.

"I've outgrown it as a pastime."

"That's foolish of you. It's bad enough to outgrow pleasures, you lose so much. I'm going to do a night-club crawl, and I'm told that I ought to have outgrown that a long time ago, but I still get a kick out of it. Are you a night owl?" She turned to look at him searchingly. "No, I don't think you are. I should say you are happily married, with three children, and you hate being home half an hour after your promised time, that's why you were going to take a taxi instead of walking to the station—you could easily have done that; the trains run late."

Sloan laughed. "Married, one child—and my wife is away for a few weeks, recuperating after the ordeal."

"Oh! A *young* baby."

142

"Three weeks and four days, almost to the minute."

"It must have been a thrill. What are you? A commercial traveler?"

"Not exactly. A representative."

"The snob name for the same thing." She laughed, robbing the words of any sting. "Why don't you have a night out with me? I—no, I *don't* mean what George would think I do. I mean, come on the club-crawl. I could show you a lot of things you probably haven't seen before! Have you ever seen the Can-Can? It's the most thrilling dance I know."

"I did see it once, at the Palladium."

"Oh, that's nothing like intimate enough. I'm going to a night club called the Can-Can. They've brought five girls from Belgium over specially— they're quite wonderful; every time I see them I begin to throw my legs about. Later on, at the Muscat, I shall probably try the dance, I shall be quite drunk by then. Now I suppose you're going to disapprove of young women getting drunk. It does one good, occasionally—it would do you good too. Come and get drunk with me." Her voice was almost pleading.

Sloan laughed again with her, not at her.

"I don't get drunk so easily. Anyhow, they wouldn't let me in. I'm not dressed for the part."

"That wouldn't matter at all of them, but it would at the Can-Can, and I can't miss that. But— where do you live?" Her voice rose in excitement.

"Victoria."

"Wonderful! We can call at your flat, I can use one of the rooms, and you'll have everything you want. I usually go to a friend, but it's farther away

143

from the Can-Can. We haven't a lot of time, if we're going to see the show, and I don't want to miss it. What's your address?"

Sloan said: "I'm not sure that—"

"Don't be a prude! Your wife will never know, and it will be innocent fun. I've told you that George's suspicions are all wrong. Drunk or sober, I do *not* like promiscuity." Her laugh rang out, and when he didn't comment, she went on: "I suppose it is asking too much. I suppose you were brought up by dull but respectable parents, who regarded drink as an evil and dancing as the work of the Devil."

"You forget that it takes a lot to make me drunk."

"So I did. Will you come?"

Sloan said: "Well, you've asked for it."

He had a three-room flat on the fifth floor of a large block, near Victoria Street. It was simply furnished, but his wife's touches were evident everywhere. Margaret looked round as they entered the tiny hall from the bleak, stone landing, and said: "She's nice. But you haven't kept it very tidy." The doors were open, proving her words. She looked into the living-cum-dining room and then the other rooms, in turn. "What a tiny bathroom! ...And a double bed, no wonder you have babies! I—what's your name?"

"William."

"She can't call you *William.*"

"She doesn't."

"I think I should like her," said Margaret. "I'll change in the bathroom, and you—"

"You can have the bedroom," Sloan said. He

stood back and looked at her, and then suddenly laughed; because he wondered what Roger would say if he could see them now. She laughed also, without asking for an explanation, and disappeared into the bedroom, carrying her own case. Then she called out to him that he must hurry and collect his own clothes. When he went in to collect them, she was stepping out of her skirt; her long, slender legs were shapely, sheathed in nylon.

Later, he heard her humming to herself, and although he hurried, she was ready first. The black gown, flecked with tiny gold pieces, was strapless and looked as if it might slip off at any minute. She had tidied her dark hair, and wore a single flower in it; the flower looked real.

"Let me do that," she said, as he fumbled with his tie. "My father always makes a hash of his, Helen or I have to do it for him." She tied the bow nimbly, laughed into his face, and danced away. "It's twelve, I think, not twelve fifteen, we'll just do it. Is it all right to leave my things here?"

"Yes, no one else will come here, until I do."

"Good old Bill! You know, you're much more fun than I thought you were going to be. Come on. Would you care to drive? I hate driving in a long dress."

The small room of the Can-Can club was in darkness when they arrived, except for a spotlight which shone on to the tiny circular dance floor. Five girls, dressed in the frills and furbelows of the dance, tripped out from a doorway and threaded their way through the crowded tables. A rustle of applause ran round the room. The head waiter had found a table near the front for Margaret, and she

145

whispered to him as to an old friend. She watched the dancers intently, her eyes glistening. The girls were small and pretty, with legs just made for this dance; and they put their heart into it, seeming to enjoy it as much as the audience did. There was a breathless hush each time they sprang up for the splits; then a rustle of applause. The light, skillfully planned, showed up the youthful freshness of each one.

Margaret didn't take her eyes off the dancers; and when they finished and bowed, and the lights went up, she stood up and clapped and kept crying out: *"Wonderful! Perfect!"*

When Sloan looked round, there was champagne on the table.

"I'm not a millionaire," he said.

"Don't forget that I've just seen your home," said Margaret. Her eyes laughed at him, she was really enjoying herself, as a child would. "You're my guest."

"I see," said Sloan dryly.

There wasn't an empty table. Nearly everyone wore tails, only a few were in dinner suits. Young and old, sweet and soured, young girls with old men, young men with old women—the usual crowd Sloan reflected, rather classier than most.

The waiter came up, the cork popped, they lifted their glasses, and Margaret said: "I'm dying to dance. I hope you dance well."

"Not well enough for you."

They had a snack, and then Margaret said: "Here's a rumba. Can you rumba?"

They started to dance, and soon she was beaming congratulations at him, although it was only possible to jig. "You're wonderful!" Two more glasses of champagne, thought Sloan, and every-thing would be wonderful to Margaret Paterson. He bumped into a man who apologized gruffly. Sloan looked round to smile an acceptance—and missed a step.

"Now, Bill, don't—why, what is it? Oh, *damn!*" She looked vexed. "You've seen someone you know. Let's get out. Come on, we were going to leave soon, anyhow. Does he know your wife, too? Or is it a she?"

It was Janet West and Mark Lessing. Lessing had seen him, Janet hadn't. As they danced, the Can-Can girls mixed with them, handing all the women hats; little feathered hats. Margaret took one, but didn't put it on.

"Let's go," she whispered.

"There's no need to panic." They finished the dance, Margaret's high spirits were damped, she was on edge to leave. She touched a waiter's arm and asked for the bill. When it came, Sloan picked it up.

"Bill, I said you were my guest."

"You have your own way too much." He put down ten one-pound notes and wondered whether he could get away with it on his expense list; Roger would back him up.

Mark and Janet were still dancing, Janet in a white dress. Janet looked more excited than usual, as if she had had a lot to drink. He didn't think much about that as they went out, and got into the Alvis.

"Where next?"

"The Firefly, in Milberry Mews."

"I know the Firefly." As he drove, she leaned to-ward him, her head fell on his shoulder. She wore

147

the hat, now. He hoped she wouldn't get maudlin and romantic, but he'd asked for this; and it was almost the only way he could carry out his job successfully. They drove through the dark streets, and he found himself thinking of Janet and her excitement; a forced gaiety.

The Firefly was dull, the Moon Calf only mildly exciting, the Toucan smelly; Margaret wrinkled up her nose and said, "We won't stay." Finally, they reached the Muscat just before two o'clock. This was the largest and most modern of them all, where there was a semblance of value for money. Also it kept open later than most. The big room was painted with vineyard scenes; great bunches of grapes hung from monstrous artificial vines which stretched across the ceiling; there was a large dance floor and a ventilation system which made it possible to breathe and dance in comfort. Margaret forgot that she was going to dance the Can-Can, forgot that she wanted to be gay, looked sleepy and soon began to yawn. The band played on, waiters slipped about between the tables, Margaret's head drooped, and she looked up blankly when Sloan touched her shoulder. He paid the bill, helped her up and led her to the door, wondering what would happen next. The fresh night air, with the blustering wind, did nothing to revive her. Her head lolled on his shoulder, and as far as he could judge it was from sheer fatigue. He opened all the windows wide, and drove fast through the West End and the parks, but her head still rested on his shoulder, and she seemed to be asleep.

He went to Victoria and pulled up outside the block of flats. She didn't stir.

"Margaret, wake up."

There was no answer. He shook her gently; it was difficult to be severe with her. Suddenly he felt anxious, and slapped her face; it didn't help. He heard a car turn into the street, then saw the headlights flash on. The car slowed down, and the light shone on Margaret's face, on her glistening red lips, which seemed not to be moving as she breathed. Sloan felt a sudden surge of panic, and shouted: "Wake up!" He seized her shoulders and shook her until her head jerked to and fro, but her mouth and eyes didn't open, she was a dead weight. He let her sit there with her head drooping on his shoulder, and took her right hand; he felt for the wrist with his finger.

She couldn't be dead.

The other car had stopped a little way beyond. A man came walking toward them. Sloan averted his head, then put his arm round Margaret's shoulders and drew her closer to him; her hair hid his face. But that didn't prevent the man from stopping.

Sloan didn't look up. It wasn't a policeman, or he would have recognized the heavy, deliberate tread. Who else—

"Enjoying yourself?" asked Roger West.

Sloan opened the front door of his flat, and Roger carried the girl inside. There, her hat fell off. He went straight to the bedroom, laid her down, took off her shoes and felt her waist; she wasn't wearing a girdle, there was nothing to loosen. He sat at the side of the bed, while Sloan stood by, pale-faced and anxious, alarmed lest she had died. She seemed to be asleep, but she hadn't moved. Sloan wasn't sure whether her pulse was beating or not.

Roger dropped her hand.

"False alarm, Bill. She's all right."

"Are you sure?"

"The Press won't get another laugh out of this," Roger assured him. "You've had quite a night out." He looked at her clothes, spread out on a chair, and grinned. "I didn't think you had it in you, William!"

"Look here, if you think—"

"Queer effect the Patersons have on us; we aren't ourselves with them," said Roger. "I don't think anything, stop being an ass. Did you have much trouble becoming her escort for the night?"

"You would probably have fallen for it, too."

"Yes. She's easy on the eye, and there's something about her. Odd, this trick of losing consciousness suddenly. It's the third time she's done it. I wonder if the good Dr. Sorenson could explain it." Roger lit a cigarette, and led the way out of the room. He picked up the little hat of feathers, and said: "Was she wearing this?"

"No. They give them away at the Can-Can."

"So that's where she got the other one from. Any idea where she was going after this?"

"She said she usually changed at a friend's flat, but I didn't get the address out of her. She behaved like a kid half the time, but gave nothing away. I thought I could wait for a while, and talk to her when she was tiddly. I never expected her to drop off like that."

"No. It's damned funny. Two policemen in search of Lobo, and this is where we get! Do you think she suspects you're a busy?"

"I shouldn't be surprised." Sloan broke off, and glanced round. "Thought I heard something." He

150

went to the door and listened, actually opened it and peered out at the stone landing.

Roger went to the bedroom. Margaret's eyelids didn't flutter, she seemed to be sound asleep. He stood and watched, and felt his heart beating fast. Damn the girl! Why did she have to be so lovely?

Stop this folly! He must put his thoughts in proper order. He was a policeman; first a policeman, then a husband, then a man. Janet hated the order of precedence, but there it was. He closed the door, only to open it again stealthily. Why? To try to catch her out? Or just to see her again? She was still in exactly the same position. The curving lashes brushed her cheeks and did not move.

Sloan whispered: "Finished bo-peep?"

"Yes." Roger led the way into the kitchen, where Sloan kept his beer; he knew the little flat well. "Mind if I break into your cellar?" He talked as he opened two bottles of light ale. "We've got a lot of things out of focus, and we've got to get them back. You know the outline of tonight's business, but I can fill in the details in ten minutes."

Sloan leaned against the sink.

"I'm listening."

In eight minutes Roger finished, and Sloan poured out another glass of beer. It was then three o'clock.

"Bray nearly boxed the whole show when he put those workmen in the lane. Why don't people learn?"

Roger shrugged.

"I thought the same thing. But Bray really started tonight's show. Carney and the other servant saw the men outside, knew what it meant, and cleared out. Whether before they left they

151

robbed Paterson or not is a moot point. I don't think they did. I think Paterson's involved in this, and that the so-called robbery was a blind. But it was made to look as if one of the servants visited the study and had a good look round. It's not the only business that's phony."

"What else?"

Roger said: "If it was sheer coincidence that Maid Margaret was fired on at the moment when I was passing, I'll hand in my papers. That was done deliberately, but why?—well, I just can't guess. The pretense that they don't know the redhead is also phony; they know him as well as I know you. Whether the redhead or Margaret or someone unknown killed Lake, I wouldn't care to guess."

Sloan said: "Kick me if you like, but she doesn't strike me as a murderess."

"I know what you mean." Roger grinned. "Miss Helen Wolf doesn't strike me as a cold-blooded vixen, but I think that's what she is. Everyone we've met tonight—I've met," he corrected hastily —"has been playing a part. They may be scared and playing a risky hand boldly. Whatever the main purpose, it's also been to pull the wool over the eyes of the police. They've partly succeeded. I think we might clear some of the wool away if we charge Margaret Paterson with the murder."

Sloan pulled a face.

"Can we get away with it?"

"No, not on the evidence. We'd have to let her go. But we could hold her for a few days, and in those few days her father might crack. Against that, if she remains free, she might lead us to the red-haired boyfriend. She knew he was in the house or grounds, and skipped out to see him—probably to

shoo him away. Make sense of that, if you can—
he's the man who took a pot shot at her."

"You make the sense," Sloan said. "It would be
more like you to let her tag around, and hope that
she leads us to the youngster. Sure he's young?"

"Yes, I wasn't the only one to see him."

The talk brightened Roger; he was sharpening
his wits on Sloan, felt better than he had for some
time.

"Helen Wolf, Paterson, and Margaret all deny
knowing a redhead. There's one of the most important jobs we have to do: find out whether Margaret
has a ginger-haired friend. I gathered that she
often goes on the loose, like tonight, and Helen
gave me a list of her likely dens of vice. Where've
you been?"

Sloan told him.

"You can add The Magpie, Silver Slipper, Rock-
ing Horse, Pelican and The Devil's Bowl. Put some
men on them, Bill. I've a picture of Margaret here."
He drew out the photographs of Paterson and Margaret. "Send two reliable boys round with these, to
the clubs you've been to and I've named. If you can
get some in tonight, fine. You're chiefly after a redhead. Right?"

"Right. What about this girl?"

"She stays here."

"Who stays with her?"

"I do."

Sloan shrugged. "I'll grant it's an unusual job,
Roger, but go slow. She's smarter than she pretends. We might have been followed tonight. I
didn't see anyone on the road, but there were several other nitwits doing a night-club crawl. They

153

might have been after her. No, no one with red hair. Ever heard of wigs?"

Roger grinned. "I have also heard of hair dye. Get those photographs copied, Bill. Some of those clubs will be open for another hour, and we might strike lucky and pick up a lot if you step on it."

"All right. You brought her here, remember," Sloan said, glancing at the bedroom door. "Don't have me blamed for it, will you?"

"The virtuous William! Your honor shall be unsullied. You did everything at the behest of an unfeeling superior officer. How much did the trip set you back tonight?"

Sloan said: "That's a funny thing. It cost ten pounds for a sip of champagne at the Can-Can. Everywhere else, it was most reasonable. She argued with me about paying—I think she had a word with each boss, and fixed it so that the charges were light, after that. I tell you, she does a lot of odd things behind that smile of hers. Delilah could be the word for her."

Roger laughed.

Sloan put on his hat, tucked the photographs into his wallet, and went out.

The wind had risen again, and he could hear it howling along the street and feel it whipping up the stairs, even at this height. He hurried down. There was no lift at these flats, and that was going to be a nuisance when Joyce was home with the baby. They'd have to find somewhere more convenient. Another gust of wind nearly blew his hat off. He jammed it more tightly on his head, and hurried outside. Brrr! It was cold. He pulled open the door of the Alvis and slid into the driving seat. He might as well use the car; the Paterson girl certainly wouldn't want it again tonight. It was one of the oddest nights of his Yard career. Later—much later—he'd tell Joyce about it, and then—

He felt his hat tipped over his eyes, half-turned, and was struck a heavy blow on the side of the head. It didn't knock him out. He caught a glimpse of a man in the back of the car, arm upraised; then a second blow fell, and his head seemed to split.

14

The Redhead

Roger went to the bedroom and looked at Margaret. She hadn't moved. They'd thrown an eiderdown over her, only her face and one shoulder showed. She lay on her back, and he did not believe that she could be feigning sleep; this was more than sleep, she was drugged.

He went slowly and quietly to the bed and stood looking down at her. Her breath-taking beauty had a quality which made his heart beat fast; she had attracted him from the moment he had seen her. He didn't stop to argue the rights and wrongs or wisdom; just accepted the fact. No woman had moved him like this since he had first met Janet. He felt no sense of disloyalty as he looked down, only an unusual quietness of mind—unusual because he had been so restless during the day.

It was warm in the room.

He went to the window and pushed it up, glanced round to make sure that no draught caught the girl, then noticed that the car still stood outside. Sloan was a long time moving off. He could see only the glowing side lamps and the dark shape of the car.

Sloan had had plenty of time to drive away.

Margaret and his quietness of mind were forgotten. He crossed the room, switched off the light, and went out into the hall, closing the door gently behind him. He stood quite still, listening, heard nothing until suddenly a faint scratching sound broke the stillness.

If Bill had forgotten something he would have hurried back, not climbed the stairs stealthily. As the scratching sound grew louder, Roger backed into the kitchen, which was opposite the front door; the man outside was fumbling in the darkness. Roger could see without being seen.

He wished he had his gun.

The lock turned; after a brief pause the door began to open slowly. A hand appeared; then a man's face and head.

He was red-haired.

He stepped swiftly inside the hall, and stood looking round, stared at the open door of the kitchen, then at the living room. He closed the front door softly, catching his breath as the lock clicked. He was tall and slender, with wide shoulders and a pale skin; a good-looking young man whom Roger thought he'd seen before, not only the back view, but the face. Undoubtedly it was the man who had run across the grounds at Morden Lodge.

He turned again, and Roger saw the heavy spanner gripped in his left hand. He was hatless. The light shone redly on his hair, which was thick, curly, attractive. He had a well-shaped, sensitive mouth, not much of a chin; with a better chin he would have compared with Paterson for good looks. There was a hint of weakness, also of femininity about him. He moved easily. The long spanner swung loosely in his hand, then tapped against his leg.

He came toward the kitchen.

Roger moved a pace, behind the door, and pressed close against the wall; he could not see the man now.

The footsteps stopped; then a door creaked. Roger looked out again, and saw the intruder standing on the threshold of the living room. The spanner was raised; so was the right hand. He was groping for a light. He didn't press it down, but stood absolutely still, as if listening for some sound of movement. He heard nothing, and suddenly switched on the light, then stepped quickly into the room, swinging the spanner.

His shadow moved eerily across the cream-colored walls; and over a small gilt mirror.

The movements stopped as the intruder stood still. Roger stayed in the kitchen. The redhead came out, the weapon half raised; no doubt he would use that if he were threatened. He had probably knocked Bill out and stolen his keys. But Bill would have to wait. The redhead's eyes glittered, he looked tired; feverish. He hesitated in the middle of the hall again, but didn't come to the kitchen, turned to the bedroom and tried the door handle.

He thrust the door open quickly, then switched on the bedroom light.

He gasped: "Margaret!"

Then he hurried into the bedroom.

Roger slipped into the hall, stood by the bedroom door, ready to go in if the redhead threatened the girl; but nothing in the man's tone was threatening. It was a despairing cry.

"Margaret!"

He pulled off the eiderdown, flung himself on the bed, put a hand beneath her head and raised her face—and kissed her passionately, muttering all the time. He kissed her lips, her cheeks, her hair, held her tightly to him, while she lay relaxed in his arms, her face hidden, her body still. The redhead gripped her shoulders, pressed his lips into them, kept muttering her name over and over again.

Roger felt an inward coldness; a repulsion from the youth's complete surrender to his passion.

The youth drew back, but gazed at Margaret, adoringly; fondled her shoulders again, suddenly pressed his face against hers. There was something hopeless in his expression; hopeless passion. He drew away again, and his hands shook as he brushed his hair back. He didn't look round, and the spanner lay by the side of the bed, no threat now. He stroked her hair with his left hand, closed his eyes, sat very still, as if the surge of emotion were too much for him to bear. Then suddenly he cried:

"Margaret, wake up. Wake up! I must talk to you, Margaret!" His voice was low pitched, vibrant. "Margaret, it's me—it's Alec! You must wake up." He took her shoulders and shook her so that her head jolted to and fro, but her eyes didn't open. "Margaret—darling—wake up, wake up!"

There was a sob in his voice.

He stopped shaking her; and he was trembling violently.

"Margaret, I'll do anything for you, anything! I'll die for you, do anything, but talk to me. Wake up and talk to me, tell me you want to marry me."

The sleeping beauty lay still.

Alec clenched his hands, raised them, turned his head away from her, and muttered: "I can't stand it, I just can't stand it. Margaret, please wake up, tell me you still love me. That's all I want to hear, just that. Tell—"

He stopped, and stood up suddenly; a new thought had entered his mind, a thought which quieted him. His stillness, now, was as uncanny as the girl's—who could sleep through all this. He glanced round. His expression had altered, there was a cunning look in his eyes which spoiled his features. He licked his lips; red lips. He turned suddenly, and made for the door. Roger backed away swiftly into the kitchen again, his heart in his mouth; but the youth named Alec had left the spanner behind; any fight would be man against man. He turned down the hall. Roger heard a sharp sound and peered out of the kitchen in time to see Alec straightening up from the bolt of the front door. He went back into the bedroom and slammed that door behind him.

If he locked it—

No, the lock didn't turn. Roger stepped swiftly toward it, turned the handle, opened the door an inch. Alec didn't look behind him, Roger widened the opening, so that he could see the youth, the bed and the girl. Alec stood at the foot of the bed, trembling, his hands at his throat. He took off his tie, and drew it taut between his hands, then let it go slack. He said in a low, clear voice:

"If I can't have you, no one else will. No one else will."

He pulled the tie taut again and went toward the girl.

Roger felt a savage anger toward him; anger, when he should have been detached, dispassionate. He found that his hands were tightly clenched, and felt cold. Alec stood over the girl for what seemed an age, then bent down and raised her head. He put the middle of the tie at the back of her neck, and she didn't move until he let her head fall to the pillow and began to knot the tie—to strangle her.

Roger pushed the door wide open and stepped into the room.

"I think that's enough," he said.

Alec swung round, hands clenching, then backed a pace. His eyes were glaring, his lips were moist. He glanced round swiftly, saw the spanner on the floor, made as if to move toward it, but as Roger darted across the room, changed his direction and came at Roger. His first blow, wild, powerful, caught Roger on the side of the head and sent him reeling back. Alec made a noise, savage, animal, in his throat, and snatched up the spanner. He turned and swung it, Roger flung up his left arm to fend off the blow; the iron cracked against it, and pain sheered through the arm and shoulder. Alec raised the weapon to smash it down upon Roger's head. Roger kicked at his shins, brought a gasp to his lips and made him lose his balance. The spanner whistled harmlessly through the air. Roger went at him, drove his right fist into his stomach, which made him give another agonized gasp and brought the weak chin forward. Roger struck at the chin; every ounce of his weight was behind the blow, and anger, too, this wasn't just self-defense. Alec reeled back, arms waving, and the spanner dropped from his hand. Roger kicked it away, and struck him again, full on the nose. Alec squealed with the pain and cupped his face in his hands; blood trickled through his fingers.

Roger sprang at him, to strike again—

He stopped himself, and drew back, trembling. He turned away, picked up the spanner, and put it on a chair by the door. His hands still shaking, he took out his cigarettes and lit one. He had never been so near to losing his self-control. Alec was too shaken by the pain to move or take his hands away; he held his mouth wide open and took in great shuddering breaths.

Through it all, Margaret slept.

Roger said: "Shake out of it." He took the red-haired man's arm and pulled him out of the bedroom into the bathroom. Alec seemed hardly aware of what was happening. Roger dropped the plug into the hand-basin and turned on the cold-water tap, grabbed the back of Alec's neck and thrust him forward, head and face beneath the water. Alec gasped and shivered, tried to back away, but couldn't move.

Water lapped over the side of the basin.

Roger let him go, pulled a towel from the rail and flung it at him.

Alec dabbed at his hair and face. His nose still bled, but the blood thinned with the water, turning it pink. He kept dabbing, and didn't look at Roger, who stood with his hands in his pocket, watching the youth, trying to sum him up. He saw that Alec's hands still trembled, his knees seemed to wobble.

Roger went forward, took his arm, and led him into the sitting room. Leaving the door wide open, he went into the bedroom, made sure that Margaret was still asleep, switched out the light and closed the door gently. He was half-prepared for a rush from the youth; but Alec sat in an armchair, the towel drooping from his hands, water tinged with blood gathering on the end of his nose and his chin.

Roger said: "Give me your wallet."

Alec didn't move or answer. Roger went across and took the wallet out of his inside coat pocket. He found what he wanted: a letter to Alec Magee, at an address in Kensington.

He tossed the wallet aside, and said: "Well, Mr. Magee?"

Alec gulped. "Who—are you?"

"A friend of Margaret's."

"I—I didn't know what I was doing. I just didn't know what I was doing, she's driven me crazy. Crazy! I can't sleep, can't eat, I can't do anything, everywhere I go she's with me, I can't help it. She's my very life."

"You're crazy, right enough. What did you do to my friend outside?"

"Eh? Who?" The eyes, blue and flecked with gold, darted to and fro. "Oh, the man in the car! I—I knocked him out. I wished I'd killed him! He spent the night with Margaret, took her everywhere, came here with her, brought her to his flat. I wish I'd killed him!"

"You'd get hanged for that."

163

"Hanged?" Alec laughed; a thin, high-pitched sound, mirthless and ugly. "Who cares about getting hanged? I'll get hanged all right, because I—" he stopped abruptly, the cunning look came back to his eyes. "I didn't say anything." He was truculent, aggressive. "I'm talking a lot of nonsense. Margaret always makes me—makes me feel crazy. I'm all right. I'll smash your face in for what you've done to me!" He touched his nose gingerly; it was red and swollen already. "That's what I'll do, smash your face in."

Roger snapped: "Get up." Alec Magee didn't move. Roger crossed the room swiftly and yanked him out of the chair. He swung him round by the shoulder, twisted his arm in a hammerlock, and pushed him toward the hall, then to the front door. He drew back the bolt with his foot, then opened the door. He felt a savage anger, would gladly have bent that arm up until the bone snapped.

Light from the hall shone on to the landing— and on to Bill Sloan, who was coming slowly up the stairs, blood on his forehead and face, his lips clenched, his right hand gripping the handrail. He relaxed when he saw Roger, raised his left hand in greeting, and stopped halfway up the stairs. He looked near collapse.

Roger said: "Take it easy, Bill."

"I'm—all right. So you got the swine." Sloan started up the stairs again. "Go in, I'll be all right." Roger drew back, letting Alec go, but the youth made no attempt to escape, just went slowly back into the sitting room. Sloan said: "I'll be all right, Roger, but watch him, he's dangerous."

"He's tamed now." Roger took Sloan's arm and led him into the sitting room, helped him to sit down beneath the light. The wound was on the back of the head; the hair was matted with blood, blood had trickled down his neck, and there was a long dark streak on his collar, stiffening to the shape of the neck. Roger said: "Magee, I'll smash you up if you move." He pushed the man into a chair, went into the bathroom, drenched a sponge and grabbed two towels, and hurried back. Magee hadn't moved. Roger draped one towel round Sloan's shoulders, then began to sponge the wound. The skin was badly cut, but was there any damage to his skull? Roger dried the wound gently, padded it with one towel and wrapped the other round, turban fashion, scowled, and went to the telephone. Magee sat watching Sloan dully, as he leaned back in his chair, his eyes closed, breathing heavily.

"Scotland Yard, can I help you?"

"This is West. Send a doctor and ambulance to Flat 40, Langeley Mansions, Victoria—Mr. Sloan's flat. Hurry." He waited for the answer, replaced the receiver, turned and growled at Magee: "If we can't hang you, you'll go inside for a stretch."

Sloan's head lolled forward, chin on his chest. Roger put a chair in front of him, raised his legs and lowered his shoulders gently on to a cushion until Sloan lay at full length.

"Is he—is he—" Magee started to say, but couldn't finish. He looked frightened, now. "I didn't mean—didn't mean to kill him."

"Changed your tune, haven't you? Why did you try to kill Margaret?"

Alec said: "*What?* I love her, don't you understand, I love her, I wouldn't—"

He broke off again, and licked his red lips; the

cunning glint in his eye didn't look like that of a sane man. Roger stood between him and Sloan, knowing there was nothing he could do to help Sloan until the doctor arrived.

"And what had Lake done to offend you? Touched his cap to Margaret?"

"Who?"

"Lake. The victim of the Indian club."

Alec said: "I don't know what you're talking about." He closed his mouth, compressed it into a thin line; a gesture of defiance which wouldn't last long. Roger, glancing at Sloan, saw that his eyes were closed; he'd lost consciousness. His skull might be cracked. The effort of walking up the stairs might prove fatal; if there were a severe hemorrhage, he would probably die. Why didn't the ambulance and the police surgeon come? He saw Alec looking at him out of the corner of his eye, with the cunning which lunatics often show.

Alec opened his mouth.

"I didn't mean to hurt anyone, I didn't mean to do any harm. I just didn't know what I was doing. I'm not myself, I can't live without Margaret; ever since she threw me over, I've been ill. I just can't think or do anything, she haunts me. But I didn't mean to do any harm. Can't you understand? I didn't mean to hurt anyone, I just—"

Roger said: "You just smashed their skulls."

"I didn't mean it!" The voice sounded tearful, now; part of the cunning, or else a slow return to sanity, a realization of what he had done. In this mood, he might talk freely. "I didn't mean to hurt anyone. If Margaret had been kind to me, it wouldn't have happened, but she's—so hard. Hard." He sighed the word. "She's beautiful, she makes me go crazy, but she's hard. Cold. Don't you understand? She made me love her, made me believe we would get married, and then—she threw me over. Jilted me! I knew there were others, lots of others, only I thought ours was the real thing. But—it wasn't, she didn't really love me. If only she loved me, everything would be all right. I'm sorry—sorry if I've hurt anyone. I wish—I wish I were dead!"

Roger wished he could do something more for Sloan; but it might be fatal to move him again.

"What were you doing at Morden Lodge, Magee?"

"Eh? The house? Oh, this evening. I was waiting for Margaret. That's all, just waiting for Margaret. I spend hours hanging about there. Just to catch a glimpse of her as she drives in. She won't speak to me, doesn't even smile at me, but it helps—it helps if I can see her. She doesn't always see me, or else she pretends not to. I don't know. Sometimes she tells Carney to throw me out of the grounds. I know that he's got orders to stop me from worrying her, but I can't help it, I just have to see her. And if she's with another man, I—I want to smash him to pulp! Jealousy, I suppose. I tried to reason with myself, I even kept away from her for a week, a whole week—but I couldn't stay away any longer. I've watched her, everywhere. I would have killed her if she'd started gadding about again, but she's been at home all this week. Tonight—tonight was the first time she's left home. Except in the day, it doesn't matter in the daytime."

"How long were you there tonight?" asked Roger.

"Eh? Tonight? I ran away, when that shot was

fired. It scared me. At first I thought it was meant to kill Margaret, perhaps it was, but—she wasn't hurt, was she? Then some other men came up, and I ran away. I thought it was Carney and the others, they'd have beaten me up if they'd caught me."

Roger said more gently: "Did you see Carney when the shot was fired?"

"Eh? No, I didn't see anyone. Only Margaret. I was only looking at Margaret." He gave a smile, a foolish smile, yet with a lot of cunning in it. "I hid in the ditch. They couldn't see me there. I hid in the ditch, and was looking at her—and then the shot was fired."

"Who fired it?"

"I don't know."

"Are you sure you didn't see anyone else there?"

"Only the men who came running up to Margaret. I just saw them, that's all, then I ran away. They'd have beaten me up." He sighed. "Look here, I'm tired, and my nose hurts. You shouldn't have hit me like that, it still hurts. You might have broken it."

A car drew up in the street below.

Roger said: "What happened, later? Why did you return to the house?"

"I just *had* to see Margaret."

"Did you see her?"

"Yes." A fatuous smile crossed Alec's face, and he nodded with deep satisfaction. "Oh, yes, I saw her. There were a lot of strange men at the house, and I couldn't see Carney or any of the others. I crept up and listened at the window, and I heard someone say that all the servants had left. I didn't mind, provided they weren't there. If Carney had ever hit *you*, you'd know why I was so scared of him. He

168

nearly broke my arm once, and—well, they'd gone, so it didn't matter. I saw Margaret, at the window, and beckoned, and—and she came to see me. Why—*you* were in the room with her!"

Roger said: "Was I?"

"Yes," Alec giggled. "So was her father. I pointed to the gym, where we always used to meet, and she nodded. So I waited until she left the room, and then I went to the gym. She—she was there." He frowned, as if teased by some unpleasant memory, and drew his hand across his face. "I know she was there, and—oh, yes. Yes! There was someone else there. I heard him moving about. Well, I think I did. Did you mention Lake, just now?"

"Don't you remember?"

"It—it's all vague, hazy, I can't remember everything. No, I can't remember." He smiled again; but there was the old cunning in the smile, he probably remembered everything vividly, reasoned that it would be smart to pretend that he'd seen nothing. "Then I left. It wasn't any good staying, was it, when someone else was coming? I—I jumped somewhere. I think I must have jumped out of the window."

The front-door bell rang.

Roger turned toward the hall. "And what happened then? Did you lie in wait for her?"

"Eh? Oh, no. I went to the Can-Can. She always goes to the Can-Can when she's able to get away. She went tonight, with that—with *that* man."

He pointed at Sloan; and looked as if he would gladly murder him.

The bell rang again. Roger opened it to the Yard men. An hour later, he was at the Yard.

15

Happy Janet

Roger lifted his office telephone slowly, heard the operator say: "It's Dr. Faulkner," and held on. The hands of the small clock on the mantelpiece pointed to half-past four. The Yard was quiet; a heavy lorry rattled along the Embankment, but he hardly noticed it.

It was an hour since he had left the Langley Place flat. Now, a detective-sergeant and a police-woman were there to watch the sleeping Margaret, and Alec Magee was downstairs at the Yard, in a waiting room—dozing in an armchair.

Sloan was already at the hospital.

The police surgeon said: "That you, Handsome?"

"Yes, how is he?"

"I won't pretend it's good, but he's not at death's door. There's a fracture, and he'll be off duty for some time. Nothing really to get alarmed about as far as we can tell yet. I shouldn't worry too much about him, he'll pull through."

"Any need to send for his wife?"

"Not until the morning, anyhow. I'll let you

know if anything develops, but I think he'll have a comfortable night. Or what's left of it! They're operating now. It's not a serious job, take my word for it."

"Thanks. What did you make of Magee?"

"I didn't see much of him, but he was a pretty good imitation of a man who's gone off his rocker."

"Imitation?"

"Yes, he could be foxing you. You'll get someone else to have a look at him, won't you?"

"Yes, I will, thanks."

Roger put down the receiver, lit a cigarette, and yawned. Faulkner had meant to be reassuring and hadn't quite succeeded; but he'd have said if Bill were on the danger list.

Magee had already been examined by another doctor, a specialist who was always reluctant to give snap opinions. There wasn't much more to be done here. The moment Margaret Paterson came round, Roger would be told—if they couldn't find him here, they'd telephone Bell Street. He ought to go home, have a few hours sleep, and come back in the morning. When he'd slept on what had happened during the day, he'd be in a better position to assess it. He needed sleep; if he hadn't been so tired, he would never have lammed into Magee like that. Once he began to lose his self-control he would throw his hand in.

So far, there was no trace of Carney or O'Hara or either of the women missing from the Lodge. There was an unexpected report about the club with which Lake had been killed; no fingerprints of any kind on it, they'd been wiped off. Had Magee been in the frame of mind to realize what he had done and wipe off his prints? It was impossible to be sure. Was he insane? Or pretending to be? Roger would have plumped for the pretense, but for what he had seen in Sloan's flat. Magee had been hardly sane when talking to Margaret, hugging her, kissing her, and then—

He stood up, telephoned the switch room, told them to put any calls through to Bell Street, and went out. He was in the front hall when a Detective Inspector came hurrying up the steps, and stopped.

"You heard?" he asked.

"Heard what?"

"Lobo's been out again."

Roger said sharply: "Any big trouble?"

"No, nothing's reported yet. But there have been half a dozen jobs so far. They've caught a man at Wimbledon, but aren't sure whether he's a Lobo or not."

"Look at his left hand," Roger said.

He waited until the report came through; there was no wolf's head on the hand of the man caught at Wimbledon, nor were there any reports of violence. The other creepers had done their jobs swiftly and silently, and crept off.

Roger drove home while London was still asleep; although here and there it was stirring, a few early morning buses looked like lighted leviathans in the gloom. He yawned again as he reached the end of Bell Street—then started, for the rear light of a car glowed halfway along, near his house.

It looked like Mark's Talbot.

He glanced at his watch: five-fifteen.

There was a light in the front room, too, so they were still up. Had there been trouble? He felt his

172

heart pound, slowed down and pulled up just behind the Talbot. He left the door open, so as not to make any sound which might warn anyone at the house, and crept along the path.

Mark was standing near the window, with his back to it, but Roger couldn't see Janet.

The front door was closed.

There was no need for alarm, but—why were they up so late? He opened the door and stepped inside the hall.

Mark was saying: "Janet, it's time you went to bed."

"Don't want to go to bed," said Janet in a clear voice. "Want to sit here. Very happy—it's nice to be happy. *Tra-la-di-da, tra-la, tra-la-di-da, tra-la, it's nice to be hap-happy, nice to be hap-happy—* Mark sweetheart, don't look as if you'd like to put me across your knee! I haven't been so happy for a long time. Call it a represh—represh—oh, never mind. *It's nice to be—hap-happy. Tra-la, di-da—*"

Roger stood outside the room; numb.

Mark said: "In the morning you won't feel so good, and the boys won't understand you've got a hangover and expect them to be angels."

"Oh, Mark, they are angels! Both of them, absolutely-ly angelic. You mustn't say they're not." Janet giggled. "Oh, it was a wonderful night. Wonderful! Doesn't champagne give you a lift? It takes you out of this world. Right out—pop!—you feel it as soon as they uncork it. *Da-da-di-da-da-da—* come on, let's dance!"

"Janet—"

"You're as dull as Roger. Let's dance. I'll put a record on. Not—" she paused, hiccoughed, laughed, and went on: "Nothing complicated. No

173

tangos. Just a quickstep, I can manage a quickstep, and you can catch me if I fall. Can't you? Strong arms, Mark—and I haven't danced for months until tonight. *Ta-ra-ta-ra-ta-ra—*"

The sound of music came from the radiogram.

Mark laughed. "You're going to have such a head in the morning!"

"Who cares? *I* couldn't care less." Suddenly she became serious, lowered her voice so that Roger could only just catch the words. He stood there, still numb, could not have moved if he tried. "Mark, you don't understand. Roger's *never* in, he always makes an excuse to be out. I wouldn't mind if it were just work, but—is it? That's what I worry about. Is it work, or has he got a blonde?" She giggled again. "I can't imagine Roger with a blonde, but you never know. *Dance*, darling!" She was lighthearted again. "*Dance*. Wasn't that Can-Can divine?"

There was silence except for shuffling movements, and then a table crashed.

Janet laughed. "Oh, I'm hopeless. Don't let me fall! It's a wonderful feeling, Mark, my head's so light, and I haven't a care in the world. I could do silly things tonight."

"I'll go and see if the coffee's ready."

Roger backed away; Mark didn't see him. Mark went into the kitchen, but was soon back, with coffee; Roger stood close to the wall, hidden by coats on a hall-stand, until Mark was in the room again. "Jan, it's time you went to bed," Mark said.

"No can do." Janet giggled. "Can't go to bed because I can't undress myself. Just can't, Mark. I'm giddy, I don't think I could get out of this chair. Unless—you carry me. Be gallant, Mark dear, and

174

carry me. Just drop me on to my bed and kiss me good night, and take the boys out all day tomorrow. I should sleep until dinner-time, and then you could take me out on another whirr-whirr-whirl of gaiety. There! I said it! Oh, Mark! I've been so dull, so miserable, so unhappy, and it's all right now. Is it the champagne, do you think? Or is it because—"

"Yes, it's the champagne."

"I'm not sho—sho—sho *sure!* Mark, do you think Roger's got a blonde?"

"I do not. Drink this, it'll make you feel better."

"You wouldn't shay sho, if you did. You're the loyalish man I know. Roger never puts a foot wrong for you, does he? You wouldn't dream of doing anything he would disapprove of. But Mark, life's sho *dull.* Deadly. Mark—"

Her voice was low pitched, now; husky.

"Mark, why haven't you married some nice girl who would give you a good time? You ought to get married. You're rich and handsome, and—such a pet. Did I ever tell you what a pet you are? Someone ought to. Why haven't you married, Mark?"

Mark said solemnly: "I'm a misogynist."

"*A what?* A mis-mis-mis-mis-woman-hater! *You!*" Janet's laugh rang out. "Don't tell me that anyone who can dance divinely like you is a woman-hater. Nonshense, absolutely non-shense."

There was silence, except for the clink of cups; unbearable silence.

Roger turned abruptly.

He shouldn't have stayed here so long; he must slink out, so that they didn't know he had been here. This had to happen just now. No use thinking it was really important. Janet had gone out for the evening. Mark had given her a good time, she was drunk—champagne always went to her head—she was saying things that she didn't mean, although up to a point she was sensible enough. He pulled back the catch of the front door; it jammed. Confound the thing! He pulled it sharply, and it slid back and the door banged against his foot, then closed again with a snap.

Janet exclaimed: "What's that?"

"I don't know," said Mark. His voice sounded nearer, he was coming to the door. Roger turned round, making it seem that he was just coming in, took off his hat and hung it on the hall-stand. The sitting-room door opened, and Mark stood framed against the light.

"Making a night of it?" asked Roger, lightly.

"Hallo, old chap." Mark smiled, but looked ill-at-ease. "Yes, I was silly enough to feed Janet on champagne."

"Foolish!" cried Janet. "It wasn't foolish, it was the wisest thing you could have done!"

She leaned back in an armchair and waved languidly at Roger; there was a fatuous smile on her face. Her eyes looked glazed, she slumped there in an attitude of absolute prostration. An empty cup was by her side. Into Roger's mind there sprang a picture of Margaret Paterson, sleeping; beautiful.

Janet didn't look exactly at her best.

He smiled mechanically.

"Trust Mark to do the wise thing."

Janet snapped. "It was wise. *He* looked after me, even if you wouldn't. Darling, I'm *not* drunk. Not *dead* drunk. I can see the disapproving look in your eyes, and you needn't pretend that it isn't there. It would do you good to get drunk. Take you off the

176

straight and narrow path you always say you're treading. Make you unbend. Your trouble is a stern sense of duty. Too stern, *dar*ling, much, much too stern, always work, no time for little Janet. Is there time for anyone else, *dar*ling?"

Mark said: "Get her upstairs, Roger."

"Don't want to go upstairs," said Janet emphatically. "Want to speak my mind. Wouldn't dream of doing it, if I weren't pickled. If Roger really cared for me any longer, he wouldn't be out so often. Simple fact. It's silly to blink at it—isn't it, Roger? You're always refusing to blink at facts. Favorite phrase of yours: let's look at the *facts*. And the fact is, our once happy marriage is going on the rocks. Breaking up fast. Roger's never at home, even when he can get here. I remember the time when he would always telephone me if he was out late, but now—never. Isn't that true? Has he spent half a dozen evenings at home in the past six months? No. It can't be *all* work. I know the Yard too well, they don't pile everything on to one man. Roger doesn't come home because he doesn't want to. Fact. He's cooled off me. I suspect a blonde. Have you got a blonde tucked away, Roger? Have you been working hard all night, or have you been—"

"Janet!" Mark snapped. "You'll wish—"

"Never mind the morning. The truth can come out now. I am in a mood for facing facts. I—Roger." She leaned forward suddenly, her hands stretched out, her face crinkling up as if she were going to cry. "Don't lie to me. I'm sorry, terribly sorry about it, but—you're getting tired of me. Aren't you?" She raised her hands. *"Aren't you?"*

It was difficult to speak evenly.

"Don't be silly, Jan." He knew that it didn't

sound convincing, it was wooden and mechanical. "There's no blonde. I've been working at pretty high pressure. It's been miserable for you, but—"

"Miserable. It's been *hell!* Roger, can you stand there and tell me that you care for me as much now as you've always done? Face the *facts.* Can you?"

Roger drew in his breath. "Janet—"

She looked at Mark as if she were quite sober.

"You see," she said. "If you don't believe me, perhaps you'll believe him." She leaned back and closed her eyes.

Roger carried her upstairs, undressed her, and put her to bed. She was as still as Margaret had been; but she wasn't asleep. She didn't speak, and didn't open her eyes. Now and again she hiccoughed. He spread the clothes over her, and she turned her face away from him. He went out, and closed the door gently. The spare-room door was closed; Mark hadn't come up yet. Then he thought belatedly: "They must have left the boys alone in the house for hours." He hurried downstairs, his face bleak and eyes hard.

Mark was in the kitchen; a kettle sang.

"What time did you get back?" Roger asked.

"Half an hour before you."

"So the boys have reached the age of security, have they?"

Mark brushed his dark hair back from his forehead. He looked tired and pale.

"Don't be an ass. The Wrigleys are in the spare room. Janet was all set for a night club, we phoned up and the Wrigleys said they'd stay the night. They've done it before. I'm sorry you came back

178

just then. She isn't herself, and doesn't mean what she says. Damn it, I needn't tell you that!"

"I think she meant every word."

The kettle boiled. Mark made tea and got out cups and saucers, while Roger opened a tin of meat and cut some bread. "Thought you'd like a cup. Roger, you've probably left her on her own much more than you realized. She's been holding herself in, and she had to burst out sooner or later. Tonight will probably do her a world of good. I hate talking like a Dutch uncle, but—try and get home more. She's worth it, worth a lot more attention. I know the job's important, but there are other things which come first."

"Riot Act?" said Roger nastily.

"If you like." Mark poured out tea, and refused food. Roger ate hungrily. "It's been on my mind for some time. Whenever I call, you're either out, on the way out, or just in for a few hours sleep and then off again. There have been times when—"

"When what?"

"*Are* you still in love with Janet?"

Roger said bleakly: "I've a job to do, and it has to be done. I haven't changed. There was a time when Janet understood. If anyone's cooled off, it's not I. What else has she told you tonight? How misunderstood and neglected she is, of course— but what else?"

"You heard all there was to hear."

"I doubt it. I—oh, hell!" Roger forced a laugh, tossed the tea into the sink, and went out of the room. When Mark caught up with him in the living room, he was pouring himself a whisky-and-soda. He drank half of it at a gulp, stood twirling the rest round in the glass.

"Don't be a fool," Mark said flatly.

"Sauce for the goose." Roger finished the drink. "I needed that. I've had quite a night out, myself. When Janet's sobered up, you might tell her that Lobo committed a little murder a couple of nights ago— and he's still murdering. Sloan's on the operating table. This is about as tough a job as I've tackled for a long time. I couldn't pretend that Janet's helping. But before I can think about Janet, I've got to catch Lobo. If she won't accept that—" he shrugged. "It can't be helped. Have a spot?"

"No."

"But I can drink myself stupid, if I like. Eh?" He poured out another drink. "This is not one of the rules of detection, but even detectives are human."

Mark said: "All you're doing is giving Janet grounds for thinking that she's right. This isn't you."

"Let's stop sermonizing," said Roger. "This is neither the time nor the place. I came back to snatch a few hours rest. If I'd stayed at the Yard I might have got it. Better go back, I think."

"Why don't you say what's in your mind? You think I'm a heel, for taking her out and making her tight."

"Well, aren't you?"

"I thought it would do her good."

"Something wrong with your psychology. Oh, I grant the good intention. Anyway—"

The telephone bell rang. He laughed. "Duty calling again." He leaned across the chair and picked it up. "West speaking."

"Will you hold on a moment? Sergeant Weeks would like a word with you, sir."

Weeks was the sergeant with Margaret, and the

speaker was a woman; the policewoman at Bill's flat. He held on. Mark lit a cigarette, and brushed back the obstinate lock of hair. Roger thought: I'm hitting a new low; but although he admitted that to himself, he felt inwardly cold, frozen, the whisky hadn't warmed him. It wasn't because Janet was drunk; they'd had wild nights out together, champagne always went to her head, he must remember that. It was because of what she had said. His fears of the morning had been justified; she'd changed. The old, precious relationship had been breaking for a long time; now it was broken, and it was no use telling himself that he'd feel differently in the morning.

"Mr. West?"

"Yes, what is it?"

"The young woman is awake, sir, and is asking for you. She says she has a statement to make, and won't tell anyone but you."

"All right," said Roger. "I'll come over."

16

Statement

Margaret came to the door of the sitting room as Roger entered the flat, and looked at him over the shoulder of the hefty Sergeant Weeks. She was fresh and delightful, and there was a hint of eagerness in her expression; eagerness to see him. She had tidied her hair and made up a little. The policewoman behind her, tall, dressed in navy blue serge, looked like a gorgon.

"So you wake up occasionally," Roger said.

"It was the champagne," said Margaret. "It always affects me like that. I just go to sleep, and then—" she laughed. "Thank heavens, it doesn't give me a headache next morning! Do you know how I got here? This man mountain won't say a word, and my wardress just tells me to be a good girl and everything will be all right."

"She doesn't know what she's asking."

Margaret's laugh was unaffectedly gay.

"I should have known better than to try to hoodwink you. Even the man mountain can't stop me from guessing. My friend Bill is a policeman, isn't he?"

"Bill who?"

"*My* Bill. We had a gorgeous evening together, but secretly I thought he was a little too earnest. The Bill who lives here. I talked him into letting me come here and change, because it laid a false trail for my fond parent; he knows where I usually go. Bill is one of your men, isn't he?"

"Yes."

"A policeman's life is such a happy one! I hope he enjoyed part of it, anyhow, and his wife won't get angry with him. Yes, he told me all about her, *and* the baby. Did you tell him to follow me from home?"

"Yes."

"What made you think I'd probably run away?"

"I've known people who want to avoid the police before," said Roger dryly.

"*Avoid* them! After tonight, I hope they'll always keep me company. It isn't often that I feel nervous, but—it's delayed action, I suppose. I didn't feel much anxiety at home, I was anxious to get out, I can't bear it when Helen's there. Don't trust Helen." She frowned. "She is crafty as a fox, but nearly everyone gets taken in by her sweetness."

"Is that the statement you want to make?"

"What's the matter with you?" asked Margaret. "You're behaving as if I were suspect Number 1."

"You are."

"I suppose it would be a new experience to be arrested and taken to a police station! Are cells really as bare as they say?" Her eyes glowed, she took his arm and led the way into the sitting room.

The wardress backed away, the sergeant's big figure filled the doorway. "I want to tell you exactly what I know, Mr. West. It wasn't any use telling anyone else, you've been to Morden Lodge, and you know what happened last night."

"Yes. You'd better sit down while you take these notes, Weeks." Roger freed himself from Margaret's grasp, and sat on the corner of a table. Weeks sat at it, taking out a notebook and pencil. "Sit down, Miss Paterson. You know that this is an extremely serious matter, don't you?"

"You make it so obvious."

"And you know that it's not wise to lie to the police or to withhold information."

"That's why I asked you to come. It didn't start last night, it all began some weeks ago." She paused, leaned back in her chair and frowned; and suddenly her gaiety was gone, and she seemed older—not old, but no longer the carefree girl. "I suppose it really goes back farther than that. Will you think I'm just being vain if I say that men— run after me?"

"I'll agree that it could happen."

"*Could!* I can't remember when it didn't, and I— well, I love a good time! I've had plenty, too. But most of them have been spoiled because men *will* get so serious. Marriage isn't the end-all of existence—or do you think it is?"

"Not for everyone."

"And I haven't met a man I could live with for the rest of my days," said Margaret. "I've an old-fashioned notion that if you get married you should stay married. So you want to be sure of yourself before you take the plunge. Most of them—"

184

"Who are these people you're talking about?"

"My—friends. Boyfriends, men friends—don't pretend to be dull, I know you're not. Most of them have been reasonable, and I think most of them think that it would be a full-time job, being married to me. But one or two of them have been silly. Quite the silliest is Alec Magee."

She paused; Roger gave no sign that the name was familiar.

She looked at him under her lashes, and then went on: "He has red hair."

"So you've got round to that, have you?"

"Yes. I'm fond of Alec, in a way. I didn't want to get him into trouble. I know he's too intense, he's always threatened to kill himself if I don't marry him." She shrugged: "That's easier to say than do. Just talk. But I was shaken when he fired at me, although he once said that if he couldn't have me, no one else should. I didn't want him to be charged with trying to murder me, though. That's why I wouldn't name him when you first asked me. Afterward—well, I saw him in the grounds, while we were in the drawing room at home. He wanted to see me. I had to reason with him. It may have been crazy, but no one else would be able to do anything with him."

Weeks' pencil was gliding swiftly over the pages.

"We often met in the gym. I knew Alec wanted to see me there, and I got there first. He was frightened because the police were after him."

"I see," said Roger.

"He hadn't any money with him and didn't want to go home. He felt sure that I'd named him, and that you would be waiting for him. I had a few pounds in my bag and gave them to him, because

185

if I'd refused he might have got violent. I advised him not to run away again. I said that we could pretend that the shooting had been an accident. But then someone came up the stairs, and he rushed to the window and climbed out. Was it you outside?"

"Yes."

"I thought it probably was. I didn't want you to catch me in there, I thought I might be able to slip back into the house without being seen. So I stayed there in the darkness. I heard you and the others chasing Alec, and thought I'd better stay where I was until you came back. I got tired of standing—"

She paused, and her face turned pale, her eyes narrowed, her voice became very soft, as if she were living over the ordeal at the gymnasium.

"There were chairs in the bathroom. Or stools. None in the gym. I had only a little torch. If I put the light on, it would have told you someone was there, you see. I went into the bathroom. I kicked against an Indian club, and then—" she shivered, covered her face with her hands, and caught her breath.

Roger didn't speak.

She spoke through her fingers. "The light shone on Lake's head. I'd no idea anyone else was there. I saw the blood, and—"

She broke off, gripped the arms of her chair, and leaned back with her eyes closed. Weeks' pencil stopped. He was a toughened old-timer, but his eyes were soft as he looked at the girl. The police-woman cleared her throat.

Margaret said: "I was afraid Alec had been in before and killed him. I thought it was my fault. He'd killed Lake because Lake had been waiting for me, because—I'd turned his head. I couldn't think straight when you found me. I pretended to be out; I can always pretend. Then Dr. Sorenson came, and he gave me some pills. I kept them in my mouth, between my teeth and my gum. He's given me them before, when my father has wanted me to stay in—the only safe way to hold me is to make me sleep. I knew I'd *have* to go out. I had to do something, dance, drink—and not think about what had happened. When I came round, just now, and began to think, I knew I'd have to tell you. I knew it didn't matter either, because it couldn't harm Alec. He didn't kill Lake."

"What makes you say that?"

"How *could* he? He hadn't been in before, I remember he told me he'd been in the grounds. I was in the gym all the time he was there. He was outside, wasn't he? He came up, after me. Lake must have been lying dead in that room while Alec and I were talking. Please don't be harsh with Alec." Her eyes were enormous. "He's only a boy, and sometimes I've wondered if he's quite normal. There's a look in his eyes which scares me."

"We'll see that he gets a square deal."

Margaret looked up. "You haven't asked me where he lives."

"No. We've found him."

"Oh, I see," she murmured. That didn't surprise her as much as he expected it to. "You've been quick. I hope I'm not to blame for anything he's done. He's such a boy."

"He's old enough to know what he's doing," said Roger. "Are you prepared to sign that statement when it's typed out?"

"Yes."

"Have you anything to add?"

"No, I've told you everything."

"What can you tell me about Carney, Lake, and the other servants at Morden Lodge?"

"They were just servants," said Margaret. "I suppose you know that my father has a kink—he believes in the milk of human kindness to such a degree that he employs ex-criminals! But they've always behaved themselves well enough. I didn't like Carney, and he didn't like me—in fact, he didn't like anyone. He and Lake were always quarreling."

"What about?"

"Silly, petty little things."

"Why didn't you like him?"

"Because he looked a brute, and I didn't like the way that particular brute looked at me. He was a kind of jailer, too, keeping me in when I had disobeyed the parental edict. I sometimes wondered why Pat really *did* employ him. He came in useful for keeping Alec away, but—well, I just didn't like him."

"And there's nothing else?"

"What else do you expect?"

Roger said: "You've a strict parent, haven't you? and this business of shutting you up indoors and drugging you to keep you at home has an old-fashioned ring about it." He meant sinister. "Why did he do that?"

"Pat believes in ruling with a rod of iron, and I like a battle of wits! He disapproves of practically everything I do. He doesn't like my friends, and—well, it's just developed like that. We have terrific rows, and then everything quiets down until I go off on the loose again. I think it's his dearest wish that I should settle down and get married. I—"

She stopped abruptly. She looked away from him, and bit her lips.

"And what?" asked Roger sharply.

"Nothing," she said. "Nothing at all. I—I was thinking of Lake, and how I felt when I saw his head."

Was that the truth? Or only part of it? Had she suddenly seen Lake's head, battered and ugly, in her mind's eye? Or had she thought of something to do with her father, something she didn't intend to speak about?

"Must I go home?" she asked suddenly.

"Don't you want to?"

"No. It's always worse when I get back if Helen's there; she drives me to distraction. May I stay here for a while?"

"Haven't you any friends in London?"

"I don't feel like going to friends, now. I don't know *what* I want. They'd probably telephone my father and tell him where I was, anyhow. I'd much rather stay here until I've had time to make up my mind."

"You can for a few hours. Bill's wife is probably coming home today, you'd better be gone by the time she arrives." He didn't tell her what had happened to Bill Sloan. "If you think of anything to add to the statement, tell Sergeant Weeks."

"I will," she promised, submissively. He moved away, then caught sight of the feathered hat. He picked it up, and her eyes brightened.

"I love those things."

"So much that you wear them with a tweed suit?"

She frowned, then laughed as she realized what he meant.

"Oh, in the car! I'd lost my own, and I hate driving bareheaded, there's always such a draught. You do notice things, don't you?"

There were two pictures in Roger's mind. Of Janet sitting back in the chair, her eyes bleary and glazed—and Janet suddenly angry, almost spiteful, wanting to hurt him. And of Margaret leaning back in the chair, pale and beautiful, as she told him what had happened.

Why must the two merge? Why couldn't he keep Janet out of this? Why was he heavy-hearted when he left the flat and drove to the Yard? Why didn't he turn the car toward Chelsea, feeling the old eagerness to see Janet and the boys, if only for a few minutes? Of course, he couldn't be eager, that morning. She would be asleep; in a stupor; he preferred to keep away. Mark would get the boys some breakfast, and at nine o'clock their daily help would be in. No, she wouldn't; this was Sunday. Well, Mark would manage. Hard on Mark; everyone took advantage of Mark sooner or later.

An Alsatian dog, out on an early morning walk, tugged at his lead. Its head looked like a wolf's. Everywhere he went he saw the sign of the wolf. Was it becoming an obsession? The nursery-rhyme book which Richard had dropped; the skin rug at Morden Lodge; Helen's scarf, and the way she kept tossing the ends over her shoulders; Lake's hand; now the dog. Wolves' heads were beginning to affect him like pink elephants. Wolves' heads and

190

quarreling with Janet. They'd never quarreled a great deal. An occasional tiff, nothing like these bitter quarrels since the Lobo case had started. In fact, the estrangement, and he had to give it a name, had started before that, because of the pressure of work. It hadn't occurred to him that Janet would get absurd ideas. *Had* she meant that talk of a blonde? Or had it been something which had sprung to her mind because she'd had too much champagne? He didn't think so; things which had been in her mind for weeks, perhaps for months, had come out then.

It was half-past eight when he reached the office. No one was there. He telephoned the hospital, and was told that Bill Sloan was "comfortable." That might mean anything. There was another problem. How to tell Bill's wife? She would have to be told, and he would prefer to do that himself. There was nothing worse than bad news broken coldly by someone whom you didn't know well. She was staying near St. Albans. Why not drive out there and see her this morning? A drive in the country would do him good, help to clear his mind. He could have a cat nap at the Yard when he came back. The round trip wouldn't take more than three hours, and it would be better than going home; he didn't want to go home to a sick or sleeping Janet.

Yes, he'd go and see Joyce Sloan. He had the address; Sloan had left it with him because he expected to go there on weekends, and whenever there was a slack half-day. Slack! Roger felt dry, and wanted a drink. There was whisky in his desk. He had a drink; another; and was still thirsty, but warmer. He went downstairs to the canteen, speaking to no one as he drank some coffee.

Half a dozen night-duty men were there, and conversation lagged. Most of them were red-eyed and tired; everyone at the Yard seemed to be too tired; he wasn't the only one overworking. There was some talk about Lobo, and one thing shocked him; the casual way in which Lobo's gang of creepers was taken for granted. It wasn't really surprising, but he hadn't realized before that so many people at the Yard had come to regard Lobo as a continual and inevitable thorn in the flesh. The murders had changed that a little, they were even more anxious to get him, but there was a kind of fatalism in the general attitude toward Lobo. Roger heard three people discussing the man as they sat over their breakfast. They wouldn't get Lobo unless they had a lucky break. These murders might prove his undoing, but—the men shrugged. It wasn't going to be easy. The advantage was with Lobo, because he had started slowly and carefully, and his organization had become powerful almost before the Yard realized it. That was a fact. Why? Because there was too much to do, and not enough men to do it.

Someone mentioned the branding, and said it was crazy. An old-timer demurred. Once a man had that brand on, he was Lobo's for keeps. Gangsters in London had a trick of leaving their boss. That was one reason why the big gangs soon broke up. Lobo had found a way of marking his men so that they had to stay loyal. If they didn't, he would shop them. The discussion broke up into complaints about the shortage of trained men from the ranks of the police constables to the C.I.D.

It would do Janet good to hear that talk.

When Roger reached his office, the gun he'd given to Bray's man was on his desk. He reloaded it, and put it into his pocket with a spare clip of cartridges.

He was sleepier than he'd realized. There were several things that had to be done quickly, and he'd almost let them slide. See Taggart, who was watching Ma Dingle's, for one thing. Perhaps the time had come to raid Ma's. He mustn't forget that, thanks to what had happened at Morden Lodge; the case was much farther on than most people realized. The men who had been discussing it didn't know that he had discovered the training center of Lobo's creepers. A big question to be answered: where had Carney and the others gone to earth? Was there somewhere else where the men could be trained? Probably, Lobo wasn't likely to rely on one place only. But Carney had been at Morden Lodge for a long time.

Who *was* Lobo?

Paterson? He wouldn't be surprised, but the man had shown signs of cracking several times; Helen had straightened his resolve. How? Odd business, that; just the sight of her seemed to have poured fresh blood into his veins. He wasn't as strong a character as he appeared to be—and liked to think he was. What about Helen?

He must check on her life during the past few years.

There was no doubt at all that Helen was involved; she might be the leading spirit. He had always assumed that Lobo was a man, but there was no justification for the assumption. Helen could be Lobo. So could Carney. It *was* possible, although unlikely, that Carney and Helen had been working behind Paterson's back, that he had no idea of what had been going on.

No, it wasn't as simple as that. It was time to take a pencil and start to jot these points down. Roger went over what had already passed through his mind, making brief notes; then started afresh. Why had Paterson made such a fuss about those jewels, then not seemed to worry about them? When they were "missing" he had pretended that they didn't belong to him, but afterward Helen had said that he had every right to them; or a legitimate right to have them in his possession, which wasn't quite the same thing. Being a jewel merchant, it wasn't really surprising that he had been so careless with them; jewels were merchandise to the dealers, and they generally knew when it was necessary to take special precautions. The wall safe at Morden Lodge had been cleverly constructed. It was after Margaret had taken them out that the odd business about the jewels had begun. It took some understanding. So did her attitude toward them; what girl in her right senses would drop fifty thousand pounds' worth of precious stones into the bottom of a wardrobe, and then leave the room? It didn't make sense, and it wasn't good enough to say that she had thought the jewels safe because the police were on the premises. The behavior of everyone concerned over those jewels was the second real problem—another thing which couldn't easily be explained. The first remained the remarkable coincidence of the shooting just as he passed the grounds of Morden Lodge. Alec Magee might be the explanation, but—

He shrugged his shoulders, and put a large question mark beside the word "coincidence."

Things to do: See Taggart. Decide when to raid Ma Dingle's. Tell Joyce Sloan what had happened. Check the reports from Morden Lodge. Go through the whole gamut of routine work. Check on Helen; check on Paterson; and for that matter, on Alec Magee, Margaret, and Dr. Sorenson. The doctor seemed to have laughed at him a great deal, as if he secretly appreciated some joke—but what joke was it? And, of course, the most important thing: find Carney and the other servants.

He was on the last line of his notes when the telephone bell rang, and at the same time the door opened on Eddie Day, his prominent teeth bared in a smile.

"Hallo, Handsome! In this morning, then—or haven't you gone 'ome yet?" He rubbed his hands together and approached breezily as Roger lifted the receiver. "'Lo, Eddie—Hallo, West speaking.... Yes." His voice hardened. "Yes, I'll speak to him."

He held on.

"Done much during the night?" asked Eddie, sitting on the corner of Roger's desk and smoothing the gray tweed waistcoat over his capacious stomach.

"So-so—hallo, Mark."

"Not usin' *Lessing*, are you?" Eddie breathed. "Chatty won't like it if you use Lessing on the Lobo job."

Roger waved him away.

Mark said: "Hallo, old chap. I thought I'd give you a ring."

"Thanks. How's Janet?"

195

"Sleeping like a top. The boys have gone across the road to the Menzies—is that all right?"

"Of course. Glad they're not cavorting round the house; even Janet couldn't sleep through their din."

"No. Er—look here, Roger, don't take this business too seriously, will you? There's no need. It was my silly fault for letting her have so much champagne. She seemed so fed up earlier on that I thought it would do her good. If you hadn't come in when you did, she would have slept it off, and felt much better about everything by this afternoon. That's true, Roger."

"Yes, of course." It was impossible to put any feeling into his voice.

"You've been keeping up the pace too much."

"Can't be helped," said Roger. "Anything else?"

Mark said slowly, unhappily: "No."

"I'll be seeing you. Good-by." Roger rang off, and forgot that Eddie was in the room. He tightened his lips, and his eyes were bleak as he stared out of the window. Any other man would have kept silent, but not Eddie. Eddie stood up and lounged across the room.

"I say, 'Andsome! 'Ad a row with your pal Lessing?"

Roger swung round.

"No, but I'll have a row with my pal Day if he doesn't shut his silly mouth!" He jumped up and hurried out of the room, wildly angry, his face flushed. Eddie gaped after him. He went outside and slammed the door, but hadn't gone far along the passage before he felt calmer; there was no justification for letting off steam at Eddie. He went back, opened the door quickly, and saw Eddie

196

standing in the same position, looking both aggrieved and astonished.

Roger said: "Sorry, Eddie. Bill Sloan caught a packet last night. Been operated on. I'm just going to tell his wife. If anyone asks for me, I'm out at St. Albans."

"Oh, I see," breathed Eddie. "I couldn't think what had got into you, Handsome. Not like you to fly off the 'andle like that. Sure I'll tell 'em. Anything else I can do?"

"When Taggart rings up, tell him I'd like to see him here, at two o'clock."

"Okay."

"And if there's any line on Carney, ask them to call me at St. Albans."

"Okay," said Eddie, picking up Roger's memo. His eyes widened, his mouth dropped open. "Say, 'Andsome, you 'ad quite a night out, didn't you?"

Roger laughed, and left the room. That flare-up showed the red light. A doctor would agree with Mark that he had been working at too high a pressure, and must lay off for a bit; but there would be no laying off until he caught Lobo. Or Helen or Paterson or Carney. He hurried down to his car, and drove off swiftly; half an hour later, he was out of the built-up area and driving fast toward St. Albans.

He wanted speed, wished that he were at the wheel of Mark's Talbot. There were times when his Morris, in spite of its super-charged engine, seemed to crawl like an old crock. It was a bright morning. The countryside looked fresh and gay— odd, how gaiety was a keynote of the Lobo business, too. Helen and Margaret were gay—the two most unlikely people to be mixed up in a sinister

197

business like Lobo's. There was a dog in a field, a mongrel, part Alsatian, with a fine head. It loped toward a man who stood there with a shotgun under his arm, at the fringe of a small beech copse.

It was coming to a pretty pass if he couldn't see a dog's head without thinking of Lobo.

17

Magee

Joyce Sloan was staying with her sister in a small, pleasant, detached house in a quiet road on the outskirts of St. Albans, near the Roman Amphitheater. On the tiny front lawn was a cream-and-black pram, displaying its newness to everyone who passed. No one appeared at the window as Roger opened the wooden gate. He went to the pram. The baby, dark-haired, red-cheeked, slept with tiny lips pouting, one plump pink hand poking out from the thick woolen sleeve of a blue, knitted coat. The Sloans had wanted a boy, and got what they wanted. He smiled faintly, and walked along the crazy-paving path to the front door. He heard footsteps on the stairs, flurrying along the hall, and the door opened before he rang the bell.

Joyce Sloan, short, plump, full-breasted just now, cried: "Roger, what is it? Has anything happened to Bill?" Her eyes were sparkling with alarm, and she clutched at her blouse. Her sister stood at the foot of the stairs, looking over her shoulder, just as anxious.

Roger said: "Yes, but he's all right."

"Oh," said Joyce, in a low-pitched voice. "Oh, when I saw you, I was so frightened. Is he—" her voice straightened. "Is he badly hurt?"

"He'll be out of action for a bit, but I can promise you there's no danger," Roger said.

"Was it—Lobo?"

"That job, yes. We've got the man who did it."

"That's no consolation," Joyce said, but obviously she hardly knew what she was saying. "You're sure that he's all right?"

"Yes, you really mustn't worry," Roger said, and saw the tears spring to her eyes. She sniffed and turned away, going into the front room. Her sister came forward.

"You're not making light of it?" she asked.

"No."

"She'll be all right, then. She'll want to go back, of course. It's such a shame, she was getting her strength back so well. But at least they'll be able to have some time together while he's convalescing!"

So high pressure at the Yard was on top of Joyce's mind, too, she'd been talking about it. He went into the front room, and found Joyce blowing her nose vigorously. Through the handkerchief, she said: "I must see him, can you take me to London?"

"I can't this time," Roger said, "but they'll arrange a car for you at the local station whenever you want it. I've a much better idea than that, though."

"What?"

"Have Bill brought to St. Albans as soon as he's fit to travel."

"Of course!" cried Joyce's sister. "That's the very

thing! You're only doing four-hourly feeds, you can see Bill and get back between them, once a day, until he can come to St. Albans."

"It depends how long it'll be before he can be moved," said Joyce, dubiously. "I'll try it for today and perhaps tomorrow, anyhow." She looked calmer, although she blew her nose vigorously again. "I suppose it's an ill wind—he'll have to have some time off while he's convalescing."

Here it was again. "Don't you get tired of always being at work, Roger?"

Roger forced a laugh. "Tired out! And I've got to get back to do some more. Do you mind if I use your flat for a day or two, Joyce?"

She looked startled. "No. But why?"

"It'll be a convenient hidey-hole for a young woman I want to keep an eye on," said Roger. "Don't worry about it, and if you go to the flat, don't be surprised to see her in possession. With a policewoman!" He shook hands, and added quietly: "Bill's all right. No need to worry. I'll arrange for you to see him as soon as you get to the hospital."

He went back to the St. Albans station, made arrangements about the car, telephoned the Yard for them to make sure that Joyce would get straight in to see Bill, and left the country town a little after eleven o'clock. He reached the Yard at twelve-fifteen. The first thing he saw was an ambulance and a little group of men outside Cannon Row police station. Then he saw Cortland's massive figure coming out of the doorway, talking to a police surgeon. The other men were reporters. He pulled the car up inside the courtyard, and hurried toward the ambulance as a man was brought out on a stretcher. There was a sheet over the man's face.

Not—Magee?

Joe Osborne, the sergeant on duty at the cells at Cannon Row polite station, was an elderly man, only two years off his pension; he could, in fact, have retired years ago and would have done so but for the shortage of men. He was a bulky, passive man, with pallid cheeks and rather sad eyes. The jetsam of humanity passed through his hands, from drunks to murderers. He had been in charge of the cells here for more years than he could remember. Crime, as such, no longer shocked or stirred him; he dealt with bad men, he knew that most of them would remain bad, he had a simple philosophy: treat them all alike. He treated them with a rough kindliness which few appreciated. He was able, when necessary, to warn his superiors that such and such a prisoner was likely to be violent; might be a suicide; would probably talk if a certain line of approach were made. He was, in fact, a fount of wisdom, and one of the most popular men in the vicinity of Scotland Yard.

Everyone knew and talked affectionately of Old Joe.

That morning, while Roger was driving back from St. Albans, Old Joe glanced at Alec Magee. Alec had slept here during the night, had been asleep when Old Joe had come on duty. The night-duty man, also a wise old-timer, had said that he wanted watching; that was a tip from the police surgeon, too. In the next cell there was a drunk, and in the cell on the other side, an old lag who had been held for questioning the night before, and continually protested that he was being victimized. The old lag stood with his hands on the bars, glaring at Old Joe, as Joe studied Magee. Magee's face was pale except for two spots of red which burned in his cheeks; and his eyes glittered. He paced the cell, hands clenching and unclenching, muttering incoherently to himself.

"Can't you stop that guy, Joe?" The old-timer whined. "Gits on me nerves, 'e does, talkin' to 'isself all the time."

"You just go and sit down, Willy, and have a nice read," said Old Joe, glancing at him tolerantly.

"Read! You know wot you can do wiv yer ruddy books!" Willy glared at him between the bars, and didn't move. Old Joe went to his desk, hearing the constant muttering from Magee's cell. The desk was at the end of the cell passage: by leaning forward he could see who came along. He was restless, and after five minutes got up to have another look. As he went past Magee's cell, the muttering stopped.

The young prisoner sat on the only upright chair, now, his clenched hands on his knees and his eyes staring toward the blank wall.

"Thank Gawd 'e's packed up," said Willy hoarsely.

Old Joe went stolidly back to his desk and telephoned a crony who worked at the Yard.

"Sam, is Handsome about?"

"No. Having a joy ride somewhere. Might not be in again until tonight; he's doing nights, now."

"Pity," rumbled Old Joe. "I'm on me own 'ere, or I'd ask the Super to do this. Well, better speak to Cortland, I suppose. Put me through, will you?"

"Okay."

Cortland's voice soon rasped into Old Joe's ear. "Yes, what is it?"

"Sergeant Osborne speaking, sir, from Cannon Row. About the prisoner Magee. Thought I ought to tell you, sir, he's behaving very queer. Very queer. Ought to be in hospital, in my opinion, and I'd be happier if the doctor saw him again. I would have reported through the usual channels, but—"

"Never mind that. Watch him, and I'll see to the rest."

"Thank you, sir."

Old Joe replaced the receiver, picked up his empty pipe and sucked it, and listened for any sound from Magee. The silence remained, welcome and yet in no way easing the sergeant's mind. He knew loonies when he saw them, and this chap wasn't all there. But Cortland would see to it, Cortland was a quick worker.

Better make sure he'd taken everything from Magee that he could use to injure himself with. Penknife; two penknives, that's right. A pipe-cleaning tool, with a small pointed piece, which could do a lot of damage. That was all. He had been allowed to use a knife and fork, for breakfast, but Old Joe had watched him eat every mouthful. Wallet, the usual oddments from his pocket, everything was in the locker. Only things he had left were his tie and shoelaces. It might be wise to take them, a man could hang himself.

He heard footsteps coming along the passage; rather quick, not like those of a policeman. He leaned forward and saw a constable whom he didn't recognize, walking toward him.

"Sergeant Osborne?"

"That's right. Who're you?"

"Prendergast, from 17," said the constable, a tall and ungainly man. "You've got Willy Russell here, haven't you?"

"That's right."

"I was asked to tell you that we've got something on Willy," said the constable. "A report's coming over. Had to do another job near here, so the boss said I should look in and tell you."

"That's all right," said Old Joe. It wasn't orthodox, and therefore he didn't like it, but he could hardly take exception. The constable puzzled him more by saluting smartly as he turned to go. He didn't look at Magee; or at Willy. That seemed odd, to Old Joe. If a man was interested in Willy, he would surely have a word with him.

The telephone bell rang.

Old Joe became involved in a long and complicated conversation about a man who had been held two nights ago and was lodging a complaint against his treatment while in the cells. Old Joe resented criticism against his treatment, and became heated. The conversation lasted for nearly ten minutes, and was still going strong when another man walked along the passage.

"You can tell the Super that..." Old Joe said dourly, and then jerked his head up. He heard a gasp in the passage, then a low-pitched: "*My God!*" He jumped up, dropped the receiver and rushed toward Magee's cell, as the man in the passage called: "Joe! Joe, come here!"

Magee lay on the floor, and blood oozed from a gash in his neck. A cut-throat razor lay open by his hand, the blade smeared.

205

18

One Way to Kill

Old Joe, even paler than usual, kept dabbing his face with a red-and-white handkerchief. Cortland sat at the sergeant's desk, Roger West stood by it, Old Joe looked miserably from one to the other as they checked over the list of articles taken from Magee. He didn't speak until Cortland looked up.

"Now what about this razor, Sergeant?"

"He didn't have it, I'm sure he didn't. I searched him myself, when I came in. I wasn't happy about him—I told you that, didn't I, sir? That's a big razor, he couldn't have hidden it anywhere about his person. I made a thorough search. He didn't say anything, just stood there while I did it, as if he didn't care what happened. I decided his behavior was unusual, sir, and he needed very careful watching. Until I was called to the telephone, I passed his cell every few minutes. I was most uneasy in my mind about his behavior, sir. And that razor was not on his person when I searched him."

"Did you search the cell?"

"Yes, every corner. Nothing was hidden there. I turned over the mattress, sir."

"Then how the hell did he get it?"

"I—I can only think of one thing," said Old Joe, and dabbed his forehead frantically. "A constable unknown to me came in just before it happened. Said he'd come from 17, and I remarked at the time that it was unusual to bring a message. Also, he said he'd come about Willy Russell, who was in the next cell—moved him quick when we found out what happened—but he didn't seem to know Willy."

Roger was already holding the telephone to his ear.

17 Division had sent no one to Cannon Row....

Old Joe wrote out a description of the phony constable in his slow, regular, and easily read handwriting, pausing occasionally to dab at his forehead.

Roger and Cortland went into Cortland's office, and Cortland grunted.

"It takes some believing."

Roger said: "We can't really say Lobo killed Magee, either."

"He gave him the instrument," Cortland said heavily.

"It was still suicide, even if it meant that he knew Magee was that way inclined." Roger lit a cigarette, blew smoke toward the window, and said: "The A.C. is going to blow up good and proper when the Press gets hold of this."

"Devil to pay." Cortland glowered.

"Anything on Magee yet?" Roger asked.

"Yes. Wealthy son of a jeweler friend of Paterson's who died years ago. Nothing against him. Good-natured lad, never had anything to do with crooks, never seemed too keen on night life, although he haunted the places where Margaret Paterson went. I—" he broke off when the telephone rang, and seemed to withdraw from the room and Roger. "Superintendent Cortland...Good morning, Sir Guy...Yes, Sir Guy." Cortland looked as if he, too, wanted to dab his forehead. "He's with me now...I ought to tell you, sir, that—"

"He's hung up," he said heavily. "Wants to see you. I'd better come along with you."

"He'll probably snarl less if I'm on my own," said Roger. "Sit tight."

For some reason, hard to understand, he was almost the only man at Scotland Yard not in awe of the Assistant Commissioner. It was not that Sir Guy Chatsworth was unpopular; there had been few better-liked. A.C.'s at the Yard. Moreover, everyone who came into regular contact with him knew that his gruffness was a pose, that he was jealous of the reputation of his men and was continually campaigning for more staff and better pay and conditions. It remained true that when anything went severely wrong, his wrath made the most hardened C.I.D. men feel timid.

Roger tapped at his door and went in.

Chatsworth didn't look up. He sat at a large, glass-topped desk, a burly man in thick brown homespun, with grizzled hair which was massed in ringlets round his head, leaving him completely bald on top. It gave him the appearance of a fat boy dressed as a man. The room was an astonishing contrast to Chatsworth, who looked as if he had brought a breath of the country into Scotland Yard. It was furnished in ultra-modern style; black glass, chromium-and-steel furniture, a black-and-white carpet with a futuristic design on it; black-and-white curtains. His arrival at the Yard had coincided with a limited refurnishing of offices which had long needed it, and he had contrived to make his own choice.

He was writing with a slim gold pencil which looked lost in his big, reddish hands.

Without looking up, he said: "I thought you were on night duty. Don't you ever rest?"

"When I can, sir."

"You're a fool. How can you be on your toes if you're dopey with fatigue? It's not the first time I've told you about it. Lobo's not going to be caught by a man who ought to be in bed. Time you learned more sense."

Roger said: "Would you like my resignation?"

Chatsworth jerked his head up. His face was brick red, deeply lined, with myriads of crows' feet at the corners of his heavy-lidded eyes. Those eyes were wide open, now; blue, often frosty, often merry—but at the moment, startled.

He said: "I thought you were serious."

"I am."

"Don't talk nonsense! Sit down." Chatsworth straightened his back and stretched his arms. Then he looked wary. "Why? What have you done now? Lost another car?"

"Lost a witness."

"Eh? Who? Don't talk in riddles." Probably the secret of Roger's success with the A.C. was his ability to get Chatsworth on the defensive; he had done so now, and knew that there might be rumblings, but no explosion. He sat down.

"Magee killed himself in his cell."

There was silence while Chatsworth eased back in his chair, picked up the gold pencil and began to twist it in his fingers. Roger wanted a cigarette and slid his hand in his pocket, but didn't take out his case.

"How?" asked Chatsworth in a smooth voice.

Roger told him.

"Newspapers got this yet?"

"There were several reporters outside Cannon Row when the ambulance drove off. I think they know. We'd better give them the story, anyhow, or they'll guess and make the situation worse."

"Hmm," said Chatsworth. "Hmm." He lifted the telephone receiver. "Backroom Inspector, hurry . . . hallo, Bream? . . . Release the Magee story as soon as you're asked for it. . . . Eh? I don't care if there are fifty in the room, tell them the story!" He banged down the receiver. "Magee was all that important, was he?"

"They didn't pass him that razor for fun."

"Don't be smart! You could have learned plenty from him."

"Probably. You can't tell with that type, he wasn't normal."

"According to the reports, he confessed to attacking Sloan but not to killing the man Lake. Think he killed Lake?"

"I think he could have, in spite of Miss Paterson's evidence. She's friendly toward him, probably tried to make out that he hadn't the opportunity." Roger spoke evenly, thinking of Margaret. "It isn't

210

much use worrying what we might have got from Magee, sir."

"No. And listen to me, you young pup, you can't make an insolent remark innocent by adding 'sir.' What's the matter with you this morning?"

"Sorry," said Roger. "Lobo's got under my skin. He's had a crack at me, too, and he's doing very nicely. But he's on the run, or he wouldn't take the chances he's taking now. Have you had time to study the report?"

"Yes. Haven't grasped everything yet, but I've a fair idea of what's been happening. Any trace of Carney and the others?"

"Nothing at all."

"They can't disappear into thin air. What have you done about Paterson and his secretary, what's her name? Wolf—yes, Helen Wolf." He looked at Roger through his lashes, and his bushy gray eyebrows almost hid his eyes. "Significant, isn't it?"

"It could be. They're being watched. I shall be surprised if they do anything unusual today, they'll lie doggo. We might get a lead from them, but we're much more likely to get one to them."

"Hmm. Been to Ma Dingle's yet?"

"No. I expect a report from Taggart any time. I may raid the place tonight." Roger took out his cigarette case at last; Chatsworth nodded, so he lit up. "I think we might get our lead to Paterson and the woman Wolf through Paterson's daughter."

"How?"

"Paterson treats her as if he were living in the reign of Queen Victoria, but the thing doesn't really add up. He's been known to give her sleeping draughts to prevent her from leaving the house—did so last night. But she was up to that, and didn't swallow the tablets. Why was he so anxious to keep her in? Possibly, because he was afraid she would notice queer things that were happening in the grounds or in the gymnasium. Last night, he pretended not to be greatly worried about her disappearance—she often runs out on him—but I think he was alarmed. She hasn't been to any friends, he probably doesn't know where she is."

"Do you?"

"At Sloan's flat, quite safe. If we keep her there, and she seems prepared to stay as long as we want her to, Paterson might get worried, and being worried, let something out. He's strangely jittery, and—"

"He broke off. He seemed to see Paterson's eyes, a muddy color clearing to clear brightness, and suddenly he guessed why.

"And what?" asked Chatsworth sharply.

"Nothing important," Roger went on quickly, doubting whether Chatsworth would force the question. "On the whole, I think we can say we're a lot farther along the road than we were this time yesterday. I don't think I shall stand off much until it's over."

Chatsworth said: "Now what's going on in that crafty mind of yours? Be careful what you do with Margaret Paterson. She could be in danger. Don't want her to go the same way as Magee."

"No, we don't," said Roger, with an emphasis which startled Chatsworth. "She'll be well looked after. If she wants to go home, we can't keep her, of course—we can question her again, but until or unless we get fresh information, we can't hold her."

"Do what you think is best."

"Thank you, sir." Roger stood up, and went out. Paterson's eyes seemed to be everywhere. He looked in at Cortland's office, and reported, learned that no fresh news had come in, and hurried downstairs. He drove swiftly along the wide embankment, past the stately buildings beyond the gardens, the last of London's trams clattering alongside. At Blackfriars Bridge he was held up by traffic, but soon he went into a chemist's shop, next door to Univex House, in Farringdon Street, near the big market.

A girl said: "Yes, sir?"

"Have you some bismuth tablets?"

"Oh, yes." She took a small bottle from a shelf behind her.

"Is there a round bottle?" asked Roger.

"I'm not sure—oh, yes. Will that do?"

He judged it to be rather larger than the bottle which Helen Wolf kept in her bag, but it would do.

"Thanks."

He took out the cotton wool at the top of the bottle, threw half a dozen tablets into the roadway, then walked up the steps leading to the front entrance of Univex House, studied the nameplates, and saw one reading: "Sixth Floor: *James Paterson and Company, Ltd.*" A C.I.D. man standing near the lift came toward him, and studied the nameplates at the same time. A porter watched from a glass-fronted office.

"Anything to report?" asked Roger quietly.

"Both upstairs."

"Thanks." Roger went to the lift, and a one-armed attendant whisked him to the sixth floor. The landing was large, the walls paneled; there

213

was an atmosphere of affluence about the building. Opposite the lift, a door with a frosted-glass panel stood ajar, marked "Inquiries." There were three other doors, all marked "Private." He heard voices coming from one of the rooms, but couldn't recognize them. He tried the handles of the "Private" doors, but all were locked. He went into the inquiry office, a small cubbyhole occupied by a smartly dressed, well-made up girl with dark, braided hair. She smiled.

"Good morning, sir."

"Good morning. I'd like to see Mr. Paterson."

"I'll find out whether he's in. Will you please sit down a moment?"

"Thanks."

"What name is it, please?"

"West," said Roger.

"Mr.—West." There was a faint pause before the "West," and he knew that she recognized the name, had been told that he might call. She pulled out one of the plugs; a bell rang three times in the office out of sight. There was a pause, before she said: "Miss Wolf, there's a Mr. West to see Mr. Paterson, do you know whether he's in?"

She smiled again, disarmingly.

"I won't keep you a moment."

"That's all right." Roger sat listening, intently, for any sound in the other rooms. He heard footsteps, but no voices; whoever was in there was whispering. He waited for a few seconds, and then suddenly jumped up.

The receptionist called: "Mr. West!"

But he opened the door and stepped on to the landing. One of the "private" doors was opening,

214

and Dr. Sorenson came out, missed a step when he saw Roger, and then grinned.

"Well, well! Night and day duty, Inspector?"

Behind him was Helen Wolf, smiling broadly; and behind her, Paterson stood frowning.

"You're having quite a send off," Roger said. "Isn't there a back door?"

"I don't want insolence!" Paterson barked.

"I'm sure that Mr. West didn't mean to be rude," said Helen Wolf. "You *do* look tired, Inspector. It must be so trying for you, working all hours. As you've come this way, you may as well come in. Good-by, Doctor. It's most reassuring, most reassuring. Pat has been so tired lately, so run down, I was afraid that he might have low blood pressure or something like that. It's a relief to know that he's all right, and I will make sure he rests. If only he weren't so worried about Margaret, he would be much better. *Good*-by." She patted the squat doctor on his shoulder, beamed at Roger, and stood back for him to pass.

Dr. Sorenson did not have his bag with him; and could hardly have tested Paterson's blood pressure without a proper instrument. Roger made no comment. Helen Wolf exclaimed: "Oh!" and hurried out after Sorenson. Paterson put a hand on Roger's arm, as if to stop him from following her.

The office was large and luxurious, more like a living room or study than a business office.

"What do you want, West?" Paterson's voice was hoarse.

"Has your daughter returned?"

"No. Haven't you found her?"

Helen came bustling back and closed the door gently behind her. She was dressed in the same old tweed suit with the short skirt, and the wolves' heads scarf still dangled over her cushiony bosom. Her fluffy hair was untidy. She tucked in a few loose strands, walked to the large walnut desk and sat down.

"Have you asked Mr. West what he wants, Pat?"

"He hasn't found Margaret. That girl—" Paterson broke off. His lips were set tightly, he did not look as if he were thinking kindly about Margaret. "She *must* learn to do what she's told! I won't have her dashing off like this, she'll have to be taught."

"She'll be all right, Pat. She *is* young, you know. You worry about her too much. Have you found Carney or any of the others, Mr. West?"

"No."

"Pat and I have been talking," said Helen, coyly. "We have been wondering how we could help you. It's rather a shock, you know, to find that these men have been carrying on their crimes under our very noses. We've prepared a list of people who have called to see them, and several men who trained at the gymnasium."

"What did they train for?"

"Why, *boxing*. Carney was an old prize fighter, he loved training youngsters—he preferred light-weights. Strange, isn't it? A big man like that always preferred to train lightweights to box, their small size fascinated him. He thought that little people were so much more *agile* than big ones, could make openings where big fellows just couldn't find a way past their opponents' defenses. Do you like boxing, Mr. West?"

Roger said: "I prefer fencing."

She laughed; a trilling, gay laugh. But she knew

216

exactly what he meant, her mind was needle sharp.

"I'm fond of fencing, too, it's so exhilarating. At all events, we've prepared a list of some of those who called, it might be a help. And we've decided that Pat made a foolish mistake yesterday, when he denied knowing about the boy with the red hair. You may not believe it, Mr. West, but Pat is such a sentimentalist. He knows that Margaret has made many young men unhappy. He blames her, too, although I don't think she should be blamed; no one can help being born attractive, any more than they can help becoming fat." She gurgled. "Look at *me!* Pat didn't want to get the boy into trouble. He's a nice lad, although rather intense, and he's worried Margaret's life out. In fact, one of the reasons why we were so anxious that Margaret shouldn't leave the house by night was anxiety lest *he* should try to do her some harm. He was so *passionate,* and he was twice heard to threaten to kill her unless she would marry him."

"Really," said Roger dryly.

"Oh, yes, and although we knew that Margaret was capable of looking after herself, we were worried because she is sometimes so reckless. Anyhow, the red-headed man whom you saw yesterday must have been Alec. Alec Magee. I think he lives in Kensington, but I'm not sure. Would you like to use the telephone?"

"Not yet," said Roger. He glanced round at her desk, which was in a corner. On it lay her handbag, big, black, and shiny. He wandered over to the desk, knowing that they were watching him closely; in spite of the front she put up, she wasn't sure of him. Paterson was the more obviously nervous of the two. "Do you carry a gun, Miss Wolf?"

"Gun? Good heavens, no!"

"Miss Paterson makes a habit of it."

"No!" cried Helen. "Surely she—Pat, did you know that Margaret carried a gun?"

"I did not!"

"It's a complete surprise. What will the child get up to next?" Helen Wolf sighed, as if in vexation, and came over to the desk. Roger picked up her handbag, and she made no comment. "I've never used a gun in my life, I'm always too frightened by the noise. I hate noise."

"So do creepers."

She looked perplexed. "Who? Oh, creepers?" She was still perplexed, or pretended that she was. "I suppose that's a joke, I can't be very bright this morning. But I don't carry a gun, look inside my bag if you like. There's absolutely nothing in it that would do you the slightest harm—except perhaps a nail file. *Has* anyone ever committed a murder with a nail file?"

"I don't recall a case." Roger opened the bag—and dropped it. The contents fell out, and the white bottle marked "Bismuth Tablets" rolled under the desk. He knelt down, and she hurried forward to help him. Her purse had opened, copper and silver rolled about, her keys, make-up, and compact lay at his feet. He turned, the bottle of tablets he had bought concealed in his palm, and groped under the desk for her bottle; found it and made the exchange, slipping the new bottle into the bag with the other things that he had collected. Helen showed no sign of vexation.

218

Paterson said: "Are you always as clumsy as this?"

"Do you know where your daughter is?"

"No."

"Have you heard from Carney or O'Hara?"

"No."

"Why don't you tell me the truth?"

Paterson flushed. "That is the truth." He looked angry enough to strike out. Helen fluttered between them, as if she were afraid there would be a fracas.

"Mr. West, you mustn't accuse Pat of lying, he's a most truthful man."

"I know. George Washington the Second. I don't believe it. Paterson, you're asking for trouble—serious trouble. You've sheltered a gang of rogues, who—"

"But he knew *nothing* about what they were doing, Mr. West! You must believe that, I beg you to believe it. Why, there has never been a breath of suspicion against Pat, never! His word is his bond, that's why I like working for him. He's not like an ordinary businessman, who says one thing and means another. Or makes a promise and then goes away and does exactly the opposite because he thinks it will get him another five per cent profit. I'm afraid you misunderstand Pat. He's not well, that's why we had the doctor. He loses his temper so easily. Pat, *please* sit down. *Please.*" She took Paterson's arm and dragged him toward an easy chair. He seemed loath to go there; and Roger saw that his eyes were a muddy color again, just as they had been when he had first met the man.

"It's that indigestion," Helen said quickly. "You must have a tablet, Pat." She took out the bottle, unscrewed the cap and shook several tablets on to

219

the palm of her hand. Paterson grabbed two. *"One!"* she cried, but he slipped the two into his mouth, and gulped them down as if his life depended on it. "Oh, you're as willful as Margaret!"

Roger said: "A couple of bismuth tablets won't hurt him. I've warned the two of you. There's something you know that you're keeping back. You realize this is a murder job, don't you? Murderers get hanged."

Paterson opened his mouth—

"Not *all* murderers," cooed Helen. "There are an awful lot of reprieves, I always think that the Home Secretary must be a very kindhearted man. Pat, *do* relax. It won't help you if you get worked up again, and the Inspector doesn't mean to be unpleasant, I'm sure. It's natural that he should be worried, with so many dreadful crimes committed and the perpetrators *still* unknown."

"Not unknown," Roger said. "Just foot-loose, for the time being."

"So confident, aren't you?" sighed Helen. "I do hope you're right. We don't know who ransacked the study and this office yesterday, I can't imagine what they were after. And I'm a little nervous, now that Carney and O'Hara are free; one can never be quite sure what they'll do, can one?"

Roger said: "Do you know who killed Lake?"

"Why, *no!*"

"I think you've a fair idea," said Roger.

He turned on his heel and went out, using the private door, which hadn't been locked again. It closed gently behind him. He pressed the bell for the lift, looking at the frosted glass all the time. No shadows appeared against it, and he heard no talking. The lift came up. Three minutes after he

220

had been in the office, he entered the chemist's shop again, went behind the counter into the dispensing department and was met by a small, long-nosed man in white smock, who blinked at him through thick-lensed glasses.

"You mustn't come in here, sir, this is for staff use only." He blinked apologetically. "The assistant will—"

Roger thrust the bottle labeled bismuth into his hand, and then showed his card. The man blinked more furiously than ever. A girl assistant came in, and he waved her away.

"What can I do for you, Chief Inspector?"

"How quickly can you make a rough test of the contents? A rough analysis?"

"What do you think I might find?"

"A narcotic."

"Well, if you could come back in half an hour, I might be able to give you an indication."

"I'd like to wait," said Roger, and smiled. "Sorry, I'm really in a hurry. You needn't try to find the different constituents, but if you can give me some idea, I'd be grateful."

"Well, you know—so much depends on the type, on the strength of narcotic content, even the resistance of the patient. Surely, as a policeman, you know a little about such things."

"Yes. I want an opinion confirmed, that's all."

"Well, perhaps a very simple, practical method will help!" The chemist took out a tablet, broke it, scraped off some powder and placed it on the tip of his tongue. He licked his lips. "It is *not* bismuth. Plain, almost tasteless, white and—h'm, I couldn't be sure. It could be cocaine. Could be."

"Thanks. Will you telephone Scotland Yard for a

man, give him some of the tablets and tell him I've asked for an analysis."

"Gladly."

"Thanks."

Roger went back to Univex House, and said to the sergeant: "Give me time to get up, then come to the sixth floor and keep an eye on the landing. There might be trouble."

Upstairs, he tried the handle of the door leading to Paterson's room; it was locked again. He went into the Inquiries, and the smile on the girl's face froze when she saw him.

Paterson shouted: "Of course he took them! Who else would, they—"

"*Please!*" cried the girl, as Roger lifted up the flap in the counter and hurried through. He didn't look at her, but saw her hand move toward the switchboard and heard three short, sharp rings; the signal that he was here. He thrust open a door, and found himself in an empty room; the door leading to another room was open, and he hurried toward it. As he reached it, Helen Wolf appeared— and stood stock still.

She wasn't smiling, gay, carefree, or whimsical; there was deadly enmity in her glance.

"Get out!" she spat. "Get out, you—"

"Unprintable," murmured Roger. He swung her aside, his fingers embedding themselves in her fleshy arms, and entered the room. Paterson jumped up from an easy chair, his eyes blazing, his fists clenched.

"Don't!" cried Helen.

Paterson flung himself forward. Roger caught his arm and twisted, and the man nearly fell. Roger pushed him away, and Helen jumped be-

222

tween them, lowered her fluffy head and butted Roger under the chin. He backed away in time to save himself from serious hurt, but it jarred his head.

"Does indigestion always take him like that?" he asked, and the malignant gleam in Helen Wolf's eyes became a glare.

19

"Bismuth"

Paterson dropped back into his chair, trembling violently. The glitter faded from Helen's eyes, but she glowered at Roger, then went to Paterson and rested a hand on his shoulder.

"It's all right, Pat, you needn't worry. I'll get some more for you."

"More what? Heroin? Snow? Marijuana?"

"Mr. Paterson has been ill, those tablets were specially prescribed for him by his doctor."

"As his daughter's sleeping tablets were. To put him out of the way when it would be inconvenient if he were around." Roger rubbed his painful jaw slowly, and didn't look away from the woman. "Supplying drugs is a criminal offense."

"They were medically prescribed, I tell you."

"Is that why you put them in a bismuth bottle? Why do you keep the supply, and not he?"

Helen said: "Dr. Sorenson is a fully qualified medical practitioner, Mr. West, and you will not alarm me by your bluster. By taking away Mr. Paterson's tablets and putting ordinary bismuth in their place, you may have caused a serious relapse. He is ill, and—"

"Your memory's not so good. You were telling the good doctor how delighted you were that this wasn't a serious illness. And remarking on a satisfactory blood pressure when Sorenson hadn't his equipment with him. You're not so good as you think you are, Helen."

She said: "You're going to laugh on the other side of your silly face before this is over. Why, you—" she drew in her breath, as if she were going to hurl a stream of invective, but broke off abruptly. "You're not wanted here. Get out."

"When I'm ready to go. Helen, my dear, we three are alone, this is informal, and I've one or two things to tell you. Lobo is on the way out. You and your precious friends are very near the dock, and that's halfway to the gallows. Throwing the blame for this and that on Alec Magee has failed. Alec was in a bad way, too. What drug did you use on him?"

Her eyes burned at him.

"We picked him up last night," Roger said. "He was in a state of collapse. He told us a lot of interesting things before he was murdered."

Paterson jerked forward in his chair.

"*Murdered?* Alec?" He turned and looked at Helen, and there was something like horror in his eyes. "Helen, *Alec* hasn't been killed. Not Alec. No one would want to kill that boy."

Roger said thinly: "He was murdered."

"No! No, it can't be." Paterson clutched the arms of his chair and pulled himself to his feet. He stared at Helen with shocked, glittering eyes. His mouth opened and closed, his slender hands quivered. He seemed to forget that Roger was there as he took a faltering step towards the woman. "Helen! Tell me the truth, was Alec—*killed*? Is he —dead?"

Roger said: "He was murdered. Just another."

"Helen!" There was shrill appeal in the cracked voice. Paterson put his hand on Helen's shoulders, and Roger could see the pressure he was exerting, and knew that he would never get Paterson nearer to cracking up than now. "Helen, it can't be true. I always told you—"

"Now, Pat." The lilting voice was back again, the sunny smile returned, but it cost a great effort. "Mr. West is trying to make you say silly things, that's all. Alec's all right. He was—"

"His throat was cut. Ever seen a man with a gash in his throat?" Roger went closer, they all stood near each other, and Paterson's tortured eyes turned this way and that, while the woman fought to retain her composure and to keep the fury from her eyes. "A cut throat bleeds. All over the place. It's not a nice way to die. It's even worse than having your head cracked like an eggshell—the way death came to Lake. The way it might happen to anyone involved in this foul business. Good-looking boy, Alec Magee. But he didn't look so good with his throat slashed. Ever wondered what your daughter would look like if *her* throat was slit from ear to ear, Paterson? Or if a man bashed her head in? Or stabbed her with a knife, like Lobo's man stabbed the woman in Hampstead?"

"Don't!" cried Paterson.

"Pat, it's all right, he's only trying to scare you. Alec is—" she suddenly stretched out her arm and slapped Roger across the face. The force of the

226

blow surprised him, and he staggered back. She came at him, and kicked him on the shins, savagely. Then she snatched a book from the desk and hit him over the head, while he was still off his balance. The book rose again, and she tried to bring it down on his head.

Roger pulled it from her and tossed it across the room. It fell to the floor with a thump. But she sprang at him, clawing at his face. Her fingers scratched his cheek, just beneath the eye; he felt the nails tear the skin. He fended her off with one hand, but she wasn't easy to keep at bay, and started kicking again.

Paterson watched as if paralyzed.

Roger grappled with the woman, fought to hold her wrists, caught one, then the other, and held her away at arm's length. She still tried to kick him. Blood oozed up from the scratches, and his head had started to ache again, but through the mists of pain, he grinned at her.

"Sheep's clothing all gone, Helen?"

"Why, you—"

"Why did you murder Alec Magee?"

"It's a lie!"

"Oh, no, it's not a lie. He was murdered, you killed him! You slit his throat—*why?*"

Paterson grabbed her shoulder, tried to turn her round, but Roger held her. Paterson pulled at her powerfully, thrust his face into hers. His eyes blazed, his mouth was working, he looked a sick man.

"Helen, if you killed that boy—"

"I didn't!" she screeched.

"He's dead," Roger said harshly. "I've just seen his body. He was—"

"He killed himself!"

Paterson dropped back a pace. Roger released the woman's wrists and smiled at her; and she realized what she had been driven to admit, and caught her breath, thrust her hand against her breast.

"Oh, did he, Helen? Who told you so?"

She didn't move or speak.

"Come on, you know all about it. Why did Alec kill himself, and how did you know what he'd done?"

Paterson croaked: "*Was* it suicide?"

"No, murder. It *was* murder, wasn't it. Helen? You made a mistake. Just a silly little mistake that anyone might make. Isn't that true?"

She licked her lips.

"Helen!" Paterson cried. "Tell me the truth, I must know the truth. If you killed him—"

"He killed himself," she said.

"Then we're back at the first question," said Roger. "How do you know?"

She said: "A friend telephoned me."

"What friend? What's his name? Where can I get hold of him? Quick, Helen! You're on the spot, you'll have to look slippy if you're going to get away with it. Who's your knowing friend?"

"A—a reporter."

"Name him. Name his newspaper."

She said: "I don't have to name him. It was confidential information. He—"

"Were you here when he telephoned?"

"I—yes, yes, of course."

"When was it?"

"Just before you arrived—after you'd been here once, before you came back." She licked her lips, backed away from him, and looked less harassed. "It's no use, West, you can't frame me with that kind of talk."

"Frame? Crook's slang, my precious, where did you learn it? And who telephoned?" He laughed at her, and went swiftly to the door leading to the empty room, pulled it open, and called: "Here! You at the switchboard."

The sleek girl appeared, pale and scared.

"Remember hearing me go away?"

"Yes," she said, in a timid voice.

"Gloria, don't say a word to this man. Don't say a word to him!"

"Gloria knows better. Did you have a telephone call after I'd left?"

"I—"

"Of course you did!" screeched Helen.

The girl's hand groped for the handle of the door, she clutched it as if she were in need of support.

"Why, yes, yes—"

Roger said: "That's got you into the mess, now. Get Scotland Yard on the telephone for me. Whitehall 1212. Put the call through into this room." He swung round, pushed Helen back into the office, and laughed into her face. Paterson stood like an image, his hands raised in front of his breast. News of the death of Magee had both shocked and frightened him. His breath was agitated; that was partly because of the news, partly because he was desperately in need of his dope. Some addicts needed it at regular intervals, if they went long without a dose, they lost their self-control at the slightest pressure of events. Roger held the woman's arm, led her to the telephone. The bell rang.

Roger lifted the instrument off its cradle. "Su-

229

perintendent Cortland, please." He waited; and Cortland's voice came harshly to his ear. "It's West. I'm at Paterson's office. According to what they say here, a telephone call was received between two-fifteen and two-thirty. Will you get the exchange to check?"

Cortland said: "What the hell are you talking about? We can't trace dialed calls as long ago as that."

"Thanks very much," Roger said. "It might make all the difference between holding the Wolf woman and having to let her go. Make it quick, will you?" He replaced the receiver, and rubbed his hands together, joyfully. "Now we won't be long!"

Helen said: "You can't trace local calls. This was a local call."

"You think we can't trace 'em," said Roger. "One of your big mistakes is that you forget how science helps Scotland Yard. It's quite an organization. You had a fool notion that if you could kill me, you could end your troubles. I'm only a cypher along there, kill me and the others get you. You've had it, Helen. We'll have that news through in half an hour. I'll wait. Do you mind?"

She said: "Get out!"

"Oh, no. There's a lot to do. Paterson—" he turned to the man, and his voice lost its mocking note. "I've come to the conclusion that you're the stooge in this business. Helen has made a complete fool out of you. She knew what Carney and his boys were up to although you didn't. Why are you so interested in Alec Magee?"

Helen cried: "Don't answer him!"

"Another squeak out of you, and I'll send for a man to hold you until the call's come through," said Roger. "Paterson—what is Alec Magee to you?"

Paterson's voice was weak and husky.

"He—he was a nice lad. I liked him. I hoped that one day he would marry—"

"Don't talk to him!" screeched Helen.

"Why did you dope your daughter with sleeping tablets?" asked Roger. "What was all the fuss about? Why didn't you want her to go into the grounds on certain nights?"

Paterson said: "She—she is a wayward girl. Very—headstrong." He paused between each word, as if he were having difficulty with the articulation. "It is the only way to treat her. The—only —way. She—means—well. There—is—no—harm—in—her. She—means—well. But—" he gulped, then began to talk more quickly, too quickly, and his words ran into one another, they took some sorting out. "She mixed with the wrong people. All these night clubs, drinking, gambling, going with different men each night. When she was a child, she was beautiful and innocent, I had great dreams for her. Then—then she grew up so fast, terribly fast, and grew away from me. She became spoiled, self-willed—wanton. Yes, wanton! I couldn't stand it. I had to try to take care of her."

"Who told you all about this?"

Helen said: "Pat, he's making a monkey out of you. You're not well. You'll feel better when you've had another tablet, and then—"

"No more tablets," Roger said. "No more, until he's told us everything he knows."

Paterson moaned: "I must have one, I must!"

"I've some in my pocket. You can have a couple

the moment you've finished answering my questions. Who told you what a bad-time girl Margaret was?"

"Well—"

"*Who?*"

"Helen—Helen did! She watched her for me. I was so busy, I couldn't do it myself."

"Who suggested drugging your daughter so that she couldn't leave the house?"

"Hel—Helen did."

"Who introduced you to Dr. Sorenson?"

"Helen—did." Paterson looked at Helen, torment in his eyes. His mind was filled with doubts, and his nerves shrieked for the drug which would make a new man of him, would work a miracle. "Yes, Helen—did. Wasn't it—true?"

"Of course it was true!" Helen cried.

"You'll find that much of it wasn't. Who first put you up to the idea of getting ex-convicts at Morden Lodge?"

Paterson licked his lips.

"Helen."

"And you fell for that! Did you know what they were doing? Did you suspect that they were using the house for training criminals?"

"No—no. That is—"

"You knew all right," said Helen.

The words carried warning, but Roger missed it. He was on the crest of a wave, convinced that Paterson would talk, that the case was unfolding fast. With the sergeant on duty outside, there was no danger. They hadn't dreamed he would come and blast their defenses down. He'd won damaging admissions by sheer weight of attack; Paterson would talk freely now, of everything he knew.

232

Blinded by that thought, Roger missed both the implication and the tone of Helen's: "You knew all right." For it was her first admission of complicity.

"I didn't," Paterson muttered. "I—I wasn't happy. I didn't like some of Carney's friends, but—"

"You knew," said Helen.

Roger said: "You keep quiet. Paterson, who ransacked your study?"

"I—"

"You knew it was being done, didn't you?"

"Yes. Helen—Helen wanted it to look as if the others had done it. I agreed, I wanted—I wanted you to think that I knew nothing about anything. And I don't!" Paterson's face worked, but all his resistance had gone. "It was—Helen's idea. She really did it. Then we hurried away."

"Who shot at your daughter?"

Paterson looked astonished. "Why, *I* don't know. I thought it was Alec. I was terribly upset. I didn't think he meant any harm. I knew he wasn't himself, and—*didn't* he shoot at her?"

"In a minute, he'll convince you that you did it yourself," sneered Helen.

Roger ignored her, but sensed the change in her manner. He moved between her and the door, so that she couldn't get out without passing him. There was no gun in her bag. If she concealed one in her clothes, he would have good time to get his out first. But he watched her warily as he spoke to Paterson.

"What about those jewels? Where did they come from?"

"I'm handling them for a Dutch firm."

"What was all the fuss about?"

"You—you wouldn't like to lose a bag of jewels like that, would you? I thought they'd gone, and—"

"Let's have the truth!"

Paterson said slowly, wearily: "Oh, all right, all right. I thought Margaret had taken them. I didn't know that she knew the hiding place. There was no reason why she should know. Then when she said they were in the wardrobe, I got scared in case she had taken them away. I didn't show it, didn't want you to guess what I was thinking. When I couldn't find them in the wardrobe, I was in a panic. But—it doesn't matter, now. It just doesn't matter."

"Has Margaret taken jewels from you before?"

Paterson licked his lips.

"She—"

"She's a thieving little bitch," said Helen thinly.

"Helen! I won't have you talking about Margaret like that! She—yes, she's taken jewels before and sold them, West. But I don't really blame her. I keep her very short of money. Very short. I haven't known what to do with her. I—I haven't been myself, ever since I started taking the—the tablets. That's the truth, West! Margaret has money in a Trust Fund, but I wouldn't let her touch it, and—and once or twice she's taken things out of the study. Or my pockets. Defiance. She sold them at those—those sewers in London. Those night clubs. But I suppose it was really my fault, if I hadn't kept her so short of money she wouldn't have wanted to take them."

"And Helen persuaded you to keep her short of money, I suppose?"

"Why—yes," said Paterson. "Yes. I always listened to Helen. I like Helen. I do like her!" His vehemence was almost childish, he thrust his face forward, as if defying Roger to deny his liking for Helen. "And—and she had the tablets, she could make me feel wonderful or—terrible. She was the only one who could get them for me. Without those tablets, it—it's like living in hell. You can't understand. It's absolute hell."

Roger said: "Yes, I believe it is." He turned and looked fully into Helen's eyes. "Nice girl, aren't you? This will sound well in court."

All the pretense was gone, now, she showed herself for the vixen she was.

"You won't get *me* in court."

"I—" began Paterson—and then his eyes widened with terror, he thrust out his hands, as if to fend off a physical threat, backed away, and missed a step.

Helen laughed.

Roger glanced over his shoulder—and saw the man with the gun. A small man dressed in gray, with his face covered by his handkerchief.

"No!" screeched Paterson.

Roger sprang to one side, snatching out his gun. The little gray man fired. Paterson coughed, and clutched his breast. Roger sprang behind a chair as a bullet tore past him. Helen ran toward the door to the outer offices, pushed the gunman outside, and slammed the door. Roger's bullet shattered the frosted glass, but he heard no cry. As he went forward, a bullet hummed into the room through the hole in the glass.

Paterson lay in a crumpled heap.

The girl in the inquiry office screamed.

Roger swung round, toward the door on to the passage, marked "Private," and as he did so the glass of the door was shattered. A bullet went close by his head, and he dodged to one side. He saw Helen rushing toward the lift, the doors of which stood open. The gunman followed her, walking backward, keeping all exits covered. Roger fired again. The bullet struck the crisscross iron of the lift gates, while they were closing. Then the wooden doors slid into place, and the lift started to drop.

On the floor of the landing, unconscious, lay the C.I.D. sergeant.

20

Woman-hunt

The porter was in his small office on the ground floor of Univex House when the telephone-bell rang. He lifted it leisurely, and a man's voiced stabbed his ear.

"A man and a fat woman, Miss Wolf, are coming down in the lift. They're armed and they're murderers. Clear the ground floor, get outside, close the doors, yell for the police. Got all that?"

The porter slammed the instrument back, and jumped from his seat. The lift doors hadn't been opened for several minutes. Two men and a girl stood by, waiting, and a man was complaining. A man peering through the little window in the wooden door, said: "Here it comes."

"About time!"

The porter shouted: "Get out. Get out, there's an armed man in that lift!" He turned toward the doorway, seeing the sunlit street, the streams of people passing by, the red buses, taxis, cars; everyday things, unflurried, unalarmed. But the porter didn't reach the steps. A little man in gray, standing by the wall, moved forward and hooked his legs from under him. The girl by the lift cried: "Look!" The lift doors burst open, and a man came out, holding a gun close to his side; his face was covered with a handkerchief. A fat woman hurried out after him.

Neither spoke.

One of the men by the lift shouted: "Stop! Come here, or—"

The man and woman ignored him, so he darted forward. The man turned and fired point-blank at him; and the girl by the lift screamed as he fell. The little man by the door kicked the porter's head.

The two gray-clad men and the fat woman ran outside.

Passers-by saw them come out and run toward a car which stood against the curb. A man at the wheel started the engine as the trio appeared, and the car moved off as a man rushed out of the Univex building, shouting: "Police! Murder! Police!" Two policemen, farther along the street, came hurrying; before they arrived, the car had lost itself in the stream of traffic. A dozen people saw it. There were three different accounts of its movements; it had gone straight on; turned left; turned right.

Men were bending over the prostrate figure of the second victim, when Roger appeared from the staircase.

The hunt for Helen Wolf started at once, and the pressure increased hour by hour.

A call also went out for Dr. Sorenson, who was missing from his house at Feltham.

Paterson was dead.

Roger opened the door of Cortland's office, and a tall, fresh-faced and fair-haired man turned round from the desk. This was Taggart, who had been watching Ma Dingle's. Cortland was speaking into the telephone, and did not even look up.

Roger said: "Anything to report, Taggart?"

"No, sir, nothing at all. The two little chaps at Ma's haven't been out."

"Who's on duty at your place now?"

"Sergeant O'Brien, sir."

"Get back at once and tell him that we're going to raid Ma's an hour after dark. Stop anyone leaving her place. I've called the Division, and asked them to have plenty of men concentrated in the area. There shouldn't be any trouble. On the way down, ask someone to send me up some food."

"Right, sir."

"Off with you!"

"The Superintendent—"

"I'll square him." Roger pushed the man toward the door, while Cortland continued to talk into the telephone as if nothing had happened. He talked for a long time. Roger went round the other side of his desk, opened a cupboard and took out a bottle of whisky, a syphon and a glass. He poured himself a drink, and gulped it down. Then another. The whisky drove off the clouds of tiredness and disappointment which were sweeping through his head. Cortland went on talking. Roger lit a cigarette, and the door opened. Chatsworth bustled in, cigarette jutting out from an amber holder.

"Cortland, I—oh, Roger!" He eyed the glass and the whisky, but made no comment. "What's all this about Paterson being dead?"

"I was there when he was shot, sir."

"Hm. Something to be proud of?"

"I didn't expect an attack from the door. Sorry." He knew that any reprimand would be justified, it would never be possible to explain why he had been so convinced that with Paterson cracking and Helen Wolf resigned to failure, he was near the end of the hunt. "I thought I'd covered the landing to stop the others getting away. But the gunman who killed Paterson caught the duty man napping. Clouted him over the head."

"Had he been drinking, too?"

Roger felt a flare of anger; fought it down.

Chatsworth growled: "How the devil do you expect to keep your mind clear if you mop up whisky early in the afternoon?"

"It's one way of keeping awake." A policeman came in with sandwiches and a mug of tea. Roger said: "Mind if I *eat*, sir?"

Chatsworth glowered, and Cortland finished on the telephone. The three men were silent for some seconds, looking from one to the other. Then Chatsworth and Cortland started to speak at the same time; both stopped.

Chatsworth started again: "What are you doing?"

"Stepping up the pace for Helen Wolf," said Cortland.

"Is that all?"

"We've surrounded Ma Dingle's and are going to raid as soon as we're sure that Helen Wolf doesn't fetch up there. Alec Magee's flat is being watched —no one has visited it since our men took over. We're still looking for Margaret Paterson's friends in London; haven't found them yet."

240

"Who's questioned her?"

"I've been over there this morning," Cortland growled. "She's an impudent piece."

"Why doesn't she give her friends' address?"

"She says she doesn't see why her friends should be involved as she didn't go there. Can't find an answer to that one," Cortland said. "On West's suggestion, we're checking up all the night clubs which she visits regularly. Might be a line there."

"Think the girl's in it, too?" Chatsworth asked Roger, still aggressively.

"She could be. But that's not the only reason for checking the night clubs."

"What's the other?"

Roger schooled his voice. "One of the puzzles is why Helen Wolf persuaded Paterson to stop his daughter from going out, and why Carney used to patrol the grounds to make sure she didn't go. The obvious explanation is that they didn't want her to see what was going on in the gymnasium. I don't like the obvious. They may have had a special reason for not wanting her to visit one of these clubs."

Chatsworth said grudgingly: "Well, you haven't altogether dulled your wits. How long are you going to wait for the raid on Ma Dingle's?"

"Until after nightfall. If Helen's waiting to go there, she'll prefer to go after dark. No use in closing up the funk hole too soon. If it's raided in daylight, a message might reach the woman."

"What are you going to do next?"

"Visit Magee's flat."

"Doesn't the same need for caution apply?"

"No. Helen knows that we'll be watching Magee's flat; she won't go there."

Chatsworth grunted, and turned. "Let me know

how you get on, and don't sit on the report until morning." He went out, and Cortland gave a smile which made him look like an amiable ape. Roger didn't trust his voice.

Magee's flat was in a short, crescent-shaped street near Kensington High Street. The terraced houses were tall, red-faced, Victorian; and yet they had a touch of grace which so much of the period lacked. The street was wide, a quiet little backwater which had once been one of the better residential parts of London. Policemen were watching from either end of the crescent when Roger arrived with two sergeants named Owen and Rugg. Owen was the older; he had worked his way up from the beat, would never rise much higher, but was as tough and shrewd as they grew at the Yard; and looked it. Rugg was a sleek, well-dressed man, public school and Hendon Police college. His beat was London's night life, and he knew Magee as a regular patron of clubs like the Can-Can.

There were four flats, all self-contained. The street door of the house was open, all the doors of the flats locked. Roger led the way, with keys from Magee's pocket in his hand. He listened outside the flat for a few seconds, but heard nothing. Neither of the C.I.D. men outside had seen anyone enter the house or leave it since they had been watching.

Roger opened the door, pushed it back a few inches, and hesitated. He sensed that both Rugg and Owen thought that this was excessive caution; they hadn't been at Paterson's office.

The room seemed to be in darkness, as if the blinds were drawn.

Roger said: "Wait a minute." He slipped inside

the room, a small one furnished as a lounge, and crossed to a room at the front of the house. Yes, the curtains were drawn, daylight crept in only at the sides. He pulled back a curtain.

It was a long, narrow room, furnished in modern style; wildly untidy. Beer bottles lay in a corner, several empty glasses stood on a table. Rings of dried beer smeared the table, the ash from innumerable cigarettes littered the floor and was heaped up in all the ashtrays. An empty whisky bottle lay on its side.

"He's had quite a party," Rugg said.

"Have a look at the other rooms, will you?"

Both men went out. Roger stood by the window and looked round this one, eyes narrowed. He couldn't imagine Alec Magee throwing this kind of party; or smoking the Wild Woodbines that were among the cigarette ends. The air smelt of beer and stale tobacco; he wrinkled up his nose and thrust open a window.

Rugg came back. "Two bedrooms, bathroom, and kitchen. No one's about. The bed in the bigger room isn't made, the other is."

"Yes." Roger looked at the rumpled cushions, the litter, and said slowly: "Too bad we didn't find this place twenty-four hours before, or we'd have caught Carney and his friends."

"*Carney?*"

"Yes. He smoked Wild Woodbines, and—"

"So do a lot of people."

Roger said: "All right, we won't argue. Go over the place for prints, will you. You've a set of Carney's with you, for comparison, I hope?"

"Oh, yes."

"Then get a move on."

Rugg opened his case, and remarked: "You ought to have a look in the bedroom, skipper," and began to take out the fingerprint equipment. Owen joined him. Roger went into the bedroom—and stopped abruptly. On the walls were pictures of Margaret Paterson; not one or two but dozens. Magee had surrounded himself with them. There were three on the dressing table, a beautifully colored enlargement on the bedside table. Wherever there was room for a photograph, there was one of Margaret.

He felt the familiar quickening of his pulse.

She looked at him from every corner; sometimes head only profile and full face; sometimes head and shoulders; or sitting down; or full-length. In most of the full-length ones, she was in a swim suit; the briefest of swim suits. Her beauty wasn't only of the face. Here and there, she was in a group; Alec Magee was always in the group, and Roger remembered where he had seen Alec before: in the photographs at Morden Lodge.

He turned away from the rumpled bed, but couldn't get away from Margaret's face. She seemed to be laughing at him—except in one photograph, above the bed. There, she was asleep; and she looked exactly as she had done when he had put her into Bill Sloan's bed.

Magee had been obsessed; no doubt of that.

Roger looked through the drawers and cupboards, found nothing of interest, and went into the spare room. There was nothing here, either. He glanced into the kitchen and bathroom, and went back to the living room. Owen stood by the window, comparing the prints on a beer bottle with those on a sheet of paper. He looked around with a glint of excitement.

"Carney's been here all right."

"You'll find they were all here—they came straight here from Morden Lodge." Roger went to a pedestal desk in a corner. It was modern, square, made of yellowish wood. There was no pictures of Margaret here, only in the bedroom. He sat at the desk, and pulled out the top drawer. At the front was a slip of paper, with one word printed on it: "Hurlingham." Beneath were dozens of slips of paper, on each a printed word or two; place names. Golders Green, Wimbledon, Tufnel Park, Wembley—he counted slowly. There were fifteen. He put the slips aside and picked up a small loose-leaf notebook. On the page he opened was a date; beneath the date, a list of place names in the Greater London area.

The last date but one was Thursday's; the date of the murders, when young Peter had been orphaned. He glanced down the list and found Hampstead.

"Anything useful?" Owen asked brusquely.

"Plenty." Roger pulled open a deep drawer in the desk, and caught his breath. The handles of dozens of knives were there. They were thrust into slots, specially made for the purpose, blades downward. Rugg and Owen came over as Roger took one of the knives out of its slot. The wide, thin blade had been freshly sharpened; and the maker's name had been ground out on a buffing wheel.

"*Now* we're moving," breathed Rugg.

"We're a bit late on this, but it helps. Magee was the man who took the instructions round to the creepers. Or prepared the packets before they were delivered."

Owen said: "Yes, but there were some raids last night. He couldn't have taken them round last night, could he?"

"They've a stand-in." Roger rubbed his eyes, which felt as if they had sand in them. Even this couldn't keep him awake. He glanced at the empty whisky bottle. "I don't think I need stay any longer. I'll take some of these and look in at the Yard, then get home for a bit."

"Right, sir."

He took the notebook, the slips of paper and one of the knives, and was at Scotland Yard within half an hour. He couldn't clear his mind enough to make a detailed report, just talked to Cortland, and left. Much of the satisfaction he should have felt from the discovery was spoiled by what had happened to Magee; but one of Lobo's chief operatives and two of their workshops had been closed down.

Lobo couldn't be feeling too good.

Who *was* Lobo?

Not Magee; not Paterson. But judging from all reports, Carney had the kind of mind which could organize such a thing as this. So had Helen. Sorenson. He couldn't rule Sorenson out, just because he didn't know much about the man. Nor could he assume that he knew Lobo; the real criminal might still be in the background. Any one of these night clubs could be his headquarters. The job was not over yet, there was still danger.

A saloon car which he didn't recognize stood outside his house. Mark's Talbot wasn't there. He pulled up in front of the car, and as he did so, heard Scoopy call: "Daddy!" Scoopy was at the garden gate of a house on the other side of the road, waving vigorously. Roger strolled across to him. Richard came running from the back garden, his nose smeared with dirt, his hands black.

"Hallo, you scoundrels! Having a good time?"

"Umm," said Scoopy.

"Yes, thank you," said Richard. "Can we have a ride?"

Roger laughed. "Not just now, old chap, but we'll have a lot of rides, one day, I—"

"Scoop!" A girl, two years older than Scoopy, came running from the back garden. "I've got a good idea, will you—oh, hallo!" Her face was dirtier than Richard's, and there was fresh dirt in her golden hair. "Oh, Mr. West, you aren't going to make Scoopy and Richard go home, are you?"

"No, unless your mother—"

"Mummy says they can stay *all* day."

"Then that's fine," said Roger. "Off you go." He stood and watched them tear round the corner— the boys knew this garden as well as they knew their own.

He walked back to the house, frowning, heavy-hearted. Janet would probably still be in bed, and they wouldn't know what to say to each other. He saw her dark hair at the top of his chair, which had its back to the window. So she was up, and Mark was probably reasoning with her. But it wasn't a thing which could be settled by reasoning; it was emotional, and—

Mark was in the kitchen; probably acting as a skivvy.

Better see Janet, alone.

He hesitated outside the door. If only there were

some way in which the ice could be broken, so that they could at least talk freely. Why not creep upstairs? He just wasn't in the mood to argue, but Janet probably would be. He touched the handle of the door, still hesitating.

Mark came out of the kitchen.

"Hallo! Roger, will you—"

"Leave this to me, will you?" Roger thrust open the door, anxious that Mark shouldn't be with them at this meeting.

Margaret Paterson looked at him from the depths of the armchair.

21

New Threat

She didn't get up, but smiled at him radiantly.

"Hallo, Roger! I wondered how long you'd be."

She hadn't called him "Roger" before, even in jest. And she spoke the name warmly, as if it were familiar, as if he meant a great deal to her. Warning flashed through his tired mind; that she had a fatal fascination for men. Remember Alec Magee —but why compare himself with young Magee?

He said: "What are you doing here?"

"I just had to come. I couldn't stay away from you any longer!" She raised a hand. "I had to talk to you."

"How touching," said Roger.

"Why behave like a boor?" asked Margaret, and then her eyes widened, as if in alarm, and she jumped up. "You poor dear, you look tired out! You didn't have any sleep at all last night, did you? I oughtn't to have kept you up."

Roger said: "You didn't—"

He heard voices outside; whispers. He turned,

and saw Janet, disappearing up the stairs. Mark appeared; he looked sick; dismayed.

Margaret said; "But I wouldn't have missed last night for anything in the world. It taught me how exciting policemen can be."

"Oh, did it."

Janet had heard all this; so had Mark. It was as if Margaret had chosen her words because she knew the situation here and wanted to aggravate it. But that was a nonsensical thought; she would talk like this to any man.

He said: "Now, what's the idea? How did you get away from the flat?"

"I just walked out."

"There was someone there to stop you doing that."

"Oh, yes, the man mountain came with me," said Margaret. "I think he's in the kitchen here. He didn't seem to mind when I said I wanted to see you again. He telephoned, and was told you were out, but I thought I'd rather see you here than at Scotland Yard. It's charming here, Roger. Policemen seem to be lucky with their wives."

"Why have you come?"

"You *are* gruff." She looked quickly away from him, reminding him of the moment, last night, when she had seemed about to say something relevant, and had then said she remembered Lake's body with the battered head. When she turned again, her eyes were moist, and the radiance had gone from her face; she looked young, helpless. "Roger, I've heard—about Alec."

"Oh."

"I asked for a newspaper. It was in the stop press. Did he—really kill himself?"

"Yes. But he had help."

"I don't understand you," she said, and waved her hand as if that didn't matter. "I feel responsible, I didn't believe that he'd actually do it."

"You can save your reproaches. It was something else that drove him to suicide. How well did you know him?"

"Very well, of course."

"How often did you go to his flat?"

She looked away. "After the first time I wouldn't go. He showed me that room with all my photographs, and was so sentimental and amorous that—" she broke off. "Of course, I've been there to parties."

"How well did your father know him?"

It dawned on him, then, that she didn't know that her father was dead. The realization came to him with a shock; he would have to break the news, and that meant dealing with her sympathetically. Janet wouldn't know that, and couldn't be blamed for jumping to conclusions. He had to get Lobo. Anything that helped him to get Lobo, had to be done. If he antagonized Margaret, it would add to his difficulties. He'd be wise to ruffle her, at first, and gradually soften, lead up to his news. He didn't trust himself to act rationally, but he must.

Margaret was speaking.

"Quite well, in fact father introduced him to me. I think Alec was a son of an old friend of father's."

"Did Alec ever come to Morden Lodge before you got to know him well?"

"No," she said. "Why are you asking all these questions? Alec's dead, and—"

He said: "And you're sorry, because you feel

251

partly responsible for the way he died, not because you were fond of him. Is that right?"

She didn't answer.

"Look here, you came to see me, and now you have to answer my questions. I'm a police officer, and I'm inquiring into several murders. You're mixed up in them. You may not have known much about it, but I think you could have known quite a lot. You're no fool, even though you often act like one. Now, stop behaving as if I'm a long-lost friend, which I'm not, and remember that I'm a policeman. Is that all clear?"

"Yes," she said submissively, and the reproach in her eyes stung sharply.

"Now, why are you sorry about Alec's death?"

"He was a friend, and he was in love with me."

"Were you in love with him?"

"No. *Must* you ask questions when you know the answers?"

"I don't know all the answers. I don't even know why you came here to see me, unless it was to tell me more about Alec—information you preferred to keep to yourself while he was alive but can't do him any harm now that he's dead. Is that it?"

"No. I wanted to talk to you about it."

"Why me, in particular?"

"I thought you'd help me to get my thoughts clear about it. You seem more confused than I am. I was *not* in love with Alec. Is that straightforward enough?"

"Are you in love with anyone?"

She hesitated.

"Are you?" he barked.

"Not at the moment," she said, and the softness

of her words and the look in her eyes made the comment sincere, not flippant. "At least not quite."

"Who are you nearly—" he broke off, realizing what she would answer! He darted a glance toward the door, which was wide open. He'd left it open because he didn't want Janet or Mark to think he was anxious to shut himself up in the room with the girl; but now she might do more damage than had already been done.

"The most handsome man I know," she said.

"That's fine." He took out cigarettes, and tossed her one. "You've been in and out of love like a jack-in-the-box. All these nice boys. That's about right, isn't it?"

"I suppose so. I wasn't infatuated, just fond of them. I've told you that I have never met a man I wanted to marry."

"Is there any one you're genuinely fond of? What about Helen Wolf?"

"I detest her."

"There's a certain Dr. Sorenson."

She looked astonished, then laughed, as if he had at last succeeded in breaking her tension.

"Don't be quite absurd," she said.

"Have you known him for long?"

"All my life."

"Was he a friend of the family?"

"I suppose he was, in a way. Lately, he's been more of a friend of Helen's. They lived together for a while, I don't know whether they still do."

"How well did Sorenson know your father?"

It was the second time he had used the past tense about Paterson. The first had passed without being noticed. Now a frown etched lines in her forehead, but she answered as if she had noticed nothing significant.

"He is father's doctor. I believe they do some business together."

"*Does* Sorenson know Carney?"

"As a servant, yes." She'd noticed the emphasis on that "Does." She stood up, slowly, the lines deepened on her forehead and were joined by a vertical little groove between her eyes. "I don't think they were close friends. Why?"

"Did Alec know Sorenson?"

"Yes." The word came sharply, she caught her breath. "He did."

"*Was* he Alec's doctor?"

"Yes."

"I see. So now we've been through the whole business. You were fond of all these boyfriends, but not in love with them. You detest Helen, don't particularly care for Sorenson, haven't a lover at the moment, and are really fond of no one."

She came close to him, stretched out a hand to touch his. Her fingers felt cold. He glanced over his shoulder, thinking he heard a sound; but he saw no one, and neither Janet nor Mark would peep round corners. Or would Janet, in her present mood? He felt Margaret's fingers move along his, and she gripped his hand tightly. She didn't speak for a few seconds; she looked as if she were having difficulty in marshalling her words. Then:

"Are you trying to tell me that there's something the matter with my father?"

He couldn't keep up the harshness any longer.

"I'm afraid so."

"What's happened?"

"According to Helen, you ought to be glad. You'll

be able to do exactly what you like now, instead of stealing odd jewels and money, and defying him day after day. The fight's over, because he won't be able to fight any more."

"Oh, no!" she cried. "No!"

Tears flooded her eyes, and she fell against him, her hands tightening on his arms, her head on his shoulder as she looked toward the door—and toward Janet.

Mark said: "Jan!"

Roger heard him, but didn't turn round. Margaret wasn't crying aloud, but her shoulders were heaving, and he knew that tears were streaming from her eyes. He wondered whether he had been unnecessarily brutal; whether he could have broken it to her more gently, or whether this was the wisest way. Better to break down than be icy cold inside—as he had too often felt, lately, about Janet. He had expected Margaret to take it coolly, perhaps too coolly.

He knew that Janet was coming into the room; that was why Mark had called out to her, entreatingly. Well, if she wanted to assume the worst and make a scene, there was nothing he could do about it. He wondered how much Janet was to blame for the way he had talked to Margaret.

Janet passed him, stood behind Margaret, and looked into his face. She said: "You were a bit harsh, Roger."

Her voice was quiet; she looked calm and, although not made up, nearly at her best. She was Janet, not the woman of last night with a brittle voice and a malicious intent to hurt.

He said: "I had to be harsh."

"I think you went too far. Who is she?"

"Mixed up with the Lobo business, but I don't know how closely. She's Margaret Paterson."

He broke off.

Janet put a hand on Margaret's arm, but spoke to Roger.

"I think you've done all you can. You'll fall asleep standing up if you don't get some rest. I'll look after her. Go upstairs for a couple of hours, please."

She took Margaret away from him, and the girl's head fell on her shoulder. He could see the tears streaming down the smooth cheeks, now, see the way her shoulders heaved convulsively.

He said: "Thanks, Jan."

He realized, now, that it had been a strain standing here and talking to Margaret, a physical effort to support her. His eyes felt as if they were made of hot stones. He turned away and faltered toward the door. Mark appeared, suddenly, and said in a bright, cheerful voice: "That's fine! Want any help?"

"I'm not dead on my feet." Roger walked upstairs, determined not to use the banisters, but he had to before he reached the landing. The bedroom door was open, and the bed was turned down for him. He kicked off his shoes, took off his collar and tie, and began to yawn. Come to think of it, he hadn't had a full night's sleep for nearly a week; not more than three hours at a stretch for four days—and not many stretches of any length of time. He flopped down on the bed. This was good; this was rest. He pulled the eiderdown over him and smiled to himself; it wasn't a smile of amusement, but of bewilderment. You couldn't tell with women; you just couldn't tell. When Janet should have stormed and walked out on him, she'd just taken charge of the situation, saying: "I'll look after her." She would.

No, you couldn't tell with women.

In the kitchen Janet said to Mark: "She'll be all right. It was the way he told her that did most of the damage, but I think he was probably right. She's lovely, isn't she, Mark?"

"Yes, but—"

"Mark, you're still a pet, but I know Roger. And Roger knows that she's lovely. Roger's been comparing her with me, and I haven't shown up to much advantage. But I don't think I can forgive him, if—"

"Look here, Jan—"

"Let me finish. If he's really known her for a long time. If she's only just appeared on the scene, well, it won't matter much. It depends how long he's felt like that about her, and how often he's had to be savage because he's afraid of letting his feelings interfere with his job. I'll say this—whatever comes or goes, he would always put his job first. No doubt about that."

"You first," said Mark.

"It used to be like that. I—but never mind. I came to make a cup of tea. She's all right, she isn't crying now. She talked for a few minutes, and said she quarrelled with her father when they last met, and she's wishing she hadn't. Do you think her father was Lobo?"

"I don't know. Roger hasn't told me a thing about this case."

"Mark, can you manage her for a bit? Take the

257

tea in, and—oh, I know we've been heaping everything on to you, I don't know what I'd have done if you hadn't come, but just this little extra—will you?"

"If it will help."

"I want to go off on my own for a bit. I shan't be long. A drive will do me good, and Roger won't need the car. I don't think the telephone would wake him now if it rang in his ear—but it won't, I've switched off the extension upstairs. Mark, will you?"

"Yes, of course."

"I won't be long," promised Janet.

She went upstairs and crept into the bedroom, for the door was open. Roger was sleeping on his back, snoring faintly; it was exactly the sound he had been making when the telephone had rung that night when she had dropped the instrument. It seemed an age, but was really only a few days ago. She didn't go near the bed, but stood looking down at him for some time. Then she took her coat from the wardrobe and tiptoed out. She didn't wear a hat. Soon, she was driving along the road toward Fulham and Putney. The windscreen was a nuisance, she had to take care; and it told her how near Roger had been to death.

At Wimbledon Common she turned toward Roehampton. The sun still shone, the Common was almost deserted, only a few small groups of children and some odd couples walked about the grass and along the cart tracks which led to the windmill; and in the distance, more people moved slowly against the background of the trees. It was quiet and peaceful. She drove a little way along, then stopped the car and walked away from it. It was here that she and Roger had spent so much time before they were married. The car was always parked near this spot, and they had walked aimlessly, idly, happily—so deeply in love. It hurt to look back over the years; and yet she knew that she had exaggerated many things, and that she was as deeply in love with him as ever she had been.

When she had seen Margaret Paterson look at him, she had realized that.

She spent twenty minutes strolling about, going to a spot from which she could see the sails of the windmill. Then she turned back, and a freshening wind blew into her face. She breathed deeply. She already felt better; not happy, but better. She would never cease being grateful for the impulse which had made her go in and help Margaret. Had she done the wrong thing then, it might have been fatal.

She reached the car, looking acrosss the road at a woman who was pushing a pram; two small children ran along by the curb, and the woman said, mechanically: "Don't go into the road." Janet smiled; the words, the tone, were so familiar, exactly like her own when she was out with the boys.

She started to climb in.

A little man straightened up from the back of the car and showed a gun which he held under his coat.

"You're doing fine," he said. "Close the door, then drive straight on. I'll tell you where to go."

22

Ma Dingle's

Roger lay between sleeping and waking. A man with a familiar grating voice talked downstairs, Mark's voice alternated with it. Why was that grating sound so familiar? He opened his eyes and blinked up at the ceiling. It was dark except for a glow of light from a street lamp. Gradually, his mind got into focus. Margaret, Janet, Mark—any of one of those could be expected to talk, but he didn't hear either of the women.

Then footsteps sounded on the stairs, and Mark said: "I've let him sleep on."

"Quite right," said the man with the harsh voice.

Cortland, of course; Roger was stupid with sleep, or he would have known at once. But why was Cortland here? Cortland was one of those officers who seemed to have no private life. One knew him well at the Yard, but had little idea what he did in his spare time. He was married, and—never mind what Cortland did away from the Yard. Why was he here? Why did Mark's "I let him sleep on" have an ominous ring?

Roger sat up abruptly.

Had anything happened to Margaret Paterson—here? It wasn't possible, surely. He pushed back the bedclothes as the door opened slowly. Light from the landing showed Mark in front of Cortland's vast figure. Cortland looked sinister.

"Now what?" Roger asked, and put on the bedside light. This made Cortland look brutal and Mark ghoulish, because of the odd way it fell upon them. But it didn't hide Mark's anxiety.

"Well, what is it?" Roger asked, and shied away from the inevitable answer. Was it murder? Had Lobo made a daring raid here, knowing that Margaret could betray him?

Mark said: "It's a bad business, Roger. I feel like hell about it. If I hadn't let her go—"

"So it didn't happen here?"

"No. It isn't certain where it happened. She—"

Cortland pushed him aside.

"Your wife's been kidnaped, West. She went out five hours ago, and hasn't returned. She was last seen on Wimbledon Common, and nothing has been heard of her since."

Your *wife*.

Blackness clouded Roger's mind; the blackness of disbelief and shock. He fought against it, but felt paralyzed; it was the last thing he had expected, and it turned his world upside down. But out of the dark cloud there shone a bright glow, far off.

Mark was saying something; he didn't catch the words.

Cortland said: "We've got every man we can out on the job, Roger. We'll find her. And we'll knock hell out of Lobo for this."

That made sense.

"Yes." Roger pushed the bedclothes farther back and swung his feet out of bed. "Anything else?"

"Nothing."

"Margaret Paterson?"

"She's gone off into one of her comas," Cortland said.

"She hardly said a word after you came upstairs," Mark remarked. "Just sat back in her chair, looking as if she'd been knocked pretty badly. I left her for half an hour, and when I came back she was asleep."

"Better have a doctor for her." Roger pulled on his shoes. "She may take a drug. Nothing I've been able to place, probably one of the rarer narcotics. It wouldn't be surprising. There's nothing natural about these sleeping fits. She says she can fake 'em, but I'm not sure. Watch her—they may have a stab at her yet, and we shall probably need her evidence before we've finished."

"We're not going to have anyone else die on our hands," Cortland growled.

"Nice resolution, anyhow." Roger put on his collar and tie. He felt oddly detached and in command of himself. "Raided Ma Dingle's yet?"

"No, we waited for you."

"Ma's is the first job, I think. There's just a chance they'll take Janet to Ma's." *Could* this have happened to Janet? Fear was closing in on him. "What about the boys, Mark?"

"They're still across at the Menzies'—sleeping there for the night. You're lucky with your neighbors."

"Need some luck." Yes, it was true. "Janet say anything before she left?"

"No. She wanted a breath of air. I let her take your car. If I'd dreamed—"

"You couldn't have dreamed of this. But she was to have been watched. One of our boys fell down on the job, Cortland." Roger ran his hand over his stubbly face before straightening his collar and tie.

"The house was watched—your wife wasn't."

"My fault," said Roger. Yes, he could blame himself for this and for a lot of things. But he must keep cool. "I won't be two jiffs." He hurried out of the room, and Cortland looked at Mark with a frown.

"He's taking it pretty well."

"You'd expect him to."

Roger heard the tail ends of the words and guessed the rest. He doused his face in stinging cold water, dried vigorously, and called out to the others. He was in the hall, shrugging into his overcoat, when they came down. He gave Mark a quick, taut smile.

"Hold the fort, will you?"

"Yes. Roger, I—"

"We can talk about it later. Lots to talk about." Roger opened the front door and led the way to the two cars standing outside. A constable was near them, as if on guard, and a sergeant stood by the side of Cortland's. "See you at the yard," Roger said.

He got into the second car and started off.

He wanted to be alone for a few minutes; and he believed he knew how Janet had felt and why she had gone for a drive. He felt much fresher, and knew that he hadn't fully realized what had happened, even yet. It was as if he were watching this thing happen to someone else, to someone who wasn't quite real. He was able to be dispassionate again, was not emotionally involved. The facts were simple. Lobo was on the run, which meant Helen Wolf and others. They had every reason to hate his guts, and they hated them. They could no longer hope to remain free and active for long; at best, they could go to earth, which probably meant out of the country, with whatever fortune they'd gathered together. They would be good haters, as Helen was; and although their hatred would be directed toward the police in general, they would have singled him out to hate most. Nothing surprising about that. They were all set to hurt; they'd hurt in every way they could. They were ruthless killers and they'd kidnaped Janet. Therefore, the chances of seeing Janet alive again were small.

Yes, he had to face that.

He felt a a spasm of pain across his chest, fought it back, and went on thinking.

They were crazy; they must have known that this would be the final challenge. Their swan song. Moreover, they were getting mixed up. Their one hope was to get out of danger; yet they had struck again and so increased that danger. There was something unnatural about the whole setup. From the mental condition of Alec Magee to the drugged folly of Paterson and the sleep which overcame Margaret from time to time. Magee might have been a drug addict; it was possible that his mental condition had been due either to an excess of drugs or to having the supply withdrawn where he was in desperate need of it. Drug addicts denied their poison, and left to run around loose, went to pieces mentally; it was one of the great tragedies of drug addiction. In England, drugs were hard to get, except through a doctor. The one medical man known in the Lobo organization, or even connected with some of its members, was Dr. Sorenson. He'd been introduced to Paterson by Helen.

Helen had had Paterson under her thumb for a

long time. The more he thought about it, the more likely it seemed that she was Lobo. But it was silly to jump to conclusions. Sorenson was another possibility, so was Carney. Catch Carney—that was one of the most urgent tasks. Catch Carney, and—find Janet.

Another spasm of physical pain went across his chest, and this time it lasted longer. He was conscious of it when he swung into the Yard and pulled up with a squeal of brakes at the foot of the steps. He didn't wait for Cortland, who was just behind, but hurried upstairs. Cortland caught up with him at the entrance to the lift.

"Thought you'd go straight to Ma's," he said.

"Two or three things to do," said Roger. The lift arrived, and they went up, Roger looking bleakly at the wall. The pain was there all the time now. "You coming to Ma's?"

"No."

"Look after Margaret Paterson and don't forget that doctor——Jenkins is the best man, he knows more than anyone here about dopeys."

"I'll see to it."

"Thanks." Roger forced a smile. "Sorry if I'm talking out of turn."

"We'll find her."

"Shall we?" Roger asked bleakly. The lift stopped and they hurried along to Cortland's office. As he entered the room, Roger thought: I probably shan't see her again. He picked up the sheaf of reports on Cortland's desk and began to run through them, talking as he read. "The most important job is catching Carney. After that, this doctor—Sorenson. Helen goes without saying, but I fancy that Carney is the Achilles heel. He won't stand up to pressure, and he probably knows all there is to know about the Lobo business. Right?"

"Yes. I've sent urgent calls out for all of them to be picked up. We've had the usual string of reports that they've been seen here, there, and everywhere, but nothing's come to anything, yet."

"What about the Press?"

"Well, what about them?"

Roger said: "Find out if there's anyone in the Back Room, will you?" He finished scanning the reports, which could not have been more useless, while Cortland telephoned.

"There are several reporters with the Back Room Inspector," Cortland told him a moment later.

"Thanks. I'll phone you as soon as we've finished at Ma's," Roger said. "I doubt if they'll have taken Janet there, but Ma may be in the know."

He hurried out and saw the burly figure of Chatsworth coming out of a room. He didn't stop; he didn't want to talk to Chatsworth. He reached the Back Room Inspector's office—the Inspector, there, Bream, was a kind of Public Relations officer to the Yard. There were five Fleet Street men waiting for a new development; they had a nose for news, were sure that something was about to break. One or two of them spoke when Roger entered; most stared at him, as if startled by his appearance. Bream certainly was.

"What's up, Roger?"

Roger said: "Listen, boys. Lobo has kidnaped my wife. You know something about my wife. I'm going after him with everything I've got. This is a personal feud now, as well as a job of work. And you'll want a human slant. Our two boys are all right—with neighbors. I see them occasionally, even though this blasted job ties me to the desk or keeps me away from home ten times as much as it should. You can say that a policeman's home life is a hell of a business, and that all policemen ought to stay single."

"Roger—" began Bream.

"They know what I mean. Get behind the Yard this time, instead of snarling at it."

He turned and hurried out, and five minutes later was on his way to the East End.

Chatsworth went into Cortland's office, and said gruffly: "What's the matter with West?"

Cortland told him.

Chatsworth said: "Hmm. *Hmmm.*" The shock hit him hard.

"He seems detached from everything that's happened; as if he's all frozen up inside," Cortland said. "I don't understand it, but I shall be sorry for Lobo if West catches him tonight. And it would take a lot to make me sorry for Lobo."

Roger drove slowly along Marsten Street, and saw no sign of a police guard. Lights blazed from the Rose & Crown. The lamp under which he had last seen Squinty glowed brightly. A small car stood a few doors away from Ma Dingle's, and there were lights at two of the windows of her house, and a light at the house opposite, where Taggart stayed. Two or three people lounged about the corner, none of them particularly small men like Lobo's creepers, none of them looking like a policeman. He drove to the end of the road, reversed the car, and knew that he was being watched.

A man came out of the shadows of a doorway, and said: "That you, West?"

"Yes." Roger recognized the Superintendent of the Division. "Nice neat job—I can't see a busy anywhere."

"We've got everything covered, don't worry."

"Anyone visited Ma's?"

"No report—the usual boarders have gone in and out, that's all. Ready to go?"

"Yes. What's the signal?"

"Five blasts on a car horn. I'll come with you, we've left our cars in the side streets."

"Right." Roger drove back toward Ma's and pulled up outside the Rose & Crown. When he turned off the engine, he could hear the babble of voices from the pub. He glanced at the Superintendent, who nodded, and blew the horn of his car five times. The short blasts screamed in the quiet night. Roger climbed out of the car and hurried across to Ma's, and as he did so, men materialized out of the gloom. By the time he reached Ma's, Taggart and three other men had gathered round the doorway. He went up to the front door and knocked.

The knocking echoed up and down the street.

Shuffling footsteps sounded, as if from a long way off. Roger didn't knock again, but kept his right hand in his pocket, about the handle of his gun. The other men were also armed; there was a chance that Lobo's men, still here, would try to fight it out. The shuffling continued for a long time. Then he saw a glow of light at the side of the door. He knocked again.

"Wot's the 'urry, wot's the 'urry." That was the whining voice of Ma Dingle. The bolts were drawn back, and Ma appeared.

She was short, squat, slatternly. Her gray hair was in metal curlers, there were smears of lipstick on her thin lips and of rouge on her raddled face. She had a silver fox round her shoulders, and her plumpness bulged in a flowered silk dress which might have been suitable for a woman half her age. Whisky fumes emanated from her as if she had been soaked in the spirit. She stood outlined against the hall light, and so her face was is shadow.

" 'Oo is it?" she demanded shrilly.

"Okay, Ma, you've had it," Roger said.

"Police," said the Superintendent.

"Police?" Ma made the second syllable sound like "lice." I'll 'ave you know this is a respeckable 'ouse. I got my register in order, everyfink's—"

"Take her in there," Roger said to Taggart, who came in behind them. There was a front room on the right. Ma protested shrilly, but Taggart took her arm and bustled her inside. Roger and the Superintendent hurried along the passage to the kitchen. It was empty. There was no one else on the ground floor. Roger turned back.

"They're inside, or I'd have seen them come out," Taggart said.

Roger grunted. "I'll lead the way," and took out his gun. He knew that both Taggart and the Superintendent were puzzled by his brusqueness; this wasn't the West they knew. He didn't dwell on that, but hurried up the narrow stairs and on to the landing, switched on another light. There were four rooms up here. Lights showed beneath two of them. He motioned to Taggart to stay at the head of the stairs, and glanced into the dark rooms; each was empty.

The Superintendent said: "Think they'll be rough?"

"Could be." Roger tapped at one of the doors of the lighted rooms. "They'd have been out to see what it was all about if they weren't as scared as hell. Open up! Police!"

Someone moved inside. Roger thrust the door open, and covered a little, gray-clad man with his gun. Behind this man was another, almost his twin. One of them was rubbing his eyes, as if he had been asleep. The other was round-eyed, wary; neither held a gun, and four hands were in full view.

"Wot the 'ell's all this?" asked the nearer man.

Roger said: "We're after Lobo and his wolves. You're under arrest. Burglary with violence. And if you like, I'll tell you that anything you say may be used in evidence." He surveyed the room. It was tidy, clean, and well furnished—not the kind of room which one would expect at Ma's. Both men were well dressed. On a table were half a dozen bottles of beer and two of gin, and there were two decks of cards and some loose silver. On another table was a telephone.

"You're crazy!" exclaimed the nearer man. Roger grabbed his hand, forced it open, and saw the mark of the wolf.

"Am I? Take 'em downstairs, Taggart," said Roger. He waited until they'd gone, and then went into the other lighted room.

An elderly woman was there, in bed; a woman as painted and raddled as Ma. She didn't speak. She was reading a colored weekly periodical, and Roger read the title of the story: "FATE'S PLAYTHINGS."

"We'll need a woman officer to look through here," said Roger.

The woman in bed glanced at him, but still said no word. Roger went out, and a C.I.D. man took his place. He led the way downstairs with a feeling of acute disappointment and with that physical pain more hurtful than ever. True, the Lobo men were caught, but he'd hoped to find others, hoped for a miracle. He wouldn't get it. Ma would refuse to talk, except to declare that she knew nothing. The raid was a flop; he'd always known it would be, he had never set much store by Ma Dingle's— except the possibility that some more important members of Lobo's gang would be here.

A Divisional Inspector was questioning Ma, and her querulous voice was raised in protest. Briggs and Milsom, two little men dressed in gray, stood in the hall, silent, almost sorrowful; they did not look dangerous, it was hard to believe that they were. But not all of Lobo's men were killers.

Then he heard the telephone.

He raised his head and looked up the stairs. The ringing coming from there. He hurried up. He didn't say a word to the Superintendent or anyone else, and he knew that they were silently criticizing him; he was antagonizing them, and couldn't help it. He hardly trusted himself to speak.

The telephone bell kept ringing.

He crossed the room in three long strides and snatched the receiver from the cradle; and then his mind cleared. He didn't speak at first, but put the mouthpiece against his chest.

The Superintendent stood in the doorway.

Roger put the receiver to his ear.

"'Allo?" His voice had a nasal whine—like the man who had spoken to him when he'd come into the room. "'Oo's that?" It would be folly to introduce himself as Briggs or Milsom.

A woman said: "Is that you, Milly?"

He couldn't mistake that voice, with its lilting note, its forced gaiety: *Helen*. He motioned to the Superintendent, and his eyes blazed. The Super

271

turned and rushed downstairs, knowing what that meant, desperately anxious to trace the call.

Roger said: "Yeh. Now wot?"

And Helen laughed.

"You know what," she said. "You're not *bad*, West, not bad at all, but I happen to know that you've been most unkind to my friends. Most unkind. If it hadn't been for that, I might have thought you really were Milsom. Don't be hard on Milsom or Briggs, will you? They're good boys— very clever. Done twenty-five jobs at least, each of them, and the busies didn't catch them. That's a good record, isn't it, West?"

Roger said: "Not as good as yours. They won't be hanged."

"And *I* won't be hanged," said Helen Wolf, without the slightest change in her voice; and she laughed again. "You'll see to that, Handsome. They do call you Handsome, don't they? And you might be interested to hear that Margaret agreed, she thinks you're quite the most handsome thing in London. Personally, I don't like good-looking men. I think they stink. But we mustn't waste time, must we, or you'll try to find out where I'm calling from. That wouldn't do, would it? I just wanted a word with you, Handsome. About Mrs. West. *Isn't* she sweet?"

23

Bargain and Threat

The Superintendent appeared in the doorway again. There was a murmur of conversation downstairs, but Roger hardly noticed it.

Helen Wolf said: "I always knew she must be, Handsome, and I can understand you being fond of her, and her being fond of you. But I've been talking to your wife, and telling her what Margaret thinks about you. She pretends that she doesn't mind, but I feel sure that she's *jealous*. Would you believe it? Jealous of Margaret!"

Roger said: "What do you want?"

"Yes, I suppose it is time to get down to business, but there's no need to worry, your men won't be able to trace this call. You see, it's a private line from here to Ma Dingle's. We never did believe in trusting the Post Office Telephones, it's much better to have our own line installed. Don't you agree? And Lake was *such* a good mechanic. He was in Signals during the war. I want to make a bargain with you, Handsome."

"What bargain?"

"I *thought* you would be interested," said Helen, and gave a little clucking laugh. "There had to come a time when you were first a human being and a policeman afterward, hadn't there? It's quite simple. I want Margaret. There's so much I would like to talk to her about. You know what a willful child she is, don't you? And how much I like her—but she needs correction and chastisement. Her father didn't know how to handle her, but *I* know. She's asleep, now. Isn't it strange that I should guess that? I haven't really guessed, it's a process of deduction. Whenever Margaret gets into an awkward position, she goes to sleep! She uses veronal, I think, which is so effective. I knew that as soon as she was told that your wife was missing, she would be afraid of questions and wouldn't want to answer them. She hasn't much confidence in herself, really, and positively *hates* being in an embarrassing position. So she goes to sleep. It's simple and feline, isn't it? There's something very catlike about Margaret. Like her looks—have you ever noticed that she's sleek and lovely, just like a great cat?"

Roger said: "Don't keep wasting time, or I'll ring off. If you've got anything to say, say it."

"How impatient! But I suppose there's something in that, Handsome. Well, it's very simple. Just a matter of exchange of prisoners. You have Margaret. I want her. I have your wife. You want her. Margaret might do me a lot of damage when she wakes up, and so I want to make sure that you're not with her. What about it, Handsome? Your wife, in return for Margaret Paterson. I know it's difficult, you'll have to make up your mind which you *really* prefer? I—just a moment, Handsome!"

She went off the line. The Superintendent whispered: "Hold her on, we're bound to get her." Roger nodded; there was no point in explaining that they'd need mechanics out to trace a private line; and Helen must be sure of herself, or she wouldn't stay talking so long.

She was somewhere in London; they couldn't run a private telephone line over many miles, it would be too big a job.

"Anything I can do?" the Superintendent asked.

Roger shook his head, and then heard a sound at the other end of the wire; Helen was picking up the receiver again. He heard her laugh; and then came Janet's voice.

Janet stammered: "Roger, *can*—can you come?"

Helen said something to her which Roger couldn't quite catch. "*Can* you come?" The phrase meant nothing and everything.

Janet spoke again.

"Roger, she wants me to beg you to exchange Margaret for me. I c*a*n't do that. I just c*a*n't do that." She made it a short "a," which didn't sound like Janet, although there was no doubt it was she. "*Can* you get here in time to—"

She stopped abruptly; and there was a sound, as of a slap, sharp and clear. Then Helen came on to the line again.

"I wonder what it is about women, Handsome, they *never* do what they're told. I've just had to smack her face. I don't want to hurt her, but I may have to. I want Margaret Paterson, you see. I *must* have Margaret, and once I get her, you can have your sweet wife back. You can manage it, if you want to. Just let Margaret leave, without being followed. I'll see to all the rest. It isn't difficult, is it? And if you do that, and I get Margaret safely, then you'll see your wife again. Oh, and don't forget that if I have to wait too long, I shall get bad tempered. I'm not very nice when I lose my temper. I just want to hurt people, anyone who happens to be near me. Your wife is standing right by my side, Handsome. You *will* release Margaret, won't you? And not have her followed. Don't say a word to any of your friends about it, because they aren't so fond of your dear wife as you are, are they? They would sacrifice her for duty, but you—don't be long, will you? Janet's got *such* a nice face, a pretty face, it would be a pity to spoil it."

The line went dead.

A man had come into the room and was whispering to the Superintendent, who turned, saw Roger standing with the receiver in his hand but no longer to his ear, and said sharply: "There's no telephone line laid on here, West—no such number as Mile End 8213."

"No. Private line. Better have some mechanics out, to try to trace it. Can't be far away." Roger brushed his hair back from his forehead.

"Who was it?"

"The woman, Wolf."

The Superintendent turned, gave instructions to the man who'd told him about the nonexistence of Mile End 8213, and then looked frowningly at Roger. The room was very quiet. Roger fumbled for his cigarettes, and the Superintendent came forward with a light.

"What's the matter, West?"

Roger said: "It's all right. I'm all right. They've probably used the gas mains or the sewers to put that line in. Easy enough to do after dark, I suppose. Easy." He laughed. "Thanks." He drew on the cigarette, and it burned down nearly half an inch before he took it from his lips. "Did you know that these beauties had a bright idea? The oldest, but still pretty bright. They've kidnaped my wife. Neat, isn't it?"

Then he heard Chatsworth's voice, downstairs.

He had no real freedom of action; no choice. He would have to sacrifice Janet for Margaret. Anything else was unthinkable. You couldn't bargain with Helen Wolf; Lobo; with anyone. You had a job to do, and it had to be done. You cut out all personal feelings, all emotion. You kept your eye on the ball, and that was all there was to it.

But—you could live in hell at the same time.

This was a new kind of hell; partly—mostly—of his own making. He'd needed a shock to jerk him out of it; but not a pain in his chest like a slash from a sword, or a burn from a branding iron. Like that little iron he'd found in Carney's room. You just had to stand there and let the thoughts ooze through your mind. Thoughts and facts—and the simple, damnable fact was that much as he argued with himself, he *had* a choice; the choice between the right and the wrong thing. He could keep silent about Helen's threat; could say nothing to Chatsworth, let Margaret go—yes, he could arrange that—and take a chance that Helen Wolf meant what she said. It was just about the only chance that Janet would have.

He could do it.

In so doing, he would send Margaret to her death; there was no argument about that, no possibility of argument. The hatred which Helen had for the girl had shown clearly enough at Univex House, had been evident in a dozen different ways. So he could save Janet, or at least give her a chance, and sacrifice Margaret, in all her youth and loveliness. It wasn't just an issue about people, a choice between one woman and the other, although it had been forced on him in that guise. It went much deeper. If he sacrificed Margaret, he would throw away the chance of finding out what she could tell them about Lobo; and she knew much more than she had allowed them to guess, so far.

Chatsworth came in burly, but soft-footed. Roger looked up, but made no sign that he saw him. Chatsworth closed the door, drew nearer, but didn't speak. He turned away and sat on the side of one of the two single beds; a man of deep understanding. Probably he guessed at the mental fight within Roger; he couldn't know what it was, but he could read all the signs of strain.

In his mind's eye, Roger saw two faces: Janet's and Margaret's. Margaret, while she was asleep; and Janet, when she had entered the living room at Bell Street and talked quietly, shown herself as she really was. The folly of his attitude toward Margaret showed up vividly; he'd been fascinated by her, and repulsed by Janet's manner, by the contrast between the two after their orgy of champagne. That had affected him when he was muddled and dazed by tiredness.

He stubbed out the cigarette.

Janet's voice sounded as if it were still in his ears: "*Can*—can you come, Roger?" All the appeal in the world had sounded in her voice. Was it fear that had made her falter? "*Can* you come?" Not—"can you let Margaret Paterson come"; not a note of pleading, to save her at Margaret's expense, just a plea: "Can you come?" And he'd said nothing to comfort her, because of the black shadow in his mind and the sharp pain in his chest.

"*Can* you come?" And: "I just *can't* do that."

"*Can't*" with a short "a." Did that mean anything? He was beginning to think again, not clearly but enough to show that the stupefying effect of what had happened was lessening.

"What is it, Roger?" asked Chatsworth.

Roger said: "Sorry. I just heard from the Wolf woman. She made an offer. Wants to exchange Janet for Margaret Paterson. Nice thought, wasn't it? Wants me to let Margaret go—without anyone on her tail—and promises to release Janet. Otherwise—bad for Janet. She likes to hurt. I'd like to get my hands round her throat."

Now he'd thrown the one chance away.

Chatsworth said: "She's a vixen, but don't use your hands, leave her neck for the rope, Roger. Think there's a chance of letting the Paterson girl go, and following her? It might work."

"Could try it," Roger said. "It would give us a chance, I suppose. Fact is, whatever we do, Janet's had it. She knows where they are—must know. They can't take a chance of letting her go free. But they might keep her alive until they see whether it will work. The exchange trick, I mean. Yes, I suppose anything's worth trying. We haven't searched this room, yet. We might find something here that

279

would give us a lead. We might get Briggs, Milsome, or Ma Dingle to talk, too."

Chatsworth said: "Sorry. No go."

"Time when we should find third degree useful," said Roger. "Nice, humanitarian people, the British police. Never hurt a rogue. Never be unfair to a rogue. Unfair!"

Chatsworth said: "Trailing isn't all that difficult. We needn't have her followed, but could station men at points of vantage all over London, warn all patrols and constables to look out for her, find out where they take her. It's somewhere in London, or you wouldn't have had that call."

"Oh, it's in London. Some clever little hiding place, where Carney, Helen, and all the rest of the beauties are hiding out, snug and secure. I'm bound to say that I think the right thing is to hold Margaret Paterson until she comes round, and then question her. We can exert *some* pressure. If we do let her go, and they snatch her, then it'll be our responsibility. Too big a chance."

"You'd take it, if it were anyone else instead of your wife."

"Would I?" Roger stared across the room at a drawer of the tallboy which stood open—the bottom drawer. Something poked out; a feather. He crossed the room and pulled it wider open. There was not one feather, but several, colorful and bright. He picked them up; they were fastened together, and they made a hat. There was another hat in the drawer, also a woman's; gray tweed, with an unusual overcheck of blue and green.

He'd first seen a feather hat like this one on Margaret; later Sloan had seen others at the Can-Can, and that overcheck tweed was identical with the suit Margaret had worn when he'd first met her.

Margaret had lost a hat, that was why she'd worn the feathered one. So—

But Margaret wasn't so important just now; the significance of those hats mattered most.

He jerked his head up. His voice cracked.

"Yes, let her go. *Let her* go. I know where they'll take her. And Janet—Janet *told* me." It wasn't because she was afraid that she stammered "*can—can* you come—I *can't* do that." Can-can't —*Can-Can*. "They're at the Can-Can! Yes, let the woman go." He stuffed the tweed hat into his pocket as he spoke.

Margaret was awake, and on her way. Every policeman and C.I.D. man who set eyes on her would report to the Yard, but Roger thought she would probably be snatched, and the trail crossed. And he was no longer so certain about the Can-Can. It was so obvious, because of the feathered hat and Janet's words, and might be too obvious; he distrusted the obvious as a matter of policy, and yet he'd jumped to it this time. At least, Chatsworth had agreed; so had Cortland, when they'd reached the Yard. The telephone line was being traced; it started from a gas main in Ma's place. Dozens of manholes were already being opened to find that single cable, especially those near the Can-Can, but there was no report of a discovery yet.

The Can-Can club was disappointing from the outside, even when the doorway was brightly lit; and the lights weren't on yet. It was half-past nine; the club didn't open until ten o'clock, and only a few people would drift in before eleven. It was in

281

Warren Mews, off Park Lane. The Mews had been turned into stables, garages, and flats, here and there a light glowed. One house had been taken over by the Can-Can club, which had the best reputation of any night club in London and had never been raided; a good front was half the battle.

Three roads led to Warren Mews, and there were many narrow turnings nearby, and two bombed sites, where the police could hide. Roger, with Taggart, stood in a doorway from which he could watch the club.

Traffic noises, from Park Lane and Oxford Street, came clearly. Street lights were reflected in the sky, which was overcast. There were no stars, but a blustery wind drove the clouds fast overhead, and cut along the street toward this spot. There always seemed to be wind when Roger was out at night on the Lobo job.

He was cold, but reluctant to move about, because the approaches to the Can-Can would be watched by Lobo's men, if he had guessed right. There were probably men at the windows, looking out, ready to give the alarm if the police were seen. He didn't think they had been seen, they'd made a special job of this—as they had at Ma Dingle's. If he were right, then Ma's had given him the key to the whole business, after all.

It was twenty minutes to ten, now.

Early revelers would soon be arriving. The lights would soon go up. Come to think, wasn't it usual for the lights to be on before opening time? Bill Sloan would know, so would the sleek Rugg. Rugg was here, somewhere, looking forward to this raid; he thrived on night-club raids. Never mind Rugg! It was an hour since Margaret had left Bell Street by taxi. As soon as she'd come round, she said that she wanted to go to her friends; she had seemed surprised, he was told, that there had been so little objection to her going.

Would she come here?

The wind whistled along the street, and Taggart muttered an imprecation and beat his arms gently across his breast; it didn't help much. A car passed along one of the turnings, but didn't stop. There were still no lights at the Can-Can. Supposing he were right, but had left the raid too late? Helen and anyone with her had had ample time to get away from the Can-Can; she might have realized the significance of Janet's words, have feared that Roger would understand the implication, and left in a hurry.

Another car drew near, its headlights blazing. Roger drew back into the shadow of the doorway. The car purred past.

Taggart grunted.

Roger said: "It's beginning to look as if we've had it." And then another thought stabbed into his mind. That they might all be there, including Janet; and the moment there were raided, might *kill* Janet; there was no doubt of the malignity of Helen Wolf; they might kill Janet before he had time—

A taxi came along the street and slowed down.

Taggart hissed: *"What's this?"*

The cab pulled up outside the Can-Can. A little man got out. Margaret Paterson followed, and a man followed her, holding tightly to her arm.

283

24

Raid

Roger said tautly: "Give them time to go in." But it was difficult to stand there, losing precious seconds. He saw one of the little men in the doorway of the night club, looking round as if anxious to make sure that he wasn't noticed. The taxi drove off, and the red light faded into the distance. Taggart said: "Surely—" and Roger said: "Yes, come on." The little man had disappeared. Roger moved across the road, and saw other shadowy figures approaching; if they were watched, the alarm would soon be given inside the club.

He reached the door.

It was open.

No one was on the narrow flight of stairs, but they heard footsteps. Roger took his gun from his pocket and led the way up. On the first landing were the cloakrooms and some private rooms, where patrons could do what they liked to amuse themselves. The night club proper was on the next floor. Above, was the apartment of the owner—a man named Clarke, a little, affable man, who was on the best of terms with the police. By now, the cloakroom attendants should be on duty; no one was there, and the first floor was in semi-darkness. Someone spoke on the next flight of stairs.

Roger reached the foot of them and slipped quickly into the cloakroom, out of sight. He caught a glimpse of the two small men, and saw that they were dressed in gray. Margaret was still between them.

A door opened and closed.

Roger said: "Come on." He walked up the stairs, very slowly and quietly. He could hear nothing, now, but behind him were Taggart and several other Yard men; he recognized Rugg, bright-eyed and eager; this was fun to Rugg. He reached the tiny landing. There was only one door. He tried the handle gently; it was locked, of course. It looked solid, too—not a door one could open by putting a shoulder against it. Cortland might be powerful enough to do that, but *he* couldn't. He drew back, and leveled the gun at the lock.

So much depended on speed; everything.

Men crowded on the landing with him; three of them carried guns. He motioned to them. They leveled their weapons toward the lock, and he said softly:

"Now."

Four shots rang out, deafening in the tiny space. Smoke filled it, the stink of cordite stung Roger's nostrils. The lock was shattered. He leaped at the door, thrust it open, and was suddenly afraid that he had been too careless, for he staggered into the room.

It was a small room.

Another door was open, opposite. In the doorway stood the two little men in gray. Beyond them, Margaret. Just in sight was Carney, with his apelike face—and he thought he saw the top of Janet's head, where she sat on a chair against the wall.

Carney shouted; just a bull-like bellow of alarm. Roger flung himself forward. The two little men sagged to one side, frightened by the gun, but Carney wasn't frightened, he had a revolver in his hand.

Roger fired, Carney's gun barked; the two shots sounded as one. Roger felt a sharp pain in his right arm—and saw Carney stagger, the gun drop from his grip. Margaret moved swiftly. Everything seemed to happen at once—even Helen Wolf's shout. But what Roger saw most clearly was Janet jumping up from her chair, and Margaret snatching the gun from Carney. Then he was at the door of the room, and saw Helen, behind a desk, with a pistol in her hand; raised, pointing at Margaret.

She said: "You little bitch. You brought them here. I'll—"

Margaret screamed: "No!" And she fired.

A bullet blotted out Helen Wolf's left eye.

Carney was lying on the floor, moaning; Margaret was sitting in a chair with her face buried in her hands, moving to and fro and sobbing. Roger had her gun. Janet knelt by her side. She had looked once at Roger, not uttered a word; words weren't necessary. Helen Wolf slumped forward on the desk, her hands daubed by her own blood.

The two gray men, O'Hara, and the two women servants from Morden Lodge were downstairs, under arrest; no one else had been in the flat on the second floor.

Taggart said: "Well, it didn't take long." He touched Helen's wolves' heads scarf. "That looks significant, doesn't it? She was Lobo."

Roger said: "Was she? Pity Sorenson isn't here." He looked at Janet, who was talking softly to Margaret; and his eyes were bleak. "Great pity, but he might come. Haven't made it seem obvious outside that we've raided the place, have you?"

"No, no one will be kept away."

"Go down and tell them there's a good chance that Sorenson will turn up."

Roger went to the desk. There were three drawers on one side, drawers which he could open without touching the dead Helen. He opened them slowly. One was filled with little wash-leather bags, familiar enough. He picked one up and felt it. There was cotton wool inside, together with something hard. This bag wasn't sealed. He untied it and shook the contents out on to the desk. There were a dozen little twists of cotton wool. He unwrapped one and three diamond rings lay on the palm of his hand. There was nothing remarkable about them, they weren't worth much—they were the kind of ring that Lobo's creepers often stole.

There were nineteen bags.

"Nineteen Lobo jobs last night, weren't there?" he said to Taggart. "This is the loot."

"Oh, we've got him all right."

"Yes. Any idea who he is?"

Taggart looked at Helen Wolf, then said something about the doctor, Sorenson. Roger laughed,

287

and the note sounded so strange that Janet turned her head sharply.

"No, not Helen, not the good doctor, or I miss my guess."

Taggart said: "Carney?" He didn't seem convinced.

"No, not Carney. Someone still alive and crying." He turned away from Taggart and went to Janet, put his hands on her waist, and raised her up. "All right, Jan," he said, and he didn't take his gaze from Margaret. "It's all right, Margaret, my pet, it's all over, you're through." He took the tweed hat from his pocket. "I was pretty sure when I found your hat. When Helen thought you'd ratted and tried to shoot you, I knew."

She kept her face buried in her hands.

"Absolutely through," Roger said.

"Quite safe," said Janet quickly. "Roger, don't you think—"

"But she isn't safe. She's come to the end of her run, that's all. Margaret Paterson, *alias* Lobo. No, I'm not crazy. It took a long time to sink in, that's all. Margaret Paterson—*alias* Lobo." He put his hand on Margaret's head, grasped her hair, as if he were going to jerk her head up, but didn't pull. She didn't look up at him, but took her hands away and groped for her case and opened it. He let her take something out, but as she raised her hand to her lips, he caught her wrist.

And then she sprang up, snatched the hat away, and struck and kicked at him in a wild fury. Her face was distorted, all beauty was gone. Two small white tablets dropped from her hand as she fought and screamed at him. Janet stood by the wall, pale, her eyes shocked and rounded. It was some seconds before anyone else moved. Roger fended Margaret off until he caught her wrists and held her at arm's length; then Taggart and Rugg pulled her away from him.

Cortland came in; and gaped.

Roger dabbed at his scratched skin and laughed, the first free laugh he had given for days. Then he pulled up his coat sleeve and dabbed at the slight bullet wound.

"Unexpected?" he asked.

"Unexpected! You don't mean that she's—"

"Lobo. Either on her own or with Helen and Sorenson. More likely on her own, and they worked for her but wouldn't stay at the Lodge when they knew we were watching. Her hat started me thinking. When I saw it at Ma Dingle's. It was one she said she'd lost, everything would click into place if it was the lovely Margaret. *Lovely* Margaret."

Two men held her tightly, but she tried to get away from them so as to fly at him again.

Roger said: "Janet, it's over. All over. But—what did the Wolf woman say to you?"

He was oblivious of the others; Janet was, too. She came toward him, her eyes glowing now, and took his hands. He didn't draw her close; didn't move; just looked at her, and it was all she needed.

"It doesn't matter, darling."

"It matters a lot. What did she say?"

"Oh—a lot of crazy nonsense! She said—you were—close friends with Margaret Paterson. She sent me a photograph of her."

"When?"

"Last week."

"Before I'd ever heard of Margaret," said Roger,

and he laughed again. His grip of her hands was very tight. "It explains the shot at the Lodge gates, of course, why that happened when it did. I could never swallow that as a coincidence." He knew that some of them didn't know what he was talking about, but that didn't matter, he was uttering his thoughts aloud. "They'd worked it up nicely. Get you worried, meaning get me worried. With domestic trouble, I wouldn't be able to concentrate so well on Lobo. Nice tactics, typical of Margaret. So she fired that shot, to attract me, to get to know me, the very moment she knew we were on to Morden Lodge. Very slick work. If she hadn't lost her hat, it might have succeeded."

Cortland said: "Break, you two. You feel all right, Roger?"

"All *right?* I feel wonderful!"

"Then tell me what's it's all about."

"Later. At the office. I'll write it all down for you. Don't they keep whisky in this place? I want a drink."

He had a drink in his hand when Chatsworth came in, and he raised it high toward the Assistant Commissioner, and then grinned as he tossed the drink down.

Before Chatsworth could speak, there was a commotion downstairs—a commotion which blasted through the quiet up here, made Cortland jump toward the door and Roger drop the glass and move after him.

A shot rang out.

"What's doing?" roared Cortland.

"We've got that doctor," a man called back.

Soon, Sorenson was thrust into the room; no longer smiling, but scared and nervous. When he

290

saw Margaret with her wrists ringed by handcuffs, he stopped dead.

"Yes, we know Lobo," Roger said.

Sorenson muttered: "I didn't think you'd get her. I just didn't think you'd get her."

They didn't go to Scotland Yard, but to Bell Street. Cortland, Chatsworth, and Taggart accompanied Roger and Janet. Margaret was lodged at Cannon Row, Sorenson at the Yard, the others at Marlborough Street. An army of officials was busy taking statements, getting them ready, even now, for the coming trials; the wheels of the law were moving fast.

At Bell Street, Mark opened the door when he heard the cars stop, and Janet called out: "All safe, Mark!"

"Thank God for that!"

"You might even think of Roger," said Chatsworth. "Hallo, Lessing. Glad he had the sense to keep you out of this job. Now don't start slinging questions at him, he's going to sit down and tell us all about it at one go. That's an order, Roger."

"Yes, sir."

"And I don't want insolence!"

"No, sir." Roger grinned, Chatsworth laughed, Cortland looked more than ever like an amiable ape. Roger sat in his armchair, and Janet on a pouffe at his knee; his fingers toyed with her hair as he talked. A lock of Mark's hair fell into his eyes as he sat at the piano. Chatsworth and Cortland stood looking down at Roger.

Roger said: "Now that we know, it's easy to see why we should have jumped at it earlier. Let's start with the most obvious sign—Alec Magee. He was desperately in love with Margaret; infatuated, hypnotized—call it what you like. He said he would do anything for her, and I believed him. Once we knew that he acted as Lobo's messenger, taking the packets to the creepers, we should have asked: Why? How did he become involved with Lobo's mob? I couldn't find any past criminal history. He was wealthy. Yet there had to be some powerful influence. Love." He let his hand rest on Janet's head. "Margaret could make him do what she liked, and she made him do that.

"Then have a look at what happened at Morden Lodge.

"Margaret fired the shot which was supposed to have made her wreck her car. I didn't think of looking for another gun, one that had been thrown away by her. Margaret knew, by then, that we had traced Lobo to the house. She'd laid her plans carefully. Knowing I was the officer in charge of investigation, she was giving me plenty to think about by preying on Janet's mind. Then, when it was obvious that I'd soon start questioning her and probing into her family's affairs, she made herself a victim, so confusing the issue. The tactics were to prevent me from concentrating on the job. She'd already started, with Janet. Then she used her peculiar fascination to finish the work."

Janet said with a queer little laugh: "She didn't know how hard it was to make you forget you're a policeman!"

He felt her head pressing against his legs.

He went on slowly: "Then began the real fun and games, the kind of confusion which always comes when we get the beggars on the run. Carney and the other servants were stooges. They got the wind up, and Helen wanted it to look as if they'd broken into the study, to make sure we'd get after them. It nearly worked, too. The ransacking of the room was good—part of the idea to make us concentrate on Carney and forget the others.

"Then came Margaret's big mistake."

"She went out after Alec Magee. She had to see him, so as to tell him what to do. They talked confidentially, no doubt the fact that she was Lobo was freely mentioned. And when he'd gone, she discovered that Lake was hiding in the bathroom of the gymnasium. He hadn't been able to get away. So Lake knew who she was. She killed him, and afterward had the nerve to point out that she was almost the only one with a real opportunity! Remember the report, Sir Guy?"

Chatsworth nodded.

"So Margaret clubbed Lake to death, and Alec escaped—and she knew that she could rely on Alec protecting her to the last. But when he was caught, she was frightened. So was Helen. Helen knew he would kill himself rather than give Margaret away, so she fixed for the phony constable to come along and give him the weapon.

"Clever, wasn't it? And daring—when someone else had to do the dirty work. Helen was really worried by me, then. She didn't think the trick was working. She was as brazen as they came—if we'd had a chance to have her examined, we'd have found that Helen wasn't altogether normal. Above all, she was vain to the point of megalomania. Well, Margaret had a trick of falling asleep suddenly; or pretending to fall asleep. I think she even fooled Helen Wolf, who thought she took drugs. Neat trick again. And she was so lovely, and had the wit to know when she seemed to be asleep she looked more lovely still.

"She had her character so nicely prepared, too. A sweet young thing, repressed by her father, just kicking over the traces. I should have known better when Paterson told me what he did about her. That she was always on the tiles; that she stole from him; that she was wayward, wanton—just the kind of character you'd expect Lobo to have, if you once accepted the possibility that Lobo was a woman, an abnormal one at that.

"We already knew he might be a woman; Helen Wolf was the best bet. But Helen wasn't the boss, only the chief executive. Helen organized so much, fixed Carney and his mob, brought them to Morden Lodge, let them train the creepers there. Paterson suspected, but Paterson was hopelessly addicted to drugs and didn't know where to get supplies except from Helen. Provided he could get it, he asked no questions. So the game went along very nicely until Morgan cracked and named Carney. That was the beginning of the end. I once thought that Bray of Hounslow made a mistake in making it obvious that he was watching the house. It was the best thing he could have done—drove them into acting hurriedly, forced them into their big mistakes. We owe Bray a lot for this, Sir Guy."

"We'll pay it. Go on."

Roger said: "There isn't much more. And we've Sorenson to fill in the gaps. He's confirmed most of this, and he'll confirm the rest. The Can-Can, Margaret's habit of night-club crawling—it all fits in so nicely. Alec Magee took the instructions out to the creepers and collected what they'd picked up —and brought it to the Can-Can. You'll find that

Paterson sold a lot of it. Helen made him—Helen being able to do what she liked with him. But he had one fear: that his daughter was involved. He put Carney on to watch Margaret, and Carney pretended to obey. Helen helped the deception, suggested the drugs to keep Margaret in—all to prevent Paterson finding out. But he still had his doubts. It changed him from a man of some distinction to a weakling. He took no pride in the house or grounds, which could have been beautiful, gave way to a craving for the only thing that gave him rest—the drugs. He was killed because without his drugs he would have given Helen away completely.

"Now, tonight's show?

"Helen knew that having got Margaret we'd keep tails on her. She had to get her free. She fooled me all along into thinking that she hated Margaret and was determined to stop her from talking. You know the terms she offered. In fact, she wanted Margaret safe, and we don't have to guess what would have happened to Janet. The *finale?* Helen thought Margaret had broken down and talked. Margaret shot Helen to prevent her from talking. No loyalty in Margaret, who hoped that she would get away with that murder under our very eyes, as self-defense. The creepers had her instructions to kill rather than be caught; yes, she herself was a killer. And if I hadn't found that hat at Ma's, I doubt if I'd have tumbled even then."

He paused, looked round, and said: "Any questions?"

"They can wait until we've talked to Sorenson and the other prisoners," Chatsworth said. "Come along, Cortland, we'll leave him in peace for a bit."

Roger said: "Sir Guy, I'm going to be insolent again. From now on I want one day in every six off, or else—"

Chatsworth said gruffly: "I know we're understaffed. I'm doing everything I can. But there's no need for you to kill yourself. Good night, Janet. Good night, Lessing."

Cortland grunted good night, they went out; and Mark went with them to the hall. He closed the living-room door firmly behind him.

Roger didn't move.

Janet's head rested on his leg, until the engine of the car outside had started up. Then she turned round, so that she could see him.

"Roger, I'm so terribly sorry. That woman told me—that you and Margaret Paterson—"

"Jan, don't—"

"And I was crazy enough to believe her!"

"Crazy," said Roger, and paused. "Don't let's talk about it." And then he went on, as if he hadn't said that: "I just couldn't get past you, Jan. I thought there was something deeper than hatred of the time I had to spend away. We were both on the wrong foot. I—I was all set to make a complete fool of myself. After the champagne party—"

"I must have looked raddled!"

"Raddled? You looked drunk. Don't ever get drunk again unless I'm with you."

There was a pause, until Janet said: "Roger, what made you realize that—we *weren't* all washed up? When you knew I'd been kidnaped?"

"No, thank God! Before that. When you came in, after I'd told Margaret about her father. That woman can act! She had me fooled completely, I could have sworn that she was heartbroken. Have you ever seen anything like it?"

Mark called: "Anyone ready for a cup of tea?"

"In ten minutes," said Roger.

"Right!" There was a cheerful note in Mark's voice as he went along to the kitchen.

Janet said: "No, I've never seen anything like it, and I don't want to. She looked too lovely to be so utterly bad. Did she persuade Carney and the others to work for her? By exerting that—"

"Sex appeal? I don't know. How she started on it, how it grew up—how can anyone tell? Wantonness started it, I suppose. First step to corruption. And she had a good mind. The creeper squad was perfectly organized. I suppose we'll know one day how much Helen did, but Margaret was the kingpin. The female of the species *is* more dangerous than the male! Everything was cunning; from the selection of small, agile men, the careful training, the branding—"

"Why *did* she brand them?"

"Once branded, you can't get rid of the mark," said Roger. "She had them once and for all. Had 'em completely in her power, once Lobo's they had to stay Lobo's, or their wives and children would suffer. She paid them fairly well, and that helped to keep them loyal. Well, it's over, and—Jan."

"Hm-hm?"

"I just have to say—"

When Mark came in, they were together in the chair; and he crept out again.

Four months later, the trials were over and everything was pieced together. The defending counsel had tried hard to use Margaret's beauty as a strong plank in her defense, and failed completely to impress either judge or jury. The world knew, now, that a craving for excitement had brought her into contact with Carney and others; a corrupt, warped mind had done the rest. She had worked in close contact with Helen Wolf and Sorenson, who supplied the drugs to Paterson. She had pretended to be just wayward and reckless and oppressed by her father, playing a game that had fascinated her.

The thing that most surprised Roger was her age—she was thirty-one.

One the day after the trials, when Margaret, Carney, and Sorenson had been sentenced to death, Roger was alone in the office when the telephone bell rang. "West here."

"Mr. West," said the sergeant in the front hall, "a Colonel and Mrs. Hambledon are here, asking to see you."

"Hambledon? Oh, Hambledon! Show them into the waiting room, I'll come down at once."

Colonel Hambledon, tall, erect, and impressive, and his wife jumped up when he entered the room.

Roger shook hands, and asked: "How's Peter?"

"That's why we're here," said Mrs. Hambledon. "We shall always remember how you handled him. I think you saved it from being a secret horror throughout his childhood, and we had to tell you how grateful we are. We're going to adopt Peter."

"That's fine," said Roger softly.

"I wish you could teach me the trick of handling him," said Hambledon gruffly. "I confess, I thought that the last person who should break the news to him was a policeman."

Roger smiled faintly.

"Well, even policemen are human. That cuts both ways. I'm glad you came today, I'm off tomorrow for three weeks. Three weeks away from this prison, and—but tell me, how is Peter?"

"He's fine. And he sent a message—a question, really. You promised to tell him how your boy Scoopy got his name."

Roger hooted.

By the year 2000, 2 out of 3 Americans could be illiterate.

It's true.

Today, 75 million adults...about one American in three, can't read adequately. And by the year 2000, U.S. News & World Report envisions an America with a literacy rate of only 30%.

Before that America comes to be, you can stop it...by joining the fight against illiteracy today.

Call the Coalition for Literacy at toll-free **1-800-228-8813** and volunteer.

Volunteer Against Illiteracy. The only degree you need is a degree of caring.

Ad Council Coalition for Literacy